BACK
TO
SOMALIA

BACK TO SOMALIA

GLENN A. BELL

ARPress
45 Dan Road Suite 5
Canton, MA 02021

Hotline: 1(888) 821-0229
Fax: 1(508) 545-7580

Ordering Information:
Quantity sales. Special discounts are available on quantity purchases by corporations,associations, and others. For details, contact the publisher at the address above.

Printed in the United States of America.

ISBN-13:   Softcover   979-8-89356-567-6
              eBook   979-8-89356-582-9
              Hardback   979-8-89356-568-3

Library of Congress Control Number: 2024902918

Glenn Bell, like the main character Ethan Breaux in his new action novel, was born in Lake Charles, Louisiana. He grew up hunting in the woods of southwestern Louisiana as well as fishing in the lakes and rivers in the confines of Calcasieu Parrish. Glenn loves the spicy Cajun cuisine of his native state. The word is that he makes one of the South's best, old fashioned Pecan pies.

Glenn has not always been an author. In fact, most of his life has been as a pilot flying helicopters and commercial jet transport airplanes. Just like his main character nicknamed Cajun, he was a Warrant Officer. He has flown most U.S. Army helicopters. Glenn has experience as an Air Mission Commander.

Ethan Breaux, a highly experienced pilot and former wing commander in the Iraq War, now CEO of his private company in England, is approached for a critical and secretive mission. A terrifying event in Africa threatens to echo the devastation of Hiroshima and Nagasaki. The United States government, determined to prevent a repeat of history, seeks Ethan, known as Cajun, to lead the mission. Ethan, now living a peaceful life in Bristol, has left his military past behind after suffering a personal loss tied to his army career. His old friend, Ryan Clayborne, arrives to persuade him, revealing not only the gravity of the mission but also a lead on the precious thing Ethan lost. What did Ethan lose? What is at stake for the U.S. government? Readers will uncover the answers in the edge-of-the-seat action-adventure novel Back to Somalia.

Readers with an interest in international politics, military operations, and the intricate dynamics between the USA and countries such as Iraq, Djibouti, Somalia, and Ethiopia will find Glenn A. Bell's book a compelling read. The book offers detailed insights into the world of Army preparations, actions, and strategic planning, while also diving deep into the aviation realm. From the cockpit to the cabin, and the cargo to the conversations between the captain and first officer during takeoff, the novel provides a rich depiction of aircraft operations. Aviation enthusiasts and those drawn to military-based narratives will find this novel a must-read.

Despite the wealth of details on secret Army operations, aviation, and geopolitics, the novel never feels dry. Two well-developed emotional tracks woven into the plot provide a refreshing balance, breaking the monotony of the technical aspects like ammunition, takeoffs, and complex political scenarios. These emotional layers add depth and keep the momentum going, making the story both engaging and relatable. From a blossoming school-day love story to a complicated, Tom-and-Jerry-style friendship, the emotional elements of the novel resonate well with readers.

The scene where Ethan asks his childhood sweetheart to wait a few days to honor his friendship with Ryan is both hilarious and revealing, offering deeper insight into his character. Similarly, the midnight bed scene where Savannah realizes that Cajun was born for the Army and that stopping him would mean losing him forever, is a powerful, clap-worthy moment crafted by the author. Ethan and Savannah are both deeply committed to their dream jobs, and it's this shared passion and relentless drive that both brings them together and keeps them apart. The dilemma throughout the lovey-dovey journey of the childhood sweethearts adds depth to the narrative, making the love track more engrossing and a standout aspect of the novel. The candid moments between Ethan and Savannah, especially after long gaps, and the playful banter where Cajun calls Ryan "Pigeon" and provokes him, showcase their heartwarming bonds, further enriching the narrative.

Overall, if you have a passion for aviation and world politics, Back to Somalia has plenty to offer. With the detailed descriptions adding a military element, and the romance interleaves throughout the story, these themes make this novel a worthwhile read, blending emotional depth with technical precision.

Amazon 5-Star Ratings

goldentwo

5.0 out of 5 stars <u>This book was recommended by a friend</u>
Reviewed in the United States on December 2, 2014
Verified Purchase

This book was recommended by a friend. Normally I am a Nicholas Sparks fan for fiction- but I am so glad that I got this book- it is timely for how it relates to current affairs. The writing is so amazing- it made me feel like I was in the co-pilots seat going along for the ride- and having a bit of a romantic piece gave it a piece of a softer side for me as a female reader. It is so evident in the detail of the book that the author writes from a view of having in depth experience about what he has written- the details about the flying experience were intriguing as well as the story line of the complexities of international governments- and their rogue players involved in political events. A great book that I could not put down.

linda

5.0 out of 5 stars <u>Not just for miliary types</u>
Reviewed in the United States on June 17, 2010
Verified Purchase

I don't have any military background or experience, but I found this to be a very exciting read. The author takes you right into the action with his descriptions of the helicopters, the cockpit, the mission, and the people he leads. He also gives the story's hero "Cajun" a unique appeal by contrasting his southern Louisiana cooking skills and his extreme expertise in all things military. He almost sounds too good to be true! A great story line with plenty of flying machines, interesting people and action - this book has it all!

JSK

5.0 out of 5 stars <u>A great read!</u>
Reviewed in the United States on July 7, 2010

I really enjoyed the storyline; adventure, military ops, current event drama and of course some romance. A real page turner and I felt like I was along for the ride; and its a fantastic ride. Strap in and hold on.

Cobra Cockpit

CONTENTS

This novel is a work of fiction. The events, characters, and military vessels described herein are imaginary and are not intended to refer to specific places or living persons. The opinions expressed in this manuscript are solely the opinions of the author and do not represent the opinions or thoughts of the publisher. The author has represented and warranted full ownership and/or legal right to publish all the materials in this book.

Aloha,

Glenn Bell

Dedication

This book is dedicated to all my friends and fellow employees of Aloha Airlines. We all worked together for many years to make Aloha a very special airline. Unfortunately, the financial maze in which we all exist consumed it. Now that we are all scattered here and asunder, I keep the memory of all of you foremost in my mind.

I would also like to dedicate this book to all the men and women of the 193rd and 1293rd Aviation Battalions of the Hawaii Army National Guard. All the old Cobra pilots who eventually transitioned into the Chinooks are very special people with very special talents. Of course, no aviation unit could survive more than five minutes without top quality, by the book, maintenance. All the personnel in these units are exemplary. This unit deserves this nation's deepest appreciation for its service during operations in Iraq.

Acknowledgements

The publication of this novel could not have been possible without massive injections of advice and character development from all my family and friends. If they had a dollar for every time they read and critiqued my manuscript, each would have earned a small fortune.I want to specially give thanks to all my pilot buddies who watched over the flying scenes to insure authenticity. To make judgments on the flying scenes required input from several pilots who have specialized in specific fields of aviation. I have had the good fortune to fly with all of them at one time or another.

Special thanks must be extended to my good friend Captain James Crockett who is not only a dual rated pilot, but also an expert on many types of weapons and military tactics. His technical assistance was invaluable. We all need to thank Jimmy for his many years of service to this country.

And last, but certainly not least, I want to thank my entire family for being so supportive during the time I was away performing military service or the many days I was gone flying passengers to and from Hawaii. Of course, there must be a special Aloha to my mother, Grace Bell, for making it possible for me to survive past ten years old.

Prologue

0500 Hours August 2007

Cajun wonders if his Moroccan informant will really help his men rescue the Greek drug addict, or get them all killed. As he makes large oval racetrack patterns five miles from the objective with his helicopter in the predawn light, the question as to whether he is placing way too much faith in Hassan nags at every fiber of his body. Cajun utters these words to himself. "Why can't I just fly planes to and from the French Riviera? Why must I continue to become involved in these missions filled with risk? Why can't I stop?"

A lone figure stands on the edge of a rooftop in the darkness. As he peers down into the alleyway below, he nervously touches the gun hanging over his shoulder. A dog barks causing him to jerk forward clutching the wall in front of him. The sky behind him is beginning to show faint streaks of pink on the horizon as the sunrise approaches, but the alley is still cloaked in an eerie darkness. He wipes sweat from his face with the sleeve of his tattered linen shirt as the muggy still air hangs on him in the predawn stillness. He is very nervous about the actions which are sure to follow, however he must make the mark so Cajun will be able to identify the rooftop.

Again, the dog barks. Hassan senses, more than sees, a slight movement in the shadows below him. The hair on the back of his neck stands up as his instinct tells him it is time to begin. He slowly turns to look across the rooftop for any sign of danger then swiftly picks up a makeshift brush and can of paint. Hassan begins to mark a large X over the rough stone surface of the roof.

Thoughts of his family consume him. Adrenalin rushes through his body causing his heart to race. His Father named him Hassan, meaning courageous. He wishes his Father could know of the acts of courage he would display today, as he is the point man for the team coming to rescue the young Greek man. With one last look at the lavender sky, he whispers a prayer to Allah as he disappears down a dark, narrow stairwell.

Below in the alley Wyatt and Geno move swiftly through the thick cover of darkness without making a sound. They approach the building with their backs against the wall. Geno enters through a door that has been left ajar by a small rock. Wyatt is right on his heels as they move in a bounding over watch tactic. They are dressed completely in camouflage with UZI Sub Machine guns with silencers raised and ready as they move into the narrow hallway. Night vision goggles rest atop their helmets. They seem to hesitate at the doorway as if waiting for something or someone. In their hands are maps with directions so they know exactly how many steps to take. They know exactly how many minutes it will take for them to complete their mission.

Wyatt and Geno move with the ease and the confidence of seasoned soldiers who have felt the pain of war. They are soldiers on a mission who are part of a covert team to rescue Nicholas, a drug addict, and the son of a rich Greek shipping magnate. The risk they face is all part of their job. This job is no exception.

Preparing for days, they know every passageway in this mazelike building. They have been informed of what obstacles they face.

Reaching an opening in the stone wall, Wyatt, and Geno slide through, all the while keeping their backs against the cold stone wall. Pressing a knob on his watch, Wyatt looks down at the faint glow then holds his hand up in a halting motion. After a few seconds he gives the "go" signal then quietly yet quickly moves down a narrow-curved stairway. At the bottom of the stairway, they come across a sleeping guard, his chin resting on his chest in a small windowless room with three doorways.

Wyatt looks at Geno and gives him the, "Can you believe this fool is sleeping on the job look." Wyatt holds his finger to his lips and whispers, "Shush." Wyatt pokes the guard in the chest once with the barrel of his UZI then waits a second or two for him to wake up. The guard is still sound asleep. Wyatt pokes him in the chest again with the gun barrel. Wyatt looks at Geno grinning from ear to ear and gives him the look like, "Watch this." This time Wyatt pokes the guard hard in the chest with the gun barrel. The guard wakes up just in time to see the butt of the weapon hit him square in the face. Geno grimaces as the guard is knocked completely unconscious, knowing the fool will have one hell of a headache when he finally recovers. He might even consider an orthodontist about that missing tooth. Geno removes a ring of keys from the waist of the sleeping beauty guard to unlock the other doors.

As the door swings fully open, a small dirty figure of a man is cowering in the corner. He is blindfolded with his wrist tied. He begins yelling in fear as Wyatt jerks him up, removes his blindfold then tells him, "We have been sent by your father to get you out of here. Do not, and I repeat, do not make another sound."

Geno whispers, "Leave the bindings on his wrist, we don't want him grabbing at us when the going gets tough."

Suddenly the charges placed earlier in the outside electrical box by Hassan explode, rocking the building. The dim, wavering lights in the building go out leaving the three men in darkness that is thick and suffocating. Unable to even see their hands in front of their faces, Wyatt and Geno flip their night vision goggles down into position. Wyatt says to the Greek man, "Nicholas, that is your name isn't it? The young man shakes his head nervously in the affirmative. "Nicholas, we're gonna shoot our way out of here to the roof, so keep as low as you can, but move when we tell you to move."

Both men grab the Greek man under his arms to stand him up. The trio swiftly begins climbing up the stairway. They encounter two of the Moroccan guards who have been alerted by both the explosion and the lights going out. The guards are flashing a couple of small flashlights, which cause the night vision goggles to flash over then shut down for at least two seconds. Wyatt and Geno shoot, killing the first two guards with very short burst of their automatic weapons.

As Wyatt and Geno make their way to the second floor, they are encountered by three more guards with flashlights. Both men dive from behind the wall, sliding onto the floor of the hallway to open fire on the guards. Two of the guards are hit. They are killed instantly, but the third dives back into one of the rooms. Wyatt jumps up from his position, charging down the hall to the room. As he races the ten yards down the hallway, he pulls a hand grenade from his ammo belt. As the grenade dislodges from the belt the pin is pulled. Wyatt throws the grenade into the room then turns to retrace his steps to Geno's concealed position as quickly as he can run.

When the grenade explodes it rocks the walls of the building. The hallway fills with grayish black smoke. A split second after the grenade explodes, Wyatt and Geno jump to their feet lifting the Greek man as well. "Come on, run up the stairs to the roof."

Just as they start into the stairwell, one of the lone Moroccan guards, hidden in a room further down on the second floor, throws a grenade down the hallway. The grenade comes to a stop in the stairwell opening. Wyatt, Geno, and the Greek are just opening the door to the roof when the grenade explodes. Fortunately, none of the three are hit by flying debris, as the bend in the staircase takes the brunt of the explosion.

The two men step around to the side of the stairway structure on the roof with their Greek drug addict just as a black Huey helicopter approaches the roof to land. Both men have a communication earpiece in his ear. They are shouting back and forth with each other and Cajun who is flying the helicopter. Cajun shouts into the microphone attached to his helmet, "Wyatt, is the landing zone safe?"

Wyatt responds, "The landing zone is safe. Five guards have been neutralized. We're in a command position above the stairway."

Cajun picks a spot on the roof thirty feet from his men opposite the structure at the top of the staircase. He lands the helicopter on the roof, taking care that he does not take all the lift out of the rotor blades. He does not want to place the full weight of his helicopter on the roof. Cajun shouts, "OK we're down, hop on board." Suddenly a rocket propelled grenade is fired at the Huey from the roof of an adjacent building. It misses the helicopter but explodes near Wyatt, Geno, and the Greek causing them to fly backward. All of them are dazed by the blast from the near miss.

Within seconds, three Moroccan guards run through the opening of the staircase to attack Wyatt and Geno, who are still on the ground. His men are experts in hand-to-hand combat, but Cajun instinctively knows they are going to need some help to fight their way back up from the ground. The guards are slashing at them with knives, while a third has control of the Greek with a knife to his neck.

Cajun begins releasing his safety harness then shouts into the headset to Jack Garrity his copilot, "Take the controls. If we lose this fight, take off then return with all our men to get us out." He knows that if any one of them is captured, they each have a small locator beacon sewn into their clothing so they can be found later.

As Cajun runs toward his men fighting for their lives, he pulls one of the Berettas from his shoulder harness then shoots the guard holding a knife to their almost rescued Greek. The guard is killed on the spot.

The Greek reels a complete half turn, falling to the ground. Cajun yells at him to stay down while he raises his Berretta to kill another guard. He fires off two rounds into the body of the guard engaging Wyatt. The guard collapses in a heap.

At the same time another two Moroccan guards rush through the stairway opening, one of them striking Cajun in the forehead with the knife blade in a glancing blow. Most of the blow seems to come from the butt of the knife. When struck, Cajun loses control of his Berretta. It falls to the ground sliding another five feet across the roof. Everything seems to be happening in slow motion.

The guard who stabbed at Cajun is regaining his footing. He is getting set to make another lunge with his knife. As it is happening, Cajun wonders why these guards do not have any handguns. He has an additional thought as he rolls over, grabs his 357-Revolver strapped to his ankle, then fires two rounds through the chest of his attacker. The guard falls on top of him. Cajun only has a millisecond to ponder the question, "Why don't these idiots bring more guns?"

When he looks up he can see that both Wyatt and Geno are starting to gain the upper hand. Geno finally has a split second where he can draw his sidearm from his waste holster. He fires two rounds through the kill zone of his attacker. At the same time, Wyatt can control the arm of another guard attacking him. He drives the knife into his attacker's torso. The guard drops to the ground.

"Come on, get him on the chopper," Cajun shouts as he runs to strap himself back in the pilot seat. Wyatt and Geno literally throw the Greek man into the Huey as they jump into the back. As Jack applies power into the rotor system, the machine rapidly lifts off the rooftop.

At that exact moment, one of the Moroccans runs to the helicopter shouting, "Wait for me! Wait for me!" The Moroccan jumps up to grab hold of the landing skids. He manages to swing one of his legs onto the skids. He reaches out grasping for something to hold onto as the helicopter banks to the right, gaining altitude. Finally, he gets his hand on the door frame then pulls himself up to where his head is slightly above the floor.

Wyatt shouts that it is their informant Hassan, who is trying to escape with them, fearing for his life. Before all the words are out of his mouth the Greek, who is lying on the floor with his hands still bound, sees the Moroccan climbing onto the floor of the helicopter. With his teeth bared he kicks him squarely in the face with all the strength in his body. Hassan loses his grip and hurls backward through the air to his death.

Wyatt yells, "Damn, this punk just killed our man Hassan. He killed Hassan." From that moment on, nobody says a word as they fly through the darkness to a small, out of the way airstrip in Sale. Cajun lands the Huey then hurriedly shuts down the engine. He methodically goes through the shutdown checklist until he gets to the "Battery OFF" notation.

Wyatt pulls the Greek along until they reach their Lear Jet. Cajun and Jack jump in the cockpit to begin the Before Engine Start checklist.

"Shoulder Harness."

"Shoulder Harness On."

"Rudder Pedals."

"Rudder Pedals Centered and Free."

"Circuit Breakers."

"Circuit Breakers Checked In."

"Overhead Switches."

"Overhead Switches On, No Fault Lights."

Captain Cajun Breaux and First Officer Jack Garrity, continue through the checklist, item for item in a professional manner, getting the Lear

Jet prepared for takeoff. Captain Breaux says, "Ok, let's set our flaps in a Flaps 10 short field takeoff configuration. We are barely going to clear the trees."

Jack responds in a professional manner, "I have the flaps lowering to Flaps 10."

"OK Captain, we are cleared for takeoff."

Captain Breaux repeats, "Roger, we are cleared for takeoff."

As Cajun responds he advances the thrust levers approximately twenty-five percent of their travel range all the while pressing his feet hard against the brake pedals. The engines spool up to forty percent turbine output. Cajun advances the thrust levers to the full forward position then removes the pressure on the brakes. The aircraft lurches forward while First Officer Garrity places his left hand behind the thrust levers to guard against any backward creep.

Jack calls out airspeeds as they speed down the runway. Garrity calls out, "Sixty knots, one hundred knots, V1, rotate, V2." Captain Breaux pulls back on the yoke to fifteen degrees pitch attitude. As the jet rotates to a nose high pitch attitude, it climbs off the runway barely clearing the trees. They climb with ever increasing airspeed, accelerating into the morning sky.

Captain Breaux commands "Gear up." At one thousand feet and climbing, Captain Breaux commands "Flaps one", then accelerates to one hundred ninety knots. After accelerating to two hundred ten knots, Captain Breaux commands, "Flaps up, let's get the After Takeoff Checklist completed."

Jack complies and says, "Roger, the engines are set at continuous climb setting. The landing gear is up with three green lights out. Pressurization is climbing normally in the AUTO Mode."

"All right, Jack, so far so good. Go ahead and give ATC a call to get us a clearance to Madrid. Once we're feet wet and they turn us over to Oceanic control, we'll change our flight plan back to Bristol, England."

Jack replies in a relaxed manner, "OK, Boss, I will get us a clearance to Madrid."

Chapter One...
The Negotiation

Mogadishu, Somalia

It is a hot, dusty day in July 2007, as three Islamic Terrorist are being driven through the streets of Mogadishu. They are dressed differently than the rag tag Muslim Somalis driving them to meet their leader. The skinny Somali soldiers seated in the front seat of the vehicle have AK-47s. The men they are escorting are dressed alike in the uniform of Hezbollah Freedom Fighters. They are being driven in an old military vehicle about the size of an American SUV. But no, this vehicle was made somewhere else in the world, perhaps Russia.

As they drive through the crowded streets they see the true face of poverty. Many people on the streets literally have rags clinging to their bodies. Beggars on the corners plead for shillings so they might exist. Everywhere one looks, people can be seen with missing limbs. The smell is terrible.

Occasionally the vehicle passes by upgraded, modern looking three-story buildings. The Somali driver pulls into just such a building. This building is even larger and more impressive than any of the previous buildings. It even has a rock wall around it. As the small open truck pulls in, five or six guards step out into the courtyard, each with an AK-47 draped over his shoulders at the ready. The three Hezbollah fighters dismount the vehicle, slowly allowing their eyes time to adjust to the obvious luxury of their surroundings. Perhaps they have come to the right place after all.

As they walk through the front entrance they are greeted by what appears to be a higher-ranking soldier, perhaps an officer of some sort. He is dressed with cleaner clothes with several weapons strapped on his body. The officer asks them in Arabic to follow him then turns to lead them through a maze of rooms until they finally arrive in a large open veranda. Behind a very large beautiful wooden desk sits a man also in full military regalia.

The pirate leader sits perfectly still gazing in the opposite direction from his guest. As the Hezbollah Freedom Fighters stand in place, seconds tick away. The fighters gaze at each other with a bit of indignation. Finally, the leader speaks without even turning around to face the visitors. "I am Abdikarim Fawzia which, as you may or may not know, means the successful one. Do you know why I am successful?" He turns around slowly in his swivel chair to face the guest. "The reason I am successful is that I do things that make me money the same way time after time. I never go out of my comfort zone, because a man could lose his hand reaching in a hole that happens to contain a snake."

As the three Hezbollah men stand there looking at each other then back at Abdikarim Fawzia, a little impatience seems to show slightly in their stare. Finally, one of the fighters says, "Our beloved and wise leader Sheik Akbar Khadduri would never ask his friend to stick his hand in a hole where a snake resides. In fact, he asks that the great and wise Abdikarim Fawzia do as he always does; capture a ship for us, nothing more. We are told that you and your men capture ships from time to time. Is this true?"

"Does a camel crap in the desert? Of course, we capture ships from time to time" ,replies Abdikarim just a little annoyed. What is your name and which ship did your Sheik Akbar Khadduri have in mind? What would it be worth to him?"

"My name is Abdul Hamid. The ship we want is not a big ship, it is just a ship that began its voyage in North Korea. Do you not capture these ships then demand payment to give the ship back?"

"Yes I do," Abdikarim fired back. "But me and my men do not normally take request. We have the luxury of having many ships sail past our shores. We don't have to capture a specific ship."

Abdikarim decides to take the edge off the negotiations by offering his guest some tea. He gets up from his chair behind the desk then approaches his guest with his hands cupped together indicating conciliatory posture. "Great fighters for the Sheik Akbar Khadduri, please forgive my impertinence. Please have a seat and let my men get you some tea?"

Abdul responds to the gesture of hospitality by turning to sit down in one of several opulent leather chairs. As he and his fellow fighters sit down he nods an acceptance to the offer of tea.

As the tea is being served by one of Abdikarim's men, Abdul accepts the cup then waits for the server to leave the room. He leans forward to say he wants to give the name and the circumstance of the ship, but he would like the number of people knowing of the details to be just Abdikarim. Abdikarim motions to his men to leave the room.

The men look directly at their boss with a little mistrust, then turn to leave the room. They close the doors behind them.

Abdul leans in closer to the pirate leader. "The ship we want will be carrying a nuclear weapon in the cargo hold. Our beloved Sheik Akbar Khadduri asks that you accept $2,000,000 American money to capture this ship then bring it here to the port in Mogadishu. We will be on shore waiting to remove the crate containing the weapon then will drive it to a location nearby until we can sail it away from your shores. You will still have the ship so that you may negotiate for your normal fee to return the ship to its owners. Please do not refuse us as we are on a mission for Allah."

As Abdul stares intently into the eyes of Abdikarim, he seems to convey a message of determination.

Abdikarim asks in an inquisitive tone, "And what will you do with this weapon when you get it?"

"When the time is right we will sail it into the harbor in the port of Haifa in northern Israel." Abdul speaks with great passion in his voice. "Great Abdikarim Fawzia, the hopes of much of the Arabic world rest in your hands. If you will do your part in this mission you will be rewarded many times in this world. Your name will be heralded for generations for your part in this blow to the Zionist. When you die you will sit at the right hand of Allah to reap your just rewards. Will you help us?"

Abdikarim replies with enthusiasm, "Yes I will help you, but you must keep your word. Give me $2,000,000 in American dollars when the ship arrives in port."

Abdul responds immediately, "You will certainly receive your payment as promised."

"How will I know where to intercept this ship" ,ask Abdikarim?

Abdul replies. "We have a GPS transmitter planted on board. When the ship enters Somali waters, we will receive its location on small GPS receivers. You will find then capture the ship. Do we have an agreement Abdikarim Fawzia?"

Abdikarim nods his head yes, while his grin slowly gets larger and larger.

The deal is finalized with a strong handshake between the two men while the other two Hezbollah Freedom Fighters look on the handshake with approval. Abdikarim is told to prepare his men then personally supervise the pirating operation to assure success. He is told the ship would be in Somali waters in three days. As they proceed at sea they will be given coordinates for the interception. The stage is set to spring the trap.

Chapter Two...
Pirates At Work

Somali Waters

Abdul Hamid stands on the deck of a small fishing ship. Abdikarim Fawzia and his men are preparing to put to sea a couple days before the North Korean freighter arrives in waters off Somalia. On board are two smaller speedboats for the attack on the North Korean vessel.

Abdul hands Abdikarim a chart of the ocean waters off the Somali coast. On the chart are several plots of GPS coordinates. Abdul points at the chart and says, "These are the locations of the North Korean ship over the past thirty-six hours. If it maintains this course and speed you should be able to locate then intercept it just about here in another twenty-four hours."

The pirate leader looks at Abdul with puzzlement in his face and ask, "What happens if it does not maintain this course? What then?"

Abdul responds, "I will call you on your radio to give you updated positions. You can do this, Abdikarim. You can do this."

Abdul turns to walk off the ship. He stands on the wharf with his fellow Hezbollah Fighters to watch the ship when it finally departs the port. After a few more minutes of preparation, the ship slowly pulls away from the wharf. As the vessel slowly motors away from the pier, Abdul raises his clenched fist to shoulder level then pumps it with exuberance. Abdikarim looks back and raises his fist in a similar manner, but with considerably less bravado.

It is not long before the ship has made it out to sea about twenty miles. The darkness starts to close in all around them. Various crewmembers are beginning to wind down their movements around the vessel. They all settle down to a more relaxed posture. The Captain of the ship, Qasim, does not normally have the big boss with him on such missions. He is a bit nervous.

Qasim, feeling a little uneasy about what his role will be on this particular trip asks the pirate leader, "A thousand pardons Abdikarim, in what direction am I supposed to proceed this evening?"

Abdikarim lays the ocean chart provided by Abdul Hamid on the navigation table. He dramatically points to the last position marked on the chart and says, "Sail to a position twenty degrees to the northwest of this position for now."

The Captain looks at the X on the chart with bewilderment. "Yes, Sir, I will chart our course to the northwest of this position you have marked on the chart."

Abdikarim departs the wheelhouse, walks down two flights of metal stairs then enters a large communal room. It is normally where the men have meals, but right now they are playing a very serious card game. Abdikarim looks on from a distance of about five feet while he pours himself some tea. A couple of the men keep glancing up nervously to gauge Abdikarim's demeanor while continuing to play. Finally, one of the men speaks up and addresses the pirate leader, "Would you care to join us, Sir?"

"No, every time I get in a game of cards with you men, my money slowly disappears. You men enjoy yourselves, but do not forget to get some rest. We have a big day tomorrow. I do not want my men sleeping on the job. Understood?" Abdikarim responds with kind authority.

Several men mumble, "Yes, Sir, we are about to turn in soon."

After drinking his tea, Abdikarim turns to leave the room for his cabin. When in his room he closes the door behind him then lies on his bunk with his hands behind his head.

Thoughts race through his mind of capturing the North Korean ship. If the North Koreans have a nuclear weapon on board, surely they will defend a capture with weapons, unlike all the other ships they had encountered. He envisions several scenarios taking place at the time of the capture that involve a fire fight the likes of which he had not seen since the days of the U.S. Military fire fights over the downed Blackhawk helicopter. His men are not really prepared for substantial resistance. Should he tell them what is at stake and prepare them for the worst? If he tells them all about the nuclear weapon, they may turn against him. For sure his men will want the money being paid by the Hezbollah Freedom Fighters.

In the middle of his private thoughts there is a knock at his door. It is a forceful knock, not the normal timid knock he is used to. Abdikarim gets up from his bed then opens the door slightly. In the hallway staring back at him in the dim lighting is his second in command, Hatim. Abdikarim asks, "What do you want, is there a problem?"

Hatim growls, "The only problem is that I don't know what is going on. Is there something you were going to tell me?"

Abdikarim answers sternly trying to gain the upper hand with his dominance. "What do you mean what is going on. Nothing is going on. Who are you to question me?"

Hatim was a very tough, experienced leader in his own right. In fact, he was one of the outstanding fighters in the streets of Mogadishu when the Americans were there in 1993. At that time Hatim was fourteen years old. He had been involved in many skirmishes with the Ethiopians in their attempt to control the towns of Dire Dawa and Gode. He has been carrying and using AK-47s since he was thirteen years old.

Hatim does not back up or seem the least bit intimidated as he stares straight in the eyes of the pirate leader. "Since when do you follow us out to sea then have our Captain sail to places on the sea we have never known before? What is going on?"

The pirate leader Abdikarim starts to say in a dominate voice, "I give you orders; you don't give me orders!"

Hatim did not let him finish his sentence when he hit the door with his shoulder knocking his boss back several steps. He already has his weapon drawn pointed at Abdikarim's face. Hatim speaks forcefully without screaming, "There is danger in this mission. I can smell it. You are going to tell me what is at stake or I am going to shoot you dead right now, then throw you overboard!"

Abdikarim's face glares with hate while he stares down the barrel of Hakim's 357 Smith & Wesson. He answers slowly but forcefully. "There is no need for you to try arresting command from me. I was going to tell you what is at stake in time. I do not want to alarm the men too early causing them to want to abandon our mission."

Abdul answers back, "Mission? What mission? Since when do we go on missions?"

"We are on a mission for Allah. We are going to make a lot of money paid in American dollars. That is right, Hatim, we will be paid by our Hezbollah brothers $1,000,000 to capture the ship that they want. It gets better, Hatim, because we get to keep the ship."

Hatim slowly lowers his weapon while keeping his distance from his leader who could himself be a fierce fighter. In his face, one could see that he was trying to digest and understand what Abdikarim was saying. "Why do these Hezbollah fighters want us to capture a certain ship only to let us keep the ship? Is there someone or something they want on the ship?"

Abdikarim responds with enthusiasm, "That's right, now you are getting it, Hatim. They want what is in the cargo hold."

Abdikarim continues on to reveal his secrets. "When I tell you Hatim, you must swear an oath with me not to tell our men, because they do not have the vision that we have. If you promise me that you can keep a secret, I will give you your half of the one million dollars. Of course, we will have to pay the men their normal wages out of our earnings. Do you swear an oath?"

"Yes, I swear an oath" ,replies Abdul.

Abdikarim knows that if Hatim will control his emotions and settle down long enough to accept his offer, he can be instrumental in keeping all the men in line. Privately he rejoices at his cleverness. He would be paid $2,000,000, but would only split $1,000,000 with Hakim. Not only would he split the lesser amount with Hatim, but all their expenses will be paid from the first million.

Abdikarim reveals that inside the cargo hold is a nuclear weapon, which is on its way from North Korea to Iran. "Our Hezbollah brothers do not want to wait years for Iran to act, they want to take the bomb as soon as possible to deliver a fatal blow to the Zionist for Allah and all Muslims." He goes on to explain to Hatim that the weapon is not dangerous to them, but it may frighten their men. In addition, there is no way of knowing what type of resistance they may face while trying to capture the ship. He asks Hatim to help control the men while preparing for a serious gun battle with the crew onboard the North Korean vessel. "Perhaps we should make up a cover story that the Americans are trying to use the ship as a cover while they move parts through our Somali waters?"

They both agree to the story. Hatim slowly leaves the cabin by backing through the door into the hallway.

The next morning, all the men are in good spirits as they go about their task of preparing for the eventual boarding of the cargo ship. Some of the men can be seen cleaning their weapons. Several of the Muslim pirates have RPGs. All of them have shoulder harnesses carrying revolvers or 9mm semi-automatic weapons.

Up on the quarterdeck someone opens the door then calls down to the pirate leader. "Sir, there is a radio message for you."

Abdikarim replies, shading his eyes from the sun as he looks up to see who is calling out to him. "OK I will be right up." As he says the words he is already in a rapid trot up the stairs to reach the wheelhouse. As he enters he reaches out to take the microphone from the outreached hand of the Captain.

"Hello this is Abdikarim Fawzia speaking."

Over the radio speakers the voice of Abdul is heard faintly, "I have some additional GPS plots for your chart. Do you have something to write with?"

Abdikarim reaches out to pick up a pencil lying on the chart table. He speaks into the microphone. "Yes, go ahead."

Abdul continues, "The two most recent positions are zero degrees, forty-nine minutes south / seventy-three degrees, eight minutes east. That position was taken when the ship passed south of the Maldives islands. They have turned north. The ship was last reported at one degree, twenty-seven minutes north / sixty-nine degrees, fifty-nine minutes east. "I have one further position to give you. This one is important so make sure you write it down correctly."

The pirate leader prepares to write down more information.

"The position is eleven degrees, three minutes north / sixty-three degrees, twenty-nine minutes east. If you stay on course and on speed you should arrive at this position before the North Korean ship arrives around midnight tonight. We will give you one more call at about ten o'clock tonight with their last position. Good hunting, Allah is with you!"

When Abdikarim finishes the conversation, he stands motionless with the microphone in one hand and the paper with the coordinates in his other hand. He looks up slowly only to be met by the gaze of the Captain. Two of his men, who are in the wheelhouse, are also staring at Abdikarim. For a few moments the wheelhouse is quiet except for the water slamming against the hull and music playing below deck. The Captain asks, "Sir, what manner of ship is it we are trying to capture?"

At first the pirate leader says nothing then the Captain asks again, "Sir, why are we sailing so far from our shores to capture a ship? Since we left port we have seen two foreign ships. Why did we not capture them? Why did your friend say Allah is with you?"

Before the Captain can ask another question Abdikarim blurts out, "The ship that we are after has special meaning to Muslims all over the world. It carries American parts in its cargo hold destined for Oman. I am told these parts are very valuable to the American government. They will pay dearly to get them back. Now make sure you sail straight to this position on this chart. If you do a good job of finding the ship you will be paid double your normal wages."

With that explanation, Abdikarim leaves the wheelhouse for his cabin. As he walks into the hallway, Hatim is waiting for him by his cabin door. Abdikarim slows the pace of his gate as he sees his second in command. "Hatim, are you here to point your pistol at my face again?"

"Not at all sir, I merely want to talk to you about our men. They have concerns about our attempt to capture the ship tonight."

"In that case, come on in my cabin."

After both men enter the pirate leader's room, Abdikarim closes the door behind them. An invitation is made for Hakim to take a seat in the small chair opposite the bed. He sits to face his leader. "What is on your mind Hatim?"

"Sir, the men are not unaware that we are on a special-mission. As we agreed I spread the word that the ship we are to capture is carrying American cargo that they will pay dearly to retrieve. I also told them to prepare all their weapons for stiffer resistance than what we are accustomed to encountering."

The pirate leader interrupted his second in command, "Well Hatim, are the men ready for a fight? Do they ask what is on the ship?"

Hatim answers with a worried frown on his face, "It's worse than that Abdikarim, they want more money. They have suspected all along that there was something special about this trip. They see you onboard leading the capture. They can see we have been traveling at sea on a single course for a whole day. When I told them we were going to capture a ship carrying valuable American cargo, it did not take them very long to guess the rest. They say that it is normally safe at sea when we capture a ship because nobody ever fires back at them. Now they fear there will be stiff resistance from the Americans. They fear some of them could be killed."

Abdikarim says in a defiant voice, "Hatim, we don't have any choice but to double their wages. I am going to walk out on deck to offer them double their wages, but at the same time I am going to demand loyalty. If I get any further back talk, there will be trouble. Follow me, we must be seen together. You must appear to back me up all the way."

Both men walk through the door into the hallway then onto the deck. Abdikarim walks up to the center of the deck with his back to the structure that supports the wheelhouse. He stands on a small crate to call the men over to hear him speak.

The pirate leader does what he always does; he uses the lure of money and the stench of fear to control those around him. As far as he is concerned, any man who does not agree to follow his plan will swim back to Mogadishu.

Abdikarim begins his speech, "Men, Hatim told me of your concerns about our mission to capture our prey. You have learned the ship is carrying American cargo. Now you want something from me. On one hand you want more money, but on the other hand, Hatim tells me you are afraid of the resistance to our capturing the ship. Something does not add up. Either higher wages will meet your concerns or you are afraid to fight. Which is it?"

The pirate leader stands there glaring down at his men. His gaze goes from man to man staring them straight in the eyes defiantly. "Well, which is it, greed or fear?" Abdikarim yells at them.

One of men toward the rear of the crowd speaks up, "Sir, now we know that the ship we are to capture will be different. We know that the American cargo will bring big money. We want our fair share."

Abdikarim fires back. "All right, there is an honest man. He says you all want more money. Is that right?"

All the men shout in unison, "Yes, we want a fairer wage. Yes, we want more money!"

The pirate leader knows he has them right where he wants them. Abdikarim shouts so all of them can hear, "Alright then, I will double your wages on this trip on two conditions. One condition is that you do not press me for more than double your wages. The second condition is that you make your weapons ready to capture the ship tonight. If you come at me again complaining, once we return to Mogadishu you and your families will be driven out of my protection. You will never work again in Mogadishu. Is that clear?"

The men moan weakly in the affirmative, as though they had better take their good fortune but not press the pirate leader any further.

Abdikarim says to his second in command, "Hatim, make sure these men are ready for action tonight as we are intercepting the ship in four hours." Hatim nods with his eyes lowered as Abdikarim storms off the deck. He too feels that the pirate leader has been pushed as far as he can be pushed. In addition, it has been demonstrated once again that Abdikarim is the undisputed leader. No question about it, he is the alpha dog.

By nine in the evening, Hatim has several men positioned high on the bow searching in the night for any sign of a ship. Abdikarim paces back and forth on the deck wondering why they have not seen the North Korean ship. Why has he not been given additional coordinates of the ship they are to capture?

At that moment, the wheelhouse door flies open. The Captain steps out with a cell phone held high in the air. He yells down to Abdikarim, "Sir, there is a phone call for you from Mogadishu."

Abdikarim races up the steps to the wheelhouse to take the phone from the Captain. "Hello, this is Abdikarim."

It is Abdul, his Hezbollah Freedom Fighter. "We could not reach you over the radio. However, we have the phone number for the Captain's cell phone. Can you hear me alright?"

"Yes, I can hear you loud and clear. Do you have more GPS position reports?"

"Yes, write down these numbers very carefully. Fifteen minutes ago, the ship was at this location, thirteen degrees seventeen minutes north / sixty-two degrees forty minutes east." That is, it, Abdikarim can see from their GPS position that they are in front of the North Korean ship. The Captain points to the chart indicating they are close to the ship's position. Excitement fills them. The pirate leader says goodbye to Abdul then points to the chart.

Abdikarim points to a position he wants the Captain to sail to. It is a position less than thirty minutes in front of them. The pirate leader rushes out of the wheelhouse then rapidly down to the deck to talk to his men. "Men, get ready to lower the two speed boats. We are almost on our prey."

All the men hurriedly do as they are told. The pirate leader is going on one of the boats to capture the ship. He does not want anyone looking at the pallet in the cargo hold. Abdikarim calls out to the men on the bow, "Men, keep a sharp lookout. You should see the ship off the starboard bow." Abdikarim orders all the lights turned off, as he does not want his ship to be seen in the darkness. As they strain in the night to see the lights of the North Korean ship, it starts to rain.

The next few minutes seem like a lifetime. Out of the night one of the men shouts, "Sir, there is a ship in the darkness off the starboard bow approximately three kilometers." Abdikarim and Hatim run up to the front of the ship to see their prey. Sure, enough they are closer than they thought. Both men run back to where the speedboats are ready to be lowered. Abdikarim jumps on one boat while at the same time Hatim jumps in the other. The speed boats are lowered in the water then away they speed toward North Korean vessel.

The two speedboat drivers know exactly what to do. They alter their course so they can approach the vessel from the left and right rear. By this time the rain is pouring down hard. Abdikarim thinks that the rain is good, making them harder to detect, but at the same time the rain could make it harder for his men to board the ship.

As they approach the rear quarter of the North Korean ship his men hurl three grappling hooks up and over the railing. The ship is only a midsized vessel at around 2,000-ton, making it easy to board. The pirates start climbing the ropes to board the ship one by one. As they climb they hear automatic weapons firing. The weapons seem to be far away and are not aimed at them. As Abdikarim and his men climb over the rail, they can see the ship's crew firing off the rear of the ship in the opposite direction at Hatim and his men.

Abdikarim and his men open fire killing several of the ship's crew in their initial volley. The other crewmembers dive out of the way of the bullets flying past them. They duck behind any and everything to protect them from the incoming fire. Within seconds they are firing back at Abdikarim and his men. As they exchange gun fire, it is not long before Hatim and his men on boat number two have circled around to the right side of the ship. They start to climb up the rope held firmly by the grappling hooks. As Abdikarim looks overboard down at Hatim, he can see that several of his men have been killed. "Oh, merciful Allah, what kind of ship is this?" They have never been fired upon boarding a ship before. "What kind of crew is this?"

The fight continues but Abdikarim has more fighters. They shoot killing several of the crewmembers. The remaining crewmembers surrender by laying down their weapons. They lie face down with their hands above their heads. As Abdikarim and his men stand they take control of the crewmembers. They can see that all the crewmembers are Asian, presumably North Korean, but they could be Chinese.

They burst through the wheelhouse door. The Captain and First Mate hold their hands over their heads fearing they might be shot right on the spot. Abdikarim tries to communicate with them in Somali but there is no chance the Captain or the First Mate have any idea what he is saying. Abdikarim then speaks to them in Arabic trying to open a line of communication, but to no avail. Finally, Hatim speaks a few broken words of English, "You Chinese? You Korean?"

"Yes, yes, Korean, " they answer over and over in broken English.

Abdikarim gestures to the Captain to turn the ship around. He points at the compass gesturing to sail in a south westerly direction. He writes down the coordinates for Mogadishu, Somalia then points to them as he hands the paper to the Captain. Hatim and another pirate in his command stay to guard the wheelhouse while the pirate leader leaves. He heads down the stairs to the deck. Abdikarim orders some of his men to board their speedboats to return to the mother ship. An order is given that they give the dead an honorable burial at sea then care for the wounded.

As soon as everyone clears the deck going about their duties, he orders several soldiers to follow him below. They go below to examine the cabins then search the ship. One by one each room is cleared looking for additional North Korean sailors. Abdikarim quickly enters a cabin he assumes belongs to the Captain as it is spacious and well furnished. Abdikarim thinks ahead. He imagines a time when this ship will effectively belong to him. There is a possibility that he will want to keep the ship because it is doubtful the North Korean government will negotiate for its return. In addition, he thinks there might come a time when he can sell it to his Israeli hating Hezbollah brothers. After all, how best to transport a devastating bomb to the Israeli coast but in a North Korean ship. Abdikarim has the Captain's belongings removed.

Abdikarim and several of his men finally work their way into the cargo hold. They find many boxes with markings indicating they are likely parts and supplies. However, in the middle is a pallet about six feet long by four feet wide. The pirate leader feels this must be the nuclear weapon but dares not open it with so many of his men around. He does not want the crew to become frightened or greedy thinking about their part of a ransom for such a treasure. Abdikarim post three guards with orders not to touch or take their eyes off the cargo until they reach the port in Mogadishu.

Abdikarim walks back to his newly acquired Captains suite. Exhaustion claims him from all the activity in the last twenty-four hours so he lies down to take a nap.. Abdikarim thinks to himself how difficult his job had been on this trip. Leading hungry men to capture a ship at sea is tiring. He feels that his most difficult task is still before him. The nuclear weapon will have to be removed from the ship. It will need to be moved to a secure location. The pirate leader wonders how all of this will be possible, all the while keeping the contents of the crate unknown to all his men. He falls asleep for several hours.

Abdikarim is awakened by a knock at his door. The knock on his door is forceful and impatient. "Yes, what do you want?"

Hatim is on the other side of the door. "The Captain has identified one of his men that can speak a little bit of English."

"So, what Hatim, we don't want to talk to them anymore, we just want them to sail the ship back to Mogadishu."

At this point the pirate leader opens his cabin door to allow Hatim to enter. He always keeps in mind that Hatim is an experienced leader in his own right. He also remembers that in a fit of anger Hatim had already pulled his revolver and pointed it at his face. However, Abdikarim opens the door then turns his back on Hatim as he walks back to the desk in the cabin to sit down. By turning his back on Hatim, he is demonstrating his complete lack of fear of his second in command. "Please have a seat, Hatim."

Hatim sits down nervously in a chair facing the desk. Even though he is a tough fighter who would not normally fear his number one, he also remembers losing his temper then pointing his revolver at Abdikarim. His boss had not gotten to where he was today by being soft. The leader did not normally allow such behavior to go unchallenged. He feels that Abdikarim might just as well pull his weapon and kill him as take another breath. Hatim wants to apologize for his actions. He wants to slowly work his way back into the confidence of Abdikarim.

Abdikarim I wanted to congratulate you for your leadership on this mission. Your guile and cunning have gained a great prize for our cause. At the same time, you have increased our value to our Muslim brothers across the sea. I want you to know how much sorrow is in my heart for challenging you yesterday in such a way in your cabin. I should have known you would include me in your plans. Please accept my apology?" Hatim slowly lowers his head.

Abdikarim, glares back at Hatim with disgust written all over his face. As much as he wants the incident to never have taken place, it did take place. Hatim had threatened his authority and his life. In years past Hakim would already be dead for such an act, but for now the pirate leader needs him. There will be a day when the score can be settled, just not today.

Abdikarim speaks between clenched teeth. "Hatim your apology is accepted. I would have a difficult time running things around here without your devoted service. What did you want to tell me about the crew speaking English?"

"The Captain is saying he wants to speak with you. He is claiming that he and his men want not to be sent back to North Korea. They want to work for us. The Koreans will do anything we ask so as not be sent back to their homeland. What should I tell him?"

Abdikarim thinks for several seconds then replies, "Tell him we will be honored that they be part of our force. We will not try to send them back to North Korea. But also tell the Captain that any breach of loyalty from any of his crewmembers will reflect badly on him. Any attempt to escape or action taken against any of our men by him or any of his crew will result in the execution of every one of them. Tell him that, Hatim, then remove our guards around them. Let's give our Korean brothers a chance to work for us, but at the same time let's keep an eye on them as well."

"I will tell the Captain at once, Sir." With that Hatim slowly rises. He departs Abdikarim's cabin, never once taking his eyes off his boss.

After Hatim departs his cabin, Abdikarim sits quietly reflecting on the latest developments. "What fools they are."

Everyone around him makes his job easy because they are such fools. First and foremost, there will be a time in the near future when he will kill Hatim. That insolent fool would not point a weapon at him and live to brag about it to his grandchildren. And what is to be done with the North Korean crewmen? They make it easy for the great pirate leader. They will gladly work for him and he does not even have to guard them as prisoners. When the time suits him, and the North Korean government pays for their release, he will send them home.

The ship sails for many hours until they reach the Port of Mogadishu. Hakim helps the Korean Captain maneuver the ship up to one of the empty positions in the port. There is not anymore activity on shore as when any other captured ship pulls up to the wharf. The only time there is ever any activity might be to unload food, which might otherwise spoil during the months of negotiations.

Abdikarim has worked out a plan for Hatim to remove the North Korean seamen from their ship. His job is to assign them other work task away from the port. He thinks that he will sit tight for a few days to make sure no one is really paying any attention to the activities taking place on the North Korean vessel. When all is quiet he will help in the unloading of the nuclear weapon for the Hezbollah Freedom fighters.

After a couple days, arrangements are made for Abdul to come aboard with his fellow soldiers. The $2,000,000 is paid to Abdikarim in his private cabin with no one else looking on. Abdikarim thanks his brothers for the transaction and the opportunity to serve them, leaving the door open for further exploits. At that point he opens his cabin door. He orders two of his men to take Abdul and his men to the cargo hold. Once the door is closed behind them, he places the money in a large money belt that straps around his waist. Once the money is hidden under his clothes, he leaves the cabin hurriedly to catch up to the inspection going on in the cargo hold.

As Abdikarim enters the cargo hold, his Hezbollah brothers are looking over the boxes of spare parts as well as the crate that contains the nuclear weapon. Abdul turns around to face the pirate leader. "Abdikarim Fawzia, please open the wooden crate so we can see what you have brought us."

Abdikarim says. "My Hezbollah brothers, no man has laid eyes on what you wish to possess, not even me. Here are a few simple tools so that you can open the crate to view your possession. My men and I will wait outside for you to crate it then call us back. In that way only your eyes will see the inside of the crate. Does this satisfy you?" Abdul looks a little puzzled if only for a moment, but soon comes to believe it is a good plan. He nods in the affirmative.

After Abdikarim and his men depart the cargo hold, Abdul orders two of his men to take the crate apart carefully. Once they remove the two sides they step closer to examine the contents. "May Allah be praised, my fellow soldiers for God," says Abdul. "Have either of you ever seen a nuclear bomb?" Both the other freedom fighters slowly shake their heads from side to side, as if to say, not only no, but hell no. "Neither have I," replies Abdul, "But if anything, I have ever seen in my life looks like it would be a nuclear bomb, it would be this monstrosity."

They quickly nail the box back together to conceal the crates contents. Abdul calls Abdikarim to return with his men. "Abdikarim, you have done well. We need our crate guarded day and night by your most loyal men until we have it removed from this ship and onto a truck. After that, we will have it moved to our location on the outskirts of Mogadishu, where we will have it guarded night and day until we decide how it will be removed from this city."

"We will guard it for a couple days. When the activity dies down on the wharf, we will help you move it."

In three days around ten o'clock at night, two trucks pull up to the wharf in front of the North Korean vessel. Using the ship's hoist, Abdikarim has his men lift the crate out of the cargo hold then lower it onto a truck along with the boxes of spare parts. After it is loaded his men pull a large canvas cover over the crate. The second truck is loaded with Abdikarim's men. The trucks drive off into the night.

They drive through several miles of streets in Mogadishu, turning left then right to insure no one is following them. Once they know they are not being followed, both trucks drive straight to the compound on the edge of town. It is a typical structure surrounded by a seven-to-eight-foot rock wall. After the crate is unloaded, it is stored in the compound. All the men board the two trucks then drive away into the night. As Abdikarim and his men drive away, the Hezbollah Freedom Fighters close and lock the gates behind them.

Chapter Three...
Back At The Office

Bristol, England

Mrs. Buckingham slowly makes her way across the room to her desk. It has often been asked of Cajun, just why he insists on keeping a seventy-three-year-old English lady as his secretary. After all, with the nonstop activity continually taking place not only in the office, but also in the lives of his employees, wouldn't a younger and better educated secretary be more in order? He always replies in the same way to all his critics.

"First of all, Mrs. Buckingham is a fairly well-educated woman in her own right," replies Cajun as he leans forward with indignation. "She has training in bookkeeping, plus a fair amount of experience in office management. Around here the most important function she plays in our organization is that daily she organizes our incoming monies, along with our expenses, then passes them on to our accountants to do their magic." While trying so emphatically to explain why she is so important, he pitches a pencil spinning in the air only to miss his intended target, a dirty coffee cup on his desk.

He further defends his choice by adding, "Mrs. Buckingham also has a hearing aid. She has very little interest in all other activities that do not directly affect her duties. You might even say she purposely avoids noticing my successes and failures because she knows that I will definitely do things the very same way the next time."

Another reason why Cajun will not trade Mrs. Buckingham for some hot, eye candy sweetheart, is that she never once complained about his Louisiana coffee. She only asked once why he did not stock a more conventional coffee like Starbucks finest or perhaps a traditional English tea. He had told her in the very beginning, "Mrs. Buckingham, I know you will never like my coffee, but I was drinking this strong, Community coffee when I was thirteen years old. I not only love the taste, but every time I sip my brew it reminds me just how much I miss Louisiana." Oh, what he would give to be back at home skiing on the infamous Lake Charles Lake.

This day is not a normal day. Mrs. Buckingham can tell immediately as Cajun limps through the office in the direction of the coffee pot, that his recent job in Morocco was nothing resembling business as usual.

Cajun slowly limps into his office then closes the door behind him. He slips timidly into his large soft leather chair with L.S.U engraved into the headrest. He opens the bottom drawer on the left side of his desk. Cajun pulls out a fifth of Southern Comfort whiskey then pours a generous amount in his coffee. Before he returns the bottle he glances at his closed office door just to make sure Mrs. Buckingham has not peeked in for any reason. She has often commented that she thought he drank too much for his own good. Hey, what she does not know will not hurt her. He leans back in his chair, closes his eyes, and holds the warm mug against his bruised head.

After just a minute, his recuperation Cajun style is interrupted by that funny little English telephone jingle that he has learned to despise so much. It especially irritates him this morning. "Hello, this is Ethan Breaux speaking, may I help you."

"Good morning Mr. Breaux, this is Mr. Papadopoulos," a voice with a heavy accent on the other end replies. "Do you have my son? Is he safe?"

"Do I have him? Is he safe?" Cajun answers with increasing anger as the words roll off his tongue. "Of course, he is safe. I told you I would get him out didn't I?," he says indignantly.

"There is something we have to discuss before I turn him over to you. We need to discuss the matter of an additional $50,000 for the damage to me, my men, and my helicopter," Cajun declares in a somewhat more contained tone.

"You said it was a small dispute between you and your creditors. You said nothing of the fact that your son is a sniveling drug addict. You did not say that your creditors were blood thirsty, drug sniffing, low life trash thugs numbering well above the three guards we were expecting." Cajun rages on. "And don't even think about calling the authorities or stiffing me because I haven't even brought him back to England yet. You give me any aggravation and I will ship his punk ass back to those Moroccans!"

"Mr. Ethan please let me assure you that I have no intention of calling the authorities. I will gladly pay what you ask plus an additional $25,000 bonus," pleads the man. "I am so very sorry that I was not able to disclose my predicament to you with more accuracy, but I was desperate to get my son back. I had it on very good authority that you were the man who could pull off such a rescue so I had to take a chance. I am on my knees thanking you, Mr. Ethan."

Cajun relaxes in his chair. He seems to be calming down a little. He replies slowly and distinctly when he speaks. "Mr. Papadopoulos, please have the money delivered here today, in cash, then our transaction will be complete. I will deliver your son to you. Should you or any of your friends have need of my services in the future, just tell me all the facts. We can deal with just about anything. When we have a job to do, we just need to fly in with enough guns a blazing," he says in more calming tones. Cajun hangs up the phone. As he leans back in his chair once more, he sips his brew then lifts the warm cup to his forehead.

As Cajun sits recovering from the night's ordeal, a well-dressed man in a suit leans in the office door. "I see you are still up to your same old tricks."

Cajun moans and groans. "As if things aren't bad enough right now, you have to show up after all these years." It is Ryan Clayborne, Cajun's old college roommate and CIA operative in Iraq in 1991.

Ryan quips back at Cajun, "Hey I would only show up here if the State Department sent me, because I don't like you any better than the last time I saw you."

Cajun says, "In case there is some doubt, I am in the aircraft charter business now. I have no business relationship with the U. S. Government."

"Yea, I can see that. You are bleeding, you need new clothes, and two of your aircraft have bullet holes in them."

Cajun sputters, "It is only because I am a Southern gentleman, plus the fact that I doubt I could get up to throw you out that I am going to offer you a seat on my couch."

Ryan laughs out loud, "You call this a couch. It looks more like a love seat. At least that is what my wife calls the one in our den. Yea, it's a love seat alright."

"Love seat? Love seat? You wish it was a love seat. I use it to take a nap on occasion. You can plainly see that it is easy to lie down and hang your legs over the edge. How is your wife, Pigeon? What was her name, Snoozy? Woozy?" Cajun asks with a sly smile on his lips.

"Her name is Snooky, and she said to tell you hello. She expects you to come over for a T-bone the very first time you get back through Virginia. She also said to tell you to bring back some of that Louisiana cooking spice. She tried to tell me the name of the spice in that little red shaker bottle. What was it, Beat your Grandmother, Whip up on your Niece? Oh, now I remember, Slap Your Momma, that is what it was, Slap Your Momma. And do not call me Pigeon," Ryan quipped.

All the guys in Cajun's unit in Iraq gave Ryan the call sign Pigeon. Since his name was Clayborne and he was always begging the pilots to fly straight and level while on missions like a clay pigeon, they named him appropriately. After all, hardly anyone in Iraq dreamed up their own call signs. In fact, Cajun himself always fancied himself as a Big Crab or Gator. Cajun was the name which stuck on Ethan Breaux, a native of Lake Charles, Louisiana.

Cajun looks at Ryan in a serious manner. "OK Pigeon, we have said our hellos, what are you doing here really?"

"The jest of it all is that we have to get back a nuclear weapon high jacked off a North Korean ship. Long story short we need someone to take on a covert mission to retrieve that nuclear weapon, which is in a crate in a small compound in Mogadishu, Somalia."

Cajun stares back at Ryan for several seconds with a dumbfounded look on his face. He cannot believe what he has just heard. "Why in the world are you telling me this? My days of having the people and equipment to take on a mission like that ended a long time ago. What about our black-ops unit from the Iraq days?"

Pigeon replied immediately, "Look I know it sounds crazy but just hear me out. First and foremost, under no circumstances can the United States military set one foot on Somali soil. It is just politically unacceptable both at home and abroad. The second and most important reason is that some crazy Islamic terrorist plan on sailing the nuke as close as possible to a port in Israel. Once the ship gets close they plan on detonating it. Do you know what that would mean?"

"Yea, I can imagine Israel would retaliate in a big way. No telling whose ass they would kick. Assuming someone was to take on a mission like that, it would require a sizeable military type organization. No way could we just sail up to the port in Mogadishu, we would have to land equipment and personnel then motor across part of Ethiopia. We would have to come in from the north to even stand a chance. It would take millions in equipment, plus I sure ain't doing it for free. I doubt even Uncle Sam would spring for the bucks I would charge for such a mission. To be perfectly honest Pigeon, I really don't think I want any part of flying missions for the CIA, the Army, the Pentagon, the President, or any other government agency." Cajun was resolute in his answer.

"All those things will be provided if and when your team provides us with a complete Mission Brief plus a list of required equipment and personnel." Pigeon replied with the utmost positive assurance.

Cajun wants to deflect any further discussion of a mission so he asks, "Why don't we go down to my local watering hole to talk it over?" Next thing you know, they walk into the pub and Cajun slings a 12pack of Budweiser onto the bar.

He says to the bartender, "Godfrey, my friend, would you please ice down my brew?" Cajun hands him a fifty-dollar bill. "Do you still have any cold ones from my last visit to your fine establishment?"

Godfrey replies while sliding two Buds toward Cajun, "Are you kidding, I couldn't pay anybody in England to drink this stuff."

"Alright, alright, no need getting personal about it. What is this, an anti-American bar?"

"No Yank, it is just a pro-England bar who takes great pride in a couple thousand years of brewing beer."

Ryan adds in his two cents. "I can't believe you still drink Bud while living in England."

"Hey, everybody has their standards. I grew up on Bud and don't see any reason to change now." Cajun defends his choice of Bud.

Cajun and Ryan find a small table next to the shuffle board table. Finally, after three more Buds plus two games of shuffleboard, the two men settle down to talk some business. "Pigeon, I can't see myself getting involved with your mission. It is just too big a job for me at this stage of my life. I am honored that you guys would even consider me and my men. However, since you made the trip all the way to visit me, why don't we head back to my place for some gumbo?"

Ryan's eyes light up. "Wow, Cajun gumbo? I would love some gumbo! I don't suppose you have some pecan pie lying around do you?"

Cajun gets up and starts walking toward the front door and says, "Well, let's get out of here. Once we get to my place I'll look around to see what we can find."

As soon as the two men enter Cajun's loft, Ryan says, "Would you look at this place. Here we are in southern England and it feels like we are back in Louisiana. May I ask where you got this alligator hanging on your wall?"

Cajun grabs a couple more Buds. He hands one to Ryan. "Never you mind where I got my gator. Just take a load off, Pigeon." Cajun picks up the remote control for his fancy music system. He punches a couple of buttons finally finding the correct one. Immediately music plays on the kitchen speakers.

Ryan listens for a couple minutes then says, "I can't believe my ears, is that Dr. John playing Such a Night?"

"Yea, I bet the last time you heard Dr. John was back in our days at L.S.U." Cajun replies while strutting an ole dance move.

Cajun goes about his business in the kitchen heating up his gumbo cooked the night before. He prepares a nice salad, and brings out half of a pecan pie. Everything is placed on his dining room table made of cypress from the swamps in southern Louisiana. "Alright Pigeon, here you are buddy. You know gumbo is always better after sitting in the refrigerator for one night."

Ryan came over in a hurry to sit down. "I must admit I had forgotten just how good gumbo smells." The two old friends sit down then proceed to devour the gumbo. They drink a few more Buds while recounting old stories of trouble they had survived.

"Hey Ryan, do you remember that black waiter who worked in Pat O'Brian's down in New Orleans? Aye man, he was the best. To this day I have never seen anyone play percussion on the bottom of a silver tray like he did."

Cajun pondered, "How he carried all those drinks on that tray filled with loose change, and played percussion at the same time will always be a mystery to me. I bet he could lift a truck with his right arm." I always wondered just how much money he made a night. Every time I was in there singing L.S.U fight songs, drinking hurricanes, I bet I put five dollars on his tray."

Pigeon says, "Well if we are going to bring up old stories about New Orleans, I must bring up the time we accidentally went in that real French restaurant. What was the name of that high-brow place? I can't remember the name to save my life, but I do remember how pissed off you made our waiter."

Cajun defends his honor, "It wasn't me who stiffed the waiter."

"Well, it wasn't my fault he didn't know how to speak English," replied Pigeon. "And besides, we were so young and poor we didn't even know how to tip."

"Hey good buddy, it's time for coffee, pie, and ice cream," Cajun says while carrying the pecan pie to the dining room table..

Cajun turns around and heads back into the kitchen to make a big pot of Community Coffee. After the coffee is ready, he pulls some Blue Bell ice cream from the freezer. "I made that pie last night so grab a big piece. Make sure you dump a big pile of ice cream on top." He sits a fresh cup of coffee in front of Ryan along with an empty plate.

Ryan replies while he is cutting the pie for his plate, "Ethan, do you mean to tell me that you have Blue Bell ice cream flown all the way to England from Louisiana?"

"Pigeon, a piece of pecan pie is just not the same without Blue Bell ice cream. My brother Mike packs it in dry ice then ships it to me from Houston, Texas."

Ryan takes a bite of pie with ice cream, sips his coffee, and says, "By golly, Cajun, you're right, it is better with Blue Bell ice cream."

Cajun grins widely and remarks, "As my Granddaddy used to say, good coffee with pecan pie and ice cream will make a rabbit hug a hound."

After dinner, right in the middle of their small talk, Cajun looks Ryan straight in the eyes. "Ryan, I don't think I am the man for this mission. Perhaps someday if you guys have a smaller project you would like me and my guys to carry out for you, come by for dinner again so I can consider it. But this mission you have in mind is a full on back in the Army mission."

"Cajun, there is another reason I thought you might be willing to take on this mission. I have it on good advice that Savannah is in Ethiopia," he said, knowing he has just played his trump card.

Cajun sits up in his chair. "Savannah, why would she be in Africa? I thought she was happily married living in Georgia."

"Well, my wife talked to her parents who were on a trip to Branson with Savannah's parents. The part that disturbed me was that she was working as a nurse with Nurses without Borders in Gode, Ethiopia.

They have not heard from her in a couple months. Gode is kind of a scary place. Just as often as not the Somali Islamic fighters will raid the town." Pigeon further stokes Cajun's interest.

For several seconds there is silence in the room. Cajun just sits there at the dining room table staring off into oblivion. Ryan can see Cajun's mind working. "I tell you what, Cajun, here is my card with a phone number where I can be reached. If you change your mind, call me. I've had too many Buds and too much gumbo for one night." Ryan walks out the front door with Cajun still sitting at the dining room table.

Cajun eventually gets up to begin a late-night cleaning of his loft. He puts the food away, washes a few dishes, all the while thinking of Savannah. He turns off the lights, picks up Ryan's business card, crumples it up then throws it on his nightstand as he crawls into bed.

Cajun lies awake in the dark for hours, eventually sitting up on the side of the bed. He opens his nightstand drawer then takes out a picture of a young couple laughing happily. A warm feeling overcomes him as he runs his thumb over their faces. After several minutes studying the faces in the picture, he places the picture back in drawer. Cajun picks up his cell phone. He opens the crumpled card then dials the number. Ryan does not answer the phone. After the answering machine message has played, Cajun says four words. "I will do the job."

CHAPTER FOUR...
L.S.U MADNESS

1981 in Baton Rouge, Louisiana

November in Louisiana can be muggy and hot. Sometimes a rare cold front can come rushing through bringing thunderstorms with heavy rain, followed by crisp, cool weather. But as unpredictable as the weather is, there is one certainty on the minds of young and old in Louisiana in November. That is L.S.U. football. This is true of roommates Ethan Breaux and Ryan Clayborne who share a dorm room located next to the L.S.U. stadium.

They become roommates by chance, both registering late for the fall semester their freshman year. Ryan grew up in an affluent neighborhood in New Orleans, Ethan in a small southwestern Louisiana town. They connect right away to become the best of friends.

On this particular-sunny Saturday afternoon, they along with thousands of football fans, make their way to Tiger Stadium. Once inside, they meet with friends and fraternity brothers as the band begins playing Tiger Rag. Ryan, the party boy of the two yells across to Ethan. "I talked to Savannah this morning. We're meeting at Kershaw's in New Orleans tonight after the game." Ethan gave him a thumbs up. "She got you a date with her friend Marie!" he added laughing. Cajun grimaces, never having met Marie. She could be the Wicked Witch of the West for all he knows. Savannah is always trying to set him up with one of her classmates.

Savannah is a nursing student at Tulane in New Orleans. She and Ryan had met years ago through mutual friends, but had not started dating until the past year. Ethan does not know her very well. He thinks she is a fun, pretty girl who is very serious about her nursing degree. She and Ryan are known as a couple, although Ethan knows Ryan is also seeing several other girls on the L.S.U. campus.

When the game is over, Ethan and Ryan, along with several other carloads of friends, head for New Orleans. The plan is to meet later in the French Quarter at Kershaw's bar, known for its loud, wild, college crowd. Tonight is no exception. By the time Ethan and Ryan arrive to meet their dates, the party is going strong. The band is playing Stevie Ray Vaughn's song, "Don't Stop Rocking." It is difficult to move on the dance floor as it is packed to overflowing. Ryan finds Savannah and her friend who have been doing their best to save a table. The group finds several tables of good friends. They all crowd together so that everybody is shoulder to shoulder playing their air guitars.

The L.S.U. crowd is partying hard, celebrating their win over Ole Miss, one of their biggest rivals. This game had been one of the most exciting games in Tiger history with a field goal win with three seconds left on the clock. Ethan, Ryan, Savannah, and Marie join in the excitement, drinking and dancing as the walls of Kershaw's seem to vibrate with the loud music.

The party parties on for hours until sometime after one in the morning. Ethan and Savannah find themselves sitting at a table together. Through the din of noise, they manage to make small talk. Both have been drinking, but the buzz is beginning to wear off.

Marie is long gone. Her sorority sisters found her dancing on top of one of the tables drunker than a two-legged skunk. They promptly removed her from the bar, taking her back to the dorm.

Ryan, who never slowed down once drinking and dancing, has been M.I.A. for some time. The last time Ethan sees him he is dancing with two dark haired Cajun girls. He looks sloppy drunk. Ethan does not know if Savannah has seen him, but thinks she probably has by her sad, quiet demeanor.

Without thinking Ethan turns to her and says, "Would you like to go get some coffee?"

Savannah replies immediately with excitement, "I'd love to."

They walk through the French Quarter in the cool night air that is such a refreshing relief after the smoky, crowded bar. Ethan is not quite sure if he has done the right thing asking Savannah to leave the bar with him, but it feels comfortable walking beside her.

They walk all the way to the French Market. Ethan grabs them a table at Café Dumonde, known for its strong hickory coffee and sweet, powdered sugar beignets. After their order arrives, they take sips of the steaming coffee. Both of them together devour a plate of the sugary doughnuts. Savannah looks across the table at Cajun with her big green eyes and whispers, "Tell me about yourself, Ethan Breaux."

"Not much to tell really. However, there is one thing you should know about me." While he speaks softly to Savannah he leans across the table to gently dust the powdered sugar off the end of her nose.

Savannah inquires playfully, "And what is that, Ethan Breaux?"

"I just love blondes with green eyes. In fact, I am quite found of blondes with green eyes from Tulane University." They both laugh out loud. "By God, I believe we are ready for another plate of beignets" ,Ethan says while doing his best to get the attention of the waitress..

Ethan begins to talk like he has never talked before. Savannah is an avid listener, never taking her eyes off his face. He tells her about his childhood, growing up in a small town with a controlling father and how that had influenced him, making him a stronger, more selfreliant person. His father, a patriot, and a veteran, had instilled in him a love for his country that was so strong Ethan hoped to serve his country one day.

Ethan tells her about his tall, beautiful Mother. He talks about how her quiet, kind voice had always tried to calm him after the numerous quarrels with his Father. He smiles when he shares that he has dated many girls but has never really had a girlfriend. Ethan shares his dreams and disappointments with Savannah. He has never opened-up to anyone like this before.

He asks Savannah about her life. She tells him she is an only child growing up in New Orleans. Her mother was a nurse and a single parent. She had a sister who died as an infant. Her parents got a divorce shortly after her sister passed away. Her father had never really been a part of her life, going to work overseas after the divorce. She wanted to dedicate her life to nursing, specializing in neo-natal intensive care. She had never gotten over the death of her baby sister. Savannah wanted to make a difference in infant health care. She tells Ethan she is not sure why she is dating Ryan. She knew about his reputation long before she knew him.

A loud clap of thunder breaks their concentration on each other. It finally occurs to them it is starting to rain. They have been sitting in the same spot for hours talking about everything imaginable, when the faint glow of pink in the east makes them aware of the time. After a few more minutes the rain slows to a slight drizzle.

They put their jackets over their heads and walk out of the French Quarter across Canal Street. Ethan and Savannah catch the St. Charles trolley that is headed toward Tulane. Savannah shivers, as the mist blows in on them. Ethan puts his jacket over her then puts his arm around her shoulders. By the time they get to her dorm there is a sliver of gold in the purple sky where the sun is coming up.

They stand at the door of Savannah's dorm for a few minutes thanking each other for the wonderful evening. The young couple is having trouble saying "goodnight." As the sun's rays get brighter, they laugh then decide it is time to say "good morning." Cajun hesitates, not sure of what he should do next. After a few seconds Savannah stands on her tiptoes so that she can take Ethan's face in both of her hands. She kisses him softly on the lips several times, turns then walks through the front door of her dormitory.

Ethan stands in the very position where she left him in front of the door for another two minutes savoring her kiss. Finally, he departs her dorm. He crosses the street to wait for the trolley, oblivious to the cold. Ethan smiles then finds himself saying "Savannah, Savannah," over and over in his head.

On Tuesday, three nights later, Ryan comes busting into the dorm room around eleven in the evening. Ethan is lying in bed reading notes from his World History class. The door slams behind him. He is cursing as he throws his car keys across the room.

"What's up, man?" ask Ethan.

"I'll tell you what's up! Savannah just broke up with me. That is what is up! I just talked to her on the phone and she freaking broke up with me. I cannot believe it!" He sits down on the side of his bed, takes off his shoes then throws them against the wall.

Ethan again asks Ryan, "What happened?"

"Nothing happened. She said we did not have the same interest or goals in life. She said that we had grown apart. You know, all that bull crap women lay on us these days."

"That's tough, man.", Ethan sympathized.

Ryan continued belly-aching", "Yeah, it's tough." After a few seconds Ryan says, "But to hell with her. I am going out!" He gets up, puts his shoes back on, retrieves his car keys then storms out the door.

Ethan places his notes on the floor then turns his light out. He lies back on his pillow with his hands behind his head. The outside lights reflect on the ceiling from the street below. Cajun lies there for quite a while without moving. Then he closes his eyes. Ethan tries to feel some empathy for Ryan, but no matter what he thinks, a big grin spreads across his face.

"Savannah, Savannah, what have you done to me?"

Ethan nervously waits several days before calling Savannah. He tells himself that he was not involved in Savannah's decision or the phone call Ryan received. But, in his heart he felt that she had broken up with Ryan for him. After mulling it over he finally makes the call early on Friday. The first thing Savannah says to him is, "What took you so long?"

On Saturday Ethan makes an excuse to Ryan about a class project he is working on then drives to New Orleans. He arrives to find Savannah waiting for him on the steps of her dorm. The smile she gives him makes him feel she has been waiting for him all her life. Ethan never felt his heart leap as it did at that moment.

Crossing St. Charles Ave., they leave the Tulane campus then walk hand in hand to nearby Audubon Park. Most of the cloudy, chilly day is spent sitting under a huge live oak tree talking and laughing. Stories of their childhoods dominate the afternoon.

Savannah turns to Ethan and says, "Ethan I want you to tell me the most remarkable story that ever happened to you when you were a kid."

"Well, when you say remarkable story, do you mean remarkable to me or my parents?", ask Ethan.

Savannah smiles, "OK, you had better tell me a story your parents might tell if they were here."

"MMMMMmmmmm, it is really hard to pick just one story. But if I had to pick just one incident, I suppose I would tell of when I was under six years old. My Dad worked in an oil refinery in the Lake Charlese area, but his real goal was to be a farmer. So that he could be a farmer he bought a five-acre place in the country outside Westlake, Louisiana. There was a low side of the property, which dropped into the surrounding marshy bayou."

Savannah asked, "You lived next to a bayou?"

Ethan says most assuredly, "Oh yea, at the bottom of our property was a little creek. On the other side of the creek was nothing but a marshy bayou. Anyway, during a major storm that flooded the area, people were cut off due to the road from the back country being under water. There were several local men in the area with small fishing boats that would motor over to the low side of the flooded road to pick up stranded residents. Three or four people would step into one of the small boats, at which point the boat drivers would motor them a couple hundred yards to where the road reached higher ground."

"One day my Dad manned a shift utilizing his friend's bass fishing boat. I was in the boat with him motoring back and forth bringing load after load from one side to the other. All the sudden a very large poisonous Cotton Mouth Moccasin snake swam alongside the boat. He was tired of swimming and desperate to find solid ground. The next thing you know that big ass snake lifted his head and made a valiant attempt to climb into the boat."

Savannah asked in amazement, "Wait a minute, you're saying a snake that can swim wanted to hitch a ride in the boat?

"Yea, when the whole area floods, they have nowhere to climb up to rest. Just like anybody else, they get tired of swimming. My Dad grabbed one of the boat paddles and whacked that Moccasin snake upside the head. Everyone in the boat was amazed at what had just happened. Lo and behold one of the male passengers felt sorry for the snake, which at this point was floating dead in the water alongside the boat. He wanted to retrieve the dead snake, then haul it into the boat to show all the people waiting at the water's edge."

"My Dad said no way to bringing the snake into the boat, however he did agree the passenger could trap the snake against the outside of the boat with the paddle then drag it onto shore."

"Once we arrived at the shore's edge the snake was dragged up onto the warm pavement where everyone marveled at its large size. Everyone agreed that the big snake was one of the largest they had ever seen and must have come from the deep marsh."

"All of a sudden, the snake recovered from his whack on the head then started to come alive. People began to scatter, getting as much distance between them and the snake as possible. It just so happened I was the one who had carried a boat paddle on shore. I was six years old, but put a severe ass whooping on that snake. When I was done, he was dead for sure."

"All the people standing around stood back a few moments looking at me seemingly amazed at how vicious I was in killing the snake. My Dad came over to put his hand on my shoulder. He looked back at the crowd of people and said, "Ethan really hates snakes.""

"OK, that is my story. Tell me a story about Savannah when she was a little girl living in New Orleans."

Savannah says with amazement still in her voice, "How can I beat a story like that?"

"You don't have to beat it, just tell me a good story.", replied Ethan

"Ok, I am going to tell you the story of the first time I rode on the Steamboat Natchez on the Mississippi River."

Ethan asks, "That's the big paddle wheeler I've seen operating tours, right?"

"Yes, the S.S. Natchez has been operating up and down the Mississippi River for well over one hundred years. It is the one that has the silver bell made from two-hundred-fifty melted silver dollars", Savannah replied.

Ethan expanded his questioning, "So what did you do, ride up and down the old Mississippi?"

"I did much better than that. What happened was that my school mate's father brought about ten of us girls onto the riverboat for a birthday party for my best friend Pamela. We were all over that riverboat, having the greatest time. When it came time for the birthday cake and Pam blowing out the candles, I played the happy birthday song on the ship's calliope."

Ethan asks, "What on earth is a calliope?"

"A calliope is a musical instrument that produces sound by sending steam through the riverboat's large whistles. It is very loud. Pamela was elated with all the attention at her birthday party, but the highlight of the day was my playing happy birthday for her so loud that it could be heard for a couple miles in every direction" Savannah explained with obvious pride.

"Wow Savannah, you have real talent. I'm not going to exchange any more stories with you because your stories will be better than mine." Ethan and Savannah laugh hysterically.

Eventually drops of cold rain bring them back to reality. Looking for shelter they jump on a trolley headed for Canal Street. Realizing they have not eaten Ethan and Savannah get off the trolley at the last stop then head down Decatur Street into the French Quarter. The rain is coming down in buckets.

Rain or no rain, they are able to run under the cover of the French Market until they reach the Central Grocery. The smell of garlic and olive oil dressing in the crowded hot deli, make their mouths water. As they get in line for a Muffaletta sandwich, Ethan wraps his arms around Savannah then kisses the top of her wet head.

Ethan suggests to Savannah that perhaps they should wait a month before dating. The delay would be out of respect for Ryan. But, Savannah shot that idea down. "Why should you feel you need to show respect to Ryan before going out with me? He never really showed me much respect. I date whoever I want. And I want to date you Ethan Breaux."

Within two weeks they are known as a couple. Ryan struts around, yelling at Ethan for a few days, accusing him of stealing his girl. But he knows it was over between him and Savannah long ago. After a couple months things get back to normal. Normal, for Ryan, is being seen around campus with two or three girls in his convertible.

These two kids who have grown up with little except for their convictions, Ethan, and Savannah work hard for what they achieve. They both earn scholarships for their educations and they both have solid, heartfelt goals. Mutual respect for each other's commitment to their dreams is paramount. Ethan knows he wants to be a pilot and serve his country. Savannah dreams of becoming an intensive care neonatal nurse.

Ethan and Savannah have overcome many negative circumstances to be where they are in life. Now, they face a new challenge. In their busy lives, working toward their goals, how will they be able to make time for each other and a life together?

Chapter Five...
Iraq Desert Storm

Baghdad, Iraq

Back in Iraq, at the beginning of the first Gulf War, Ethan Breaux was a Warrant Officer flying Cobra Attack helicopters. He loved the "Snake" as it was called back in the day. Some of the luckier guys that flew attack helicopters during that time were flying the newer, advanced AH-64 Apache Longbow Attack helicopters. Fully loaded with fuel and armament, it weighed in at 20,000 pounds. The Cobra on its best day in Iraq, weighed in at 10,000 pounds. As Cajun used to explain, it only had one engine, compared to the two engines on the AH-64 Apache Longbow. In addition, in the hot Iraqi desert the engine performance limited a fully loaded aircraft.

None of those things mattered to Cajun. He loved the Cobra because it was fast and sleek with a low profile making it harder for the enemy to see against the skyline. He had been flying it for several years. If he was finally going to be in combat, he wanted to fly something that he wore like a glove. Plus, he always bragged that the air conditioning on his Cobra was far colder than that on the Apache.

Often he would demonstrate to non-believers that when the air conditioning compressor was dialed into the high setting, small little ice chips would fly out of the vent only to land on his flight suit. He could do things in that machine that would boggle the mind of other aviators in his unit. In fact, his exploits were noticed by the top brass of the unit. The next thing he knew, he had been designated as a Unit Trainer. God he loved that Cobra.

The first Gulf War ended after the dictator Saddam Hussein signed the surrender treaty. All the troops and equipment were shipped back home. After the war Congress decided to retire many of the Cobras in favor of an increased budget to acquire more AH-64 Apache Longbow Attack helicopters. Cajun's unit was changed from the 194th Attack Aviation Battalion to the 1294th Heavy Lift Battalion. It was a unit with sixteen brand new D-model Chinook helicopters. They were stationed at Ft. Rucker, Alabama, the Army's Aviation Training Command.

The Chinook helicopter was everything the Cobra was not and vice versa. It weighed in at 50,000 pounds fully loaded. Fully loaded could mean anything from fuel plus troops, to fuel plus cargo, to fuel plus weapons. At first being transferred into a Chinook company seemed like being demoted to Cajun. However, he soon learned to respect the aircraft. All the pilots in the unit were amazed at what the aircraft was capable performing. They all trained hard. It was not long before Cajun was appointed right back into the role of Unit Trainer, training other pilots.

Cajun would tell stories of how freaked out the new pilots would get while performing sling load operations at night while wearing night vision goggles. Because the training was held in the hours of darkness, all flight crew members onboard would clear the areas visually on the way into congested landing zones.

The inexperienced pilots would always tighten up and start to "sweep" the cockpit with the cyclic flight control. The next thing everyone noticed was that the rear of the giant machine would be drifting five feet from side to side. Cajun would call out over the intercom, "Go

Around." The flying pilot would pull power into the collective causing the helicopter to climb into the night sky.

He also developed what most pilots felt was an unusual technique, or at least a new way of addressing an age-old problem while performing sling load operations. The problem was that pilots tended to line up on the load the normal twenty-five yards short, then come to a complete stop, hovering in position.

In an effort to be as precise as possible, they would creep in a little power then use that little increase in power to maneuver the cyclic forward to gain some forward flight toward the load. A little power, a little cyclic, then back with the cyclic to avoid too much forward speed repeated, again and again. The next thing one would notice was a start and stop of the aircraft. Because of the tenseness, the training flying pilot would again start to sweep the cockpit followed by the aircraft swaying from side to side.

Cajun introduced the "bombing run" technique. He taught the guys to come to a hover the normal twenty-five yards short of the load then line up the entire fuselage toward the load. It was best to take an early measure of any side loads introduced from winds coming from either side of the aircraft. As they pulled in power he would have them move forward at what many considered, too fast. But he explained that it was best to have a definite uninterrupted forward movement rather than a start and stop movement. Besides, even though the aircraft approached then flew over the load, it was at a controlled rate. As it turned out, the rate was not actually too fast, just faster than many had ever experienced.

Normal operations called for the load master to have his head down in the hole located in the floor at the center of the helicopter. He would be looking for the approaching load to appear under the belly of the aircraft. He would call out, "Twenty feet, ten feet, nine, eight, seven, six, five, four, three, two, one." As the Load Master called "one," the pilot flying was supposed to have slowed the aircraft to zero forward airspeed with the load directly under the Load Master and the hole in the floor.

The pilot was to have attained a steady hover over the load. At the moment the aircraft achieved zero forward airspeed directly over the load without sweeping the cockpit; Cajun equated it to being directly over a fictitious enemy target and dropping a bomb precisely on the target. Everybody developed a good mental picture of the technique then began executing much steadier sling load operations. They loved it.

The ground crew would then use a grounding rod to dissipate the static electricity, which was always generated by the massive dual rotors. Without dissipating the static electricity, a man could be completely knocked off his feet by accidentally coming-in-contact with the metal slings or the skin of the helicopter.

Once the slings holding the load were hooked onto the large hook under the belly of the aircraft, the pilot flying would slowly and steadily apply power to take the slack out of the slings. Once the slings were tight, more power was pulled into the collective to lift the aircraft into the dark night. Everyone agreed that Cajun was the man.

The 1294th Aviation Battalion was selected to be the first heavy lift aviation unit to learn and perform "special operations," sometimes referred to as "Black Ops."

First on the company's agenda was to paint all the aircraft black. Second on the agenda was to hook up with a unit of Special Forces. The unit was made up of crack troops from virtually all the combat forces. There were Navy Seals, Army Rangers, and Air Force Special Ops personal. These guys were bad, as in bad asses.

They would do things like dive out of aircraft at night and free fall till nine hundred feet AGL. Once they reached nine hundred feet above ground level, these bad asses would pop their shoots then glide into a precise landing zone. They would rappel into jungle terrain in any weather carrying all types of special equipment. Jumping into the ocean, then swimming under water for long distances to dry land was routine for them. Once on land they were the best trained fighting force in the world. Securing objectives with very few men was their specialty.

They were bad asses, but they needed bad ass, very skilled pilots to fly them into these environments then deliver them over their target on time. The 1294th Aviation battalion consisted of three companies, A, B, and C Companies. Cajun was assigned into what later became known as The Bad Boys of Company B.

His co-pilot was Jack Garrity originally from Oakland, California. Jack's call sign was Raider for the simple reason he would eat, drink, and sleep the Oakland Raiders. He was a Raider at heart. There simply was no other name that would do for Jack.

The skill of these flight crews was second to no other special ops aviation unit in the world. They trained in Night Hawk mode, Night Vision Goggle mode, Instrument mode, and most notably Nap of the Earth mode. Utilizing maps of the terrain they could navigate inches above the canopy, traverse many miles of terrain, then deliver their forces over a spot no wider than a chow hall.

During this time is when Cajun met and worked with the most skilled bad ass, black man of all time, Army Ranger Wyatt Madison. His call sign was POW, because every time he got anywhere near an enemy target he would blow it up, shoot it up, or otherwise dispose of it by other means. When training missions were assigned, Cajun would always make every effort to have Wyatt as part of his team. POW felt the same about the flying skills of Cajun and his crew. They became an inseparable team.

There came a time when the Company Commander called a meeting of all the flight crews to make an operational announcement. When everyone entered the room, standing up in the front of the room with the Commander were three men dressed in business suits. One of these men as it turned out was Ryan Clayborne, Cajun's old L.S.U college classmate. He had also been a rival suitor for his college sweetheart, Savannah. Cajun new that Ryan had been recruited into the CIA several years before. Could Ryan still be with the CIA? Was that what all this commotion was about?

The Commander began his briefing by saying, "Men, there is no question about it, you are the best equipped, best trained, and most dedicated special operations aviation unit in the world. You have become so proficient that you have garnered attention from the Pentagon. In fact, now the Congress of the United States is aware of your special talents. There are going to be times in the future when you will be called upon to secure then transport high value targets. To that end we have been tasked with an additional skill set. That skill will be the integration with CIA operatives with highly classified information on any number of possibilities. After we break up here this morning I will expect each company to meet with one of these gentlemen you see up here at the podium. Start your training immediately."

That was it. That began the integration of the Battalion with the CIA. At first everyone in the unit thought these men were too soft to be part of a down and dirty Special Ops company. Oh sure, they were smart guys. If you used your credit card anywhere in the world these guys knew how to track you down. They knew how to work around the world with informants. But one wondered if they were the type to get down and dirty.

The answer became apparent soon enough. The CIA were best at identifying high value human targets then devising a plan to capture and transport those targets. The dirty work was to be left up to the unit. Basically, their attitude was "Don't tread on our turf and we won't tread on yours." In any case, they were all special Americans with one goal to fulfill. The goal was to accomplish the mission at all cost then meet at the "O" Club to knock back some serious alcohol.

All the flight crew members were given extensive weapons training. They were taught how to identify, load, fire, clear malfunctions and assemble every handheld weapon in the forces. They even got extensive training on firing the Russian AK-47 and some Chinese assault weapons. It was not long before Cajun, Jack, and all the guys in back of the helicopter were some pretty bad asses in their own right. Crew members were authorized to carry their own weapons in case they were shot down.

Cajun carried two, Beretta 9mm in holsters on each side of his chest. He had a snub nosed 357 Revolver in a holster strapped to his ankle. His favorite was his pump twelve gauge, sawed off shotgun he had strapped to his seat in the aircraft. If and when he went down, Cajun would be loaded for Bear.

Chinook with sling load operations going on

Chapter Six...

Savannah, Savannah

Dallas, Texas

Cajun reaches a point in his Army career when he starts questioning his purpose in life. On one hand he is a leader in one of the most effective military aviation units ever conceived. On the other hand, the unit is in continuous training mode, which seems to have no end. And frankly, since there is no war to fight, he feels it is time to resign his commission from the Army. Once free to return to Louisiana, his plan is to find his lost love Savannah then try his hand at being a Commercial Pilot.

It only takes a few months for Ethan to be hired on with an airline operating out of Dallas, Texas. An airline pilot system is based on seniority. One may or may not be the best pilot on the face of the earth, but the starting position is as a co-pilot. First Officers, as they are called, first enroll in the company provided ground school to learn the systems on the aircraft they will be flying.

After passing the grade in the ground school, First Officer Breaux goes through a very extensive pilot training curriculum in a flight simulator. After the flight simulator phase, he spends several days flying the real aircraft during night training sessions. Finally, First Officer Ethan

Breaux starts "flying the line" in the right seat as second-in-command on a Boeing 737.

This new flying environment is a little strange to Ethan. Although he enjoys the training, he had always been the top pilot in his unit. He had been the Unit Trainer, which meant it was he who determined who made it through the training periods. Ethan thinks to himself, "Hey this is an airline flying Boeing 737s all over the country. They pretty much know what they are doing. I do not think they need an Army helicopter pilot telling them how things should be done. So, count your blessings at this opportunity and learn as much as you can from each of the Captains."

After a few months flying 737s all over the United States, Ethan decides he misses his olive-green helicopters. In addition, all he must do is to fly part-time for a few years with a National Guard unit then he will earn his twenty-year military retirement. He joins an Army Guard unit stationed at Ft. Polk Airfield in Louisiana. To meet his flying hour requirements for the unit, Ethan commutes to Ft. Polk from Dallas over the course of the next five years.

Ethan settles into civilian life as an airline pilot. It is time to locate Savannah.

When they separated the first time, Savannah worked as a Registered Nurse for a couple of years. Eventually she went back to school for two additional years. She earned her Master Degree to become an intensive care neonatal nurse.

Finally, Savannah answers one of the many letters Cajun has written her at her parent's house in New Orleans. He opens the letter to read her message to him.

"Dear Ethan, I am sorry I have not written you earlier. I must admit I have been very unhappy with you for being gone so long in Iraq. It upset me so much worrying about whether you might get seriously hurt or worse. It seems you have really and truly separated yourself from the Army and settled down in a civilian job. I really never thought I would see the day when you left the Army, but there you are flying jets out of Dallas."

"Anyway, the reason I am writing you now is that, number one, I must admit I have missed you quite a bit. There has never been anyone who could take your place. The second reason I picked this time to write you is that I have just been offered a very good job in Dallas. When I move there in about two weeks, I will give you a call once I get settled in my new apartment. Perhaps we could have dinner some evening when you are in town. Yours truly, Savannah."

Cajun could not believe his eyes. His heart turns flips. He was beginning to think she had found someone else and gotten married. But no, she had not gotten married. She still had a soft spot in her heart for him.

For the next couple of weeks Cajun cannot concentrate as well as normal. As he flies from airport to airport, thoughts of his reunion with Savannah occupy his mind. In fact, on two occasions he must apologize to the Captain for missing items on a checklist. Cajun is becoming a nervous wreck.

A full month goes by with no word from Savannah. He is beginning to wonder if she has changed her mind on giving him a call. He knows Savannah better than anyone. If she thinks about how angry she was at him originally, she could just as easily change her mind again. That lady is strong headed and Cajun knows it.

After six weeks from the moment, she had written him, Ethan is home moping around eating a TV dinner when his phone rings. Hopefully it is not the airline asking him to come in to take an unexpected trip. Maybe it is his mother Grace wondering when he would be able to find the time to visit her in Louisiana. "Hello, this is Ethan speaking."

"Hi Ethan Breaux, this is Savannah." When talking with him she always referred to him as Ethan, Mostly she just called him Ethan Breau. Cajun was the name all his military buddies called him. It was his "Call Sign."

Ethan whined, "Savannah, I thought you were going to call me when you got to Dallas."

"I told you I was moving to Dallas. Then I said I would call you after I got an apartment and got settled in. Well, I did move to Dallas, I did get an apartment then I got settled in. Now I am calling you for the dinner date", Savannah explained emphatically.

"Savannah, you always did know how to spark my interest then keep me waiting. I am just glad to finally hear from you. Once I received your letter all I have thought about is seeing you again."

Savannah asks, "Well you need not wait another day, where are you taking me to dinner?"

Ethan thought quickly about his half-eaten TV dinner but immediately decided to pitch it in favor of eating out with Savannah. "Tell me where you are and I will drive over to pick you up. Have you ever eaten at Nate's Cajun Seafood Restaurant?"

Savannah responds immediately, "I didn't mean dinner tonight, silly boy, it's already seven o'clock. I meant dinner perhaps this weekend? Will you be in town?"

Ethan's heart fell back down to the floor but he did not want to let on to Savannah how excited he was to see her. "I knew that, young lady. I was just teasing you about tonight. And yes, I will be in town Saturday then fly out Sunday around noon. How about we get together Saturday evening?"

She replies, "That would be wonderful, Ethan Breaux. How should I dress for our dinner date? This Nate's Cajun Restaurant is not the kind back home where we throw peanut shells on the floor and crawfish tails in a garbage can lid is it?"

"Girl, you need to dress fine when you go out with me. After all I am a commercial jet airplane pilot now. I do not go out with just anybody. And you are going to love Nate's. Right in the middle of the restaurant row in Dallas with restaurant after restaurant made of concrete, you will see Nate's. But instead of concrete it is a wooden structure that looks like the real Louisiana places we used to go. In fact, I think there is even a little sag to the roof line."

Savannah laughs out loud and says, "You're telling me there is a sagging roof line Louisiana food restaurant in Dallas?"

"Yes, Darling, and when you taste the food you will realize we are back home."

She asks, "Do they have red beans and rice?"

Ethan proclaims with pride, "Do they have red beans and rice? Does a butterfly have wings? Of course, they have red beans and rice. They have crawfish, catfish, fried oysters, raw oysters, and Etouffee. You name it and they have it. When you taste the food there you will immediately know that the owner Nate is from Louisiana. And if you are really nice to me I will introduce him to you."

Savannah questions him, "You know Nate?"

Ethan says, "Do I know Nate? Baby, Nate, and I are like vanilla wafers on pudding. When L.S.U plays on TV, he expects me in the bar watching with him. Of course, I am not the only one from Louisiana that goes in there, but most of his patrons are from Dallas."

"Wow, I have to see this place. I expect you to introduce me to Nate" , says Savannah.

"Consider it done. I will pick you up around seven at your place. Does that sound alright to you?"

"I'll be waiting. Bye, bye" , says Savannah in her best flirty voice.

When Ethan hangs up he is elated. For some reason, when he speaks with Savannah, his heart sings.

Savannah hangs up the phone and sits down at the kitchen table. She thinks out loud, "My Lord, he has done it to me again. We have hardly talked in years and within minutes of hearing his voice, I feel we have only been apart a few days."

She knows she loves him. She always loved him from the first time they walked through the New Orleans French Quarter. Her job now is to not be too obvious; otherwise, she might turn him off. After all he thinks of himself as a new man. What was it he said? He does not go out with just anybody because he is a big-time commercial jet airline pilot. How will she ever keep his ego in check?

Ethan stops his car one block short of the entrance to Savannah's apartment building. It is only six fifty-five He does not want to be too early. At exactly seven in the evening Ethan drives up to the entrance of her building. He cannot believe his eyes when she walks out the door. Is it possible for a lady to become more beautiful? Her blonde hair cascades over her shoulders hiding the spaghetti straps to her black dress. She did not hold back on how she dressed. Savannah is even strutting down the steps to his truck in four-inch-high heels. Ethan says to himself, "Ok big boy, just take it easy and play it slow. Do not, and I repeat do not maul her because you are so excited to see her. Just give her a little peck on the cheek. For now, get out there and open the door for this Louisiana Queen."

As Ethan walks around his truck. he grabs the door handle to open the door for her. She walks straight up to him and gives him a little peak on the cheek. "Hello, Ethan Breaux, I am so excited to see you again. I see you are still driving pickup trucks."

"I am so happy to see you again too, Savannah. Step into my chariot. And yes, it is a pickup truck, but not an old noisy one like I had before," he says. He shuts the door then walks back around to hop back in the driver's seat. As soon as he gets back inside he hits the play button on his $1,500 CD stereo system. George Strait's song "Leaving Dallas" starts playing.

The song did not play for more than ten seconds when Ethan took the time to look straight in Savannah's eyes. She was so beautiful he just could not get his arms around it. He decided to lean over to give her a little kiss on her cheek but misses and kisses her on her neck. BAM that was the match that lit the dynamite. The next thing they know is that they are in a long kiss and embrace before they even drive out of the driveway. Savannah finally withdraws from the embrace and straightens her dress and hair. "Ethan Breaux, I see you for one minute then the first thing you do is kiss me on the neck. You know I can't stand that."

She mockingly hits him on the arm and says, "Now take me to get some Louisiana seafood."

"Yes, Mama, let's go get some catfish. By God, I think I will get me a long neck Bud" Ethan says with a twinkle in his eye.

"Yea, well you might as well get us a six pack because I will need a couple beers, too", replies Savannah as she uses her hand to fan herself.

Off they drive in the general direction of the restaurant. Ethan is so happy to see Savannah and to have gotten a very serious kiss that he is not sure what he is doing. That woman affects him in unimaginable ways.

On the way to the restaurant Savannah starts to notice the interior of Ethan's truck. It is all leather. The air-conditioner is blowing nice cold air on her which helps to cool her down. "Wow Ethan, this is a really nice truck. What kind is it?"

Savannah dear, this is a souped-up King Cab Dodge Dakota with a big V-8 engine plus towing package," replied Ethan with obvious pride "Do you like it?"

"Like it? I love it. What do you need a towing package for?", she asks.

"Darling, I need that bigger radiator, battery, and suspension that comes with the towing package. It comes in handy when I tow my boat."

Savannah continues asking questions, "You have a boat? What kind of boat?"

"Well Savannah, you are not going to believe this but I got a real good deal on a small cabin cruiser" , he replies.

She continues, "You have a cabin cruiser that you tow with this truck?"

"Yes, I keep my boat on a trailer out on White Lake. Sometimes I tow it over to the Sabine River" he answers again.

Ethan knows that he needs to change the subject. The next simple question out of her mouth will be who he is taking skiing and boating. "Savannah, enough about my over-priced truck. Tell me about your nursing job. Where are you working? What is your position?"

Savannah knows that he has switched the subject on her, but plays along for the moment. "I was offered the head nurse position in the Neonatal Intensive Care Unit at the Children's Medical Center. It is located in North Dallas. They made me an offer I could not refuse."

Ethan compliments her, "That is impressive Savannah. You have really come a long way in the nursing field. You just might have to take my blood pressure after we eat all that Louisiana seafood."

As they drive by several restaurants on Restaurant Row, Savannah sees a wooden structure with a big parking lot. There are more cars in this parking lot than any of the other restaurants they pass. She says, "I didn't even have to see the sign out front. I already know this is Nate's

Seafood Restaurant. Look, the roofline does sag a little in the center. Do you think he really built it that way on purpose?"

Ethan replies, "Well, you will be able to ask the owner soon enough yourself because I'll get you introduced.

Ethan and Savannah are asked to have a drink in the large bar area while their table is being prepared. When they enter the bar area, a couple of seats open-up at the far end. It just so happens that L.S.U is playing the Florida Gators. They order a couple of long neck Buds.

After a few minutes Nate enters the area behind the bar. He looks up and sees his ole Louisiana buddy. "Ethan, I knew you would come down to help me watch L.S.U beat these Gators. Did you know that at least half the people in this bar want the Gators to beat L.S.U? I need backup down here."

"Nate, I promised I would introduce my beautiful date to you. She is originally from New Orleans, Louisiana. Savannah, this is Nate. Nate, this is Savannah."

"Hello Nate, I am so please to meet you. Ethan has told me so much about the great food you have here."

"I am very pleased to meet you Savannah. That is such a beautiful Southern name." Nate gently kisses the back of her hand.

"OOOooooyyyeee!" says Savannah. "Now I know you are from Louisiana, Nate."

"Nate, right now we are just waiting for our table. We have reservations in the dining room."

"Nonsense, you and Savannah stay with me here in the bar. I will get you all the good food you like and it is on the house. We must stick together to beat these Gators," Nate responds with a gleam in his eyes.

Ethan and Savannah look at each other questioning each other with their eyes. Savannah and Ethan wanted to be alone for the first time in a long time.. But, on the other hand, there was a great football game playing and Nate would surely show them a great time. Savannah says, "Well, Nate, that would be great. We would love to hang out here in the bar and watch the game." Ethan just looked on as Savannah takes over. After all, she was once one of the most fanatic L.S.U supporters not only in New Orleans, but the entire State of Louisiana.

Nate is pleased, at least in his mind, that Savannah is warming up to him and says, "that is wonderful. How about I start you two off with a shrimp cocktail appetizer?"

Savannah says, "Oh, that would be great." Ethan just watches at how she just wraps Nate around her fingers. Nate is just as mesmerized by her beauty and charm as anyone.

Nate returns from the kitchen area. "Here you are you two." He slides them two large shrimp cocktails with enormous shrimp sitting on the ice on the sides of the dishes. "Try my cocktail sauce. If you don't say it's the best you have ever had, I'll pay you ten dollars each."

Both Ethan and Savannah dig in, whacking one jumbo shrimp at a time, then wash them down with cold Budweiser. Ethan says, "Nate, we already need a couple more long neck Buds please."

Nate snaps his fingers and replies with a grin, "Two Buds coming right up."

Savannah chimes in, "Nate this is the best shrimp cocktail sauce I have ever tasted. Wow, it has opened up my sinus."

Just then L.S.U, backed up against their goal line, throws a pass down the sideline. Nate, Ethan, Savannah, and everyone in the bar yells in anticipation. The fast receiver runs under the ball then accelerates down the sideline for a touchdown. All the fans for L.S.U shout their approval while all the Gator fans moan at being down by a touchdown. Nate shouts, "You see what I mean, half the people in here are rooting for the Gators."

After Ethan and Savannah finished their shrimp cocktails, Nate ask, "What do you two want for dinner?"

Ethan replies, "I know what I want, but maybe Savannah wants to see a menu."

"Nonsense, all this beautiful lady has to do is to tell me what she wants the most. I will have it prepared special," Nate replies.

"Savannah says, "I know what I want. I want a seafood platter with one piece of catfish and some fried oysters. Could you please put just a small portion of red beans and rice on the side? I miss red beans and rice so much."

Nate sings out with his arms up in a touchdown pose, "Of course I could do that. It is coming right up. How about you Ethan? What can I get for you?"

Ethan says, "I want the same thing, but would you add a couple fried shrimp to mine?"

"Hang on you two it'll be out in a jiffy." Nate turns to walk into the kitchen to get their food prepared.

"Goodness gracious, Ethan, by the time we leave here I'll surely have gained ten pounds."

"Just keep in mind we can't come down here too often. We will both gain fifty pounds in a month. But for tonight, you are about to experience the most delicately fried catfish in his secret spices. They prepare the shrimp the same way. It is unbelievably good."

They both go back to watching the football game. Both he and Savannah are having a wonderful time. Here they are in Dallas, Texas, but it is almost like they are back in Baton Rouge, Louisiana dating for the first time.

After a while Nate returns with two big plates of food. He sets the plates down in from of Ethan and Savannah. "Here you go you two go ahead and dig in."

Savannah takes one bite of the catfish fillet and says, "MMMMM mmmmm, this is the best catfish I have ever had. It's fried, but the crust is so light and delicate."

Ethan goes straight for the fried oysters. "Savannah, you have never had oysters until you try one of these." He sticks one on the end of his fork and then feeds it to her.

She eats the oyster then gives him the look. It is the "I agree with you look."

They eat their dinners while continuing to watch the game with Nate. The game remains tied until the last two minutes. The Gators drive down the field pushing L.S.U further backwards. Finally, as they are about to score, one of the defensive players rushes through the line and puts a can of whoop ass on the quarterback. The ball drops out then hits the ground. Everyone can see what was happening. At the same exact moment, the ball drops out, the television announcer shouts "Fuuummmmmbbbble." One of the defensive linemen picks up the ball then starts his run toward the goal line. As this is taking place everyone is wondering if this three-hundred-pound lineman can even run all the way to the end zone, let alone outrun the Gators who are in hot pursuit.

Everyone in the bar rooting for L.S.U is shouting Run! Run! Run! Nate is jumping up and down behind the bar. Ethan is standing up pumping his arm in the air. Savannah is hanging onto Ethan's other arm jumping up and down.

The lineman is huffing and puffing as he sprints toward the end zone. Gators are catching him, but other L.S.U players are picking them off one by one with knock out blocks. As the lineman runs to within ten yards of the goal line, a Gator jumps on his back trying to bring him down. The big fella wobbles but does not fall. As he crosses the three-yard line he falls forward with the Gator on his back. The ball crosses the goal line by six inches. The referees raise their arms indicating a touchdown. The announcer on TV yells "Touchdown!" The clock reads zero time left. Everybody in the bar rooting for L.S.U jumps up and down shouting at the top of their lungs.

After the game ends the patrons in the bar settle down to talk about the game. Ethan and Savannah sit back down at the bar facing Nate. Nate says, "Do you see you brought the Louisiana mojo tonight. I haven't seen that good a game in this bar ever."

Both Ethan and Savannah feel the same way. They are trying to wind down a little but are still grinning from ear to ear.

Finally, Ethan and Savannah give Nate a big hug. They thank him profusely for such a wonderful evening. Savannah says, "I cannot remember the last time I had this much fun."

On the way back to Savannah's apartment, they cannot stop talking about how good the food is in Nate's restaurant Ethan says, "Savannah, remind me to take you back there again in about a month or so. You can see that if we were to go there a couple nights per week for dinner, our backsides would grow immensely."

Savannah raises her hand like a stop sign and says, "Oh, don't worry, I won't ask you to take me there too much. The food is too good. The next time we go out it has to be to a soup and salad restaurant."

"Yea, I have been to a couple of those in my neighborhood," Ethan replies. After a short drive, Ethan drops Savannah off at the front door to her apartment building.

"I would ask you up, Ethan Breaux, but I have to wake up in just a few hours. I need to be on duty at five in the morning."

"No problem Savannah, I have to fly out for a couple of days tomorrow morning. I will give you a call in a few days. Maybe we can get together for dinner again next Saturday night? Will you go out with me again, Savannah?"

She laughs and says, "Of course I will go out with you again, you silly boy." You had better call me in a few days. Don't make me go over to your place to pull you out by your ear." Ethan gives Savannah a long kiss then she gets out of the truck.

On the drive home to his house, Ethan feels as good as he ever has. Getting back with Savannah, watching L.S.U beat the Gators, and eating so much good food all in the same evening has him smiling from ear to ear. While he is reliving the evening the drive home takes just minutes.

The next day Ethan reports for work at noon. Within an hour he is "wheels up" flying out to the west coast. It is going to be a four-day trip so he will not be back in town until Thursday.

During the trip out to the west coast Ethan is flying with a Captain named Michael he has flown with several times. Mike is originally from Houston, Texas so they hit it off a little more than other Captains he has met. Once they level off at thirty-nine thousand feet, Mike notices that Ethan seems to be in an obviously wonderful mood. "First Officer Breaux, what are you smiling about? Did you win the lottery?"

Ethan says, "I did better than that Mike. Last night I had the best evening."

Mike asks, "Well, what are you going to do, keep it a secret? Tell me about it. You know I live vicariously through you."

"A very wonderful thing happened as I had dinner with my old flame last night," Ethan says with obvious pride in his voice.

"What is her name? Who is she? I do not remember your ever mentioning her before" ,Mike continues to probe.

"Her name is Savannah. She and I were sweethearts back in college. We were inseparable until I finally joined the Army to go into the aviation program. She did some extra schooling to become a very well qualified nurse."

Mike continues with his questioning, "What happened to her?"

"Well, when I went into the Army then finished flight training, I spent a couple years stationed at Ft. Rucker, Alabama, doing some very serious flying. We tried to stay together but I was gone all the time. Then when I was shipped off to Iraq, she went ballistic. We tried to keep it together, but finally quit writing each other" ,Ethan replies with regret in his tone.

"Damn, Ethan, that is pretty serious stuff. How did you get back together?"

"As you know, after several years of flying helicopters in the Army, I decided to get out. I thought that I should become an airline pilot then try to find her again. The thought occurred to me that maybe I could patch things up. After writing her many letters she finally wrote back to me. She had an opportunity to move up in her career by taking a supervisory role in the Neonatal Intensive Care Unit at the Children's Medical Center."

Mike, seemingly more curious by the minute ask "So you took her out to dinner last night?"

Ethan beamed, "Ah man, you will not believe how much fun we had last night."

"So, you guys really got back together?" ,Mike asked.

"No, it wasn't like that. We went to a great Louisiana restaurant. I know the owner so we ended up hanging out at the bar with him while he fed us the best food we have ever had" ,Ethan explained.

While checking the airplane's instruments and dialing in a new navigation aid frequency, Mike continued his desperate attempt to know the outcome, "Ok you had some great food, then what happened? L.S.U played the Florida Gators last night? You mean to tell me you ate good food in a bar then watched a football game?"

Ethan protested vigorously at Mike's characterization of the evening, "Football game? This was not a football game! This was L.S.U playing the Florida Gators on Saturday night nationwide TV. You should have seen the game. L.S.U won the game on a fumble return by a three-hundred-pound lineman. He carried a defender on his back then fell over the goal line. The place went wild."

Mike continued his cross examination, "All right, what happened after the game? Did you two have a late nightcap?"

"No, in fact, I dropped her off by the front door to her apartment because she had to be at work real early this morning," Ethan added with a tinge of regret in his demeanor.

"Let me see if I got this right?" You are back with your long-lost love and you watch a football game then drop her off at the front door of her apartment?"

Ethan hand waves Mike off and replies, "It's not like that. The truth is that we were once so close, now that we are back together, it is almost like we were never apart. Do you know what I mean?"

Michael looked at Ethan and smiled. "If you say so brother, if you say so."

Ethan flew the trip then called Savannah on Thursday. "Hello this is Savannah speaking."

"Savannah, this is Ethan. What have you been up to this week?"

"The only thing I have been up to is trying to get a handle on all the details in the unit I supervise" she replies sounding a little downtrodden.

Ethan answers with concern, "Is everything under control or do you have some problems to straighten out?"

"It's not that I have to get things under control, it is just that there are so many different personnel to deal with plus so many different tasks being carried out on a daily basis. I am just trying to bring myself up to speed with all the variables," replies Savannah.

Ethan asks, "Well, I am sure you will get things under control in another week or two. How about dinner Saturday night? Would that make you feel a little better?"

Savannah is quick to answer, "Absolutely, I'm ready for dinner Saturday night. Why don't we go somewhere nice and quiet this time?"

Ethan feels elated and relieved, "Ok, I'll make reservations at a nice steak house. Does that sound good to you?"

"Ethan Breaux, that sounds like a wonderful plan to me. Why don't you pick me up around seven?"

"I'll be at your front door at seven to pick you up. Bye, Bye." Ethan went about carrying out the details of his life, trying to speed up the time from day to day. Having a quiet dinner with Savannah is something to which he is looking forward.

Saturday night Ethan drove up to Savannah's front door at exactly seven in the evening. Just like the last time, she came walking out right on time. He walked around the truck to open the door for her. "Ethan Breaux, you are most definitely a Southern gentleman."

"Do you know why I really walk around to open the door for you?" It is because I do not want anyone seeing you standing out there looking so good. I am always afraid someone will try to steal you while I am sitting here fat, dumb, and happy" ,adds Ethan.

"Oh Ethan, you are the silliest man I know. Nobody is ever going to steal me" ,she says in a reassured manner.

"Well, maybe you're right. But I am going to walk around to open the door for you every time just to make sure. Now that you are in my truck, I am going to play some great music for you," Ethan says with pride. He touches the play button on his CD player. The Allman Brothers, one of the greatest Southern rock bands of all time, begin playing "Midnight Blues."

Savannah swoons, "I love this song."

"My Moma didn't raise a fool. I know you like the Allman Brothers and I know from the past you love this song in particular."

She says, "Turn it up so we can rock all the way to the restaurant."

Ethan turns the volume up so they can rock while driving to their steak dinner. After about a twenty-minute drive they arrive at the restaurant. Ethan pulls right up to the entrance so that the valet boys can park his truck.

Within a few minutes, Ethan and Savannah are seated at a booth in the rear of the restaurant. They are seated next to a small pond with colorful Japanese Koi fish swimming back and forth.

"Ethan, this place is beautiful. Thank you for bringing me to such a nice place. Would you look at these fish swimming around? They are so peaceful looking," she commented lovingly.

"Savannah you are welcome. How about a little wine to go with our steaks? Is Cabernet Sauvignon still one of your favorites?"

Savannah looks Ethan directly in the eyes, smiles and says, "Ethan, some things just never change."

After the wine is served, Ethan proposes a toast. "Here is to Savannah. I'm so glad she is back in my life."

Savannah raises her glass to clink it against Ethan's. "Here is to Ethan. I'm so glad he is back in my life as well."

Ethan and Savannah have a wonderful time drinking their wine and eating the best steaks in Dallas. They laugh hard about funny things that happened to them in their college years. In fact, at one point Ethan has Savannah laughing so hard, she must excuse herself to go to the lady's room. When she returns Savannah says, "Ok don't make me laugh anymore. Let us just talk about our life now. We have to let the old days go."

"You're right, Sweetheart. Let's just talk about today."

Ethan and Savannah take up where they left off several years before. After dating again for a few months, it does not take long for them to start living together again. Their professional schedules are quite different. She is up and off to work at five every morning, which means early to bed each night. Ethan flies in and out of town with a totally irregular schedule. Sometimes he is in town on the weekends. Then again he is gone on the weekends just as much.

To complicate their time together even more, Ethan must commute to Ft. Polk Airfield in Louisiana for the weekend once per month. He must fulfill his obligation to his Army National Guard unit. To maintain his position within the unit he must complete the same flying hour requirement as regular Army pilots. In fact, he must fly down during the week at least once per month to complete his night vision goggle iterations.

Life settles down for Savannah and Ethan, but it is obviously a busy life. They make the best of the time they can spend with each other. Boating on the weekend is something they do as often as possible. Since Ethan has free flying privileges with his airline, he and Savannah occasionally fly out for short weekend trips around the country.

Savannah is forever trying to get Ethan to take her back to New York City. Ethan, on the other hand, would rather go to somewhere quiet like Santa Fe. In fact, Ethan reminds her of the great restaurant where the waiters break off their dinner service to perform Broadway show tunes. "Remember Savannah, when our waiter Brett sang the song for us? There he was, well above six feet tall weighing in at least two hundred twenty-five pounds, and he began performing Fiddler on the Roof. If I had not seen it with my own eyes, I would not have believed it. If I were a rich man, da, da, da, da, da, da, da, da, da, da, daaaah. You ready to go back Savannah?"

Savannah replies, "No I don't want to go back to Santa Fe right now. How about we fly out to Lake Tahoe? I see the photos of the snow on the mountain peaks and it looks so beautiful."

"Well Darling, if that is where you want to go that's where we'll go," Ethan assures her.

The years start to add up for Ethan and Savannah. They have been back together for several years but they are still not married. Even though Ethan has made Captain, he is getting very bored with airline flying. Although being an Airline Pilot is a profession comes with loads of responsibility, there is just something missing.

For one thing, the friends he makes while flying in the airline industry are not as close as those he has made while flying combat missions. In addition, there is nothing like the adrenalin rush of flying into an enemy area with night vision goggles and firing off enough ordinances to level a city block. Probably the most important aspect of all is enemy return fire. There is never a time when Cajun appreciates life as much as when enemy rounds are flying all around him. That is the time Cajun feels most alive.

To compensate for his true feelings, Cajun begins to commute more and more to Ft. Polk Airfield. He flies more training missions at night to get his adrenalin fix. The next thing he hears is that Iraq is heating up again. The word going around is that the Army needs more trained experienced pilots to meet their needs in Iraq and Afghanistan.

Cajun must face the changes coming in his life. As much as he loves Savannah, he is not adapting well to civilian life. He misses the real action of flying helicopters in a combat zone. Even Cajun can see how his crazy thoughts are starting to weigh him down. On the one hand he can remain flying as an Airline Pilot and living with Savannah. On the other hand, he can be reinstated with his old Warrant Officer Commission right back into the U.S. Army. There would not be much question that within months of reenlisting in the Army he would be sent into combat in the Middle East. These private urges of Cajun are driving him nuts. How can he ever explain this dilemma to Savannah?

It did not take too many more weeks for things to start to come to a head. Savannah did not like him flying off to Ft. Polk Airfield to get in additional night vision goggle training. She knows that he is volunteering to fly those additional hours. Savannah has waited long enough for Ethan to grow up to be a man. She wants to be married and have a couple of children before her time clock runs out.

One night while lying in bed, Ethan is tossing and turning. Savannah can feel the tension in the air. "Ethan Breaux, why are you having such a tough time sleeping? Can I get you something?"

"I don't know why I am having such a tough time sleeping. It must be that my mind is thinking about all the bad weather around Atlanta. That is where I am scheduled to fly tomorrow" ,Ethan offers his explanation.

"Ethan Breaux, you expect me to believe that you are concerned about a little rain and a few thunderstorms? I happen to know for a fact that you love flying in heavy weather. In fact, if it were up to you, you would volunteer for all the bad weather flights."

Uh Oh, Ethan knows that Savannah has a bee in her bonnet. He wants to diffuse the conversation as soon as possible. "Maybe you are right. Maybe I had too much caffeine today."

Savannah is not buying what he is selling, "Too much caffeine my ass, something else is bothering you so let's hear it. What is your problem?"

Uh Oh, Ethan now knows it is time to fess up before she kicks him right out of bed. "Well, Dear, I am concerned about my job at the airline. Contract talks are not going very well. I am afraid that we will end up on strike. And regardless, whether we go on strike, the airline is not doing very well. I am fearful they will go the way of TWA or Pam Am."

She asks, "You mean to tell me, you are seriously worried you might lose your job as an Airline Pilot?"

"Well, it has happened before, Savannah. Things are not going well for airline carriers these days."

Savannah just lay there in silence pondering what Ethan has said. Is there any truth to what he is saying? Maybe the airline will fold or his union will go on strike.

The next morning Savannah leaves very early to go into work. Ethan leaves around ten in the morning for his drive to the airport. Around noon Captain Ethan Breaux is wheels up enroute to Atlanta for the first leg of his trip. The good thing about this trip is that he will be back home by tomorrow night.

When Ethan walks in the door, Savannah has the lights turned down low. She has made her favorite dinner of roast beef with mash potatoes. As Ethan walks in he asks, "Sweetpea, it looks like to me we won't be going out to dinner tonight."

Savannah says, "That's right, we will be eating at home tonight. I've made your favorite dish."

"I can already smell it and it smells so good. I think I will pour us a little drink. I bet you need one too" ,Ethan hums with anticipation.

Savannah agrees but suggest to make her drink perfect, "Yes please do, and tonight make sure you put in a twist of lime into my Goose."

Ethan is getting with Savannah's program now, "Of course, Baby, one slice of lime coming right up."

Ethan brings Savannah her drink in the kitchen while she puts the finishing touches on the mixed green salad she asks, "Ethan, will you help me carry all the food to the dining room table?"

"Ok, Sweetheart, you go sit down, I will carry all this good smelling food" Ethan replies immediately.

Savannah whines a little bit, "Thank you so much, Ethan, my feet are killing me."

Savannah and Ethan sit down to enjoy a wonderful dinner together. Ethan turns on his music center and plays a little smooth jazz. They talk and laugh about each other's trials and tribulations over the last forty-eight hours.

After dinner they make their way over to the couch to watch a little news before they go to bed. It is not long before the news focuses on the latest events taking place in Iraq. Civilian contractors have been killed and are being dragged through the dirty streets of Fallujah.

Savannah watches Ethan as he is transfixed by the news. Rage shows in his face. She can see the artery in his temple beating. She becomes very sad because she knows there is nothing she can do to change his nature. He wants to be back in Iraq with his buddies, dodging bullets and rocket propelled grenades.

As much as she loves Ethan Breaux, she knows it is time to let him go be what he wants to be the most in life, a combat helicopter pilot. Cajun resigns his airline job and joins the Army again.

It was inevitable that the U.S. Army would assign Cajun right back into his old unit. The 1294th Aviation Battalion remained stationed at Ft. Rucker, Alabama. Many of the old guys had retired out of the unit.

Chapter Seven...
Operation Iraqi Freedom

Baghdad, Iraq

Crew Chief Firing A Gatling Gun

It was inevitable that the U.S. Army would assign Cajun right back into his old unit. The 1294th Aviation Battalion remained stationed at Ft. Rucker, Alabama. Many of the old guys had retired out of the unit.

Amongst the pilot ranks are some new, wet behind the ear's aviators. However, Cajun is pleased to learn that a few of the old guard are also reenlisting. Before long he is accompanied by Jack, Jimmy, and Morley. Cotton and Booker, the two best crew chiefs in the Army, are there doing their jobs as always.

Time rolls on. The training continues until one day they receive Army orders to deploy to Iraq for the second time. It is the summer of 2002. When they are given orders to pack up to deploy, the initial few weeks of the war have already occurred.

Once in Iraq they are assigned space to operate from within the walls of the Green Zone. Almost immediately his Chinook unit is given missions considered Black Ops caliber. On the very first mission they are assigned, Cajun's crew escorted by an AH-64 Apache Longbow Attack helicopter, transports a General and one of the most prominent Shiite Clerics out of Baghdad all the way up to Kirkuk. It is a two-day trip with refueling enroute.

The sortie lands at specific coordinates out in the rocky terrain south of the city. They are met by Army Special forces that drive the Cleric and the General to a mosque to meet with other religious leaders. After staying the night, both the General plus the Cleric are flown back to the Green Zone in Baghdad. Cajun thinks to himself, "Geemanize, will all their missions be as docile as this one?"

As it turns out the first mission is only a glimpse into the future as to the serious nature of their assigned missions. The various flight crews certainly fly their share of ash and trash missions, but they also fly many hardcore missions.

In December 2003, deposed Iraqi President Saddam Hussein is captured in an operation in Al-Dawr, located south of Tikrit. Hussein is found hiding in a concrete hole inside a walled compound, several feet below ground. U.S. forces capture two men along with Hussein, identified as bodyguards. They have almost $1,000.000 in $100 bills and several weapons.

The number of Special Operation missions in direct support of the CIA, involving the movement of Saddam Hussein from place to place is tremendous. He is always moved in a Chinook, escorted by at least one Apache attack helicopter. Sure enough, Ryan Clayborne, representing the CIA, has been reassigned to Iraq. Pigeon is back onboard the old unit.

Following the killings of demonstrators in Fallujah, the population in Anbar is becoming more and more hostile towards U.S. forces. Roadside bombings on U.S. military patrols are taking place more frequently. The roads are just not safe anymore. The U.S. military decides that the safest mode of travel is with helicopters. However, an Army Chinook Helicopter is shot down with a rocket propelled grenade. Sixteen soldiers onboard are killed and another twenty-six are wounded. This is the deadliest attack on U.S. troops since the end of the invasion.

Al Anbar is the largest province in Iraq geographically, encompassing much of the country's western territory, it shares borders with Syria, Jordan, and Saudi Arabia. Al Anbar is overwhelmingly Sunni Muslim Arab

As the war in Iraq rages on, the violence becomes more wide spread. It is decided by the CIA to up the ante for Al Qaeda. Cajun's unit is being assigned more frequent special operations missions into the Anbar Province. No other unit is prepared to operate that far north, all the way to the Syrian border. They will fly out north into the desert. Some aircraft carry nothing but fuel bladders so the sortie can remain self-sufficient for days at a time. During the day the aircraft are covered up with camouflage nets. The crews rest. During the night, under the cover of darkness, is the time they intercept Al Qaeda fighters filtering across the Syrian border into Iraq. The fighting is violent. It all takes place away from the eyes of the world as no reporters are embedded with their unit.

One evening just after chow, the flight crews are advised to be at a mission brief at 1700 hours. Cajun is the Air Mission Commander. "Alright, listen up," Cajun addresses the men as he ducks his head under the camouflage netting. "I want each of you to settle down to get some sleep for a few hours. Thanks to Pigeon and his CIA boys, we have some real good intelligence on roughly one hundred ragheads that have crossed the border heading our way. They seem to be bedding down in groups of twenty to thirty men approximately three hundred yards from each other."

Cajun passes out a mission briefing card to each Pilot-in-Command who will be going on the mission. Each card has the crewmembers assigned to the aircraft. It also lists rally point coordinates, radio frequencies, as well as flight times to each check point.

Cajun begins his brief, "Now we know they are coming across already armed to the teeth with AKs and RPGs. Our orders are to surprise them at 0400 hours on the dot. We want to capture some of them then kill the rest. Do not think for a second that we are taking prisoners because we are not. We are going to capture then bring back two or three Al Qaeda fighters so Pigeon and his CIA guys can interrogate them. Our main mission is to get so nasty with them as to cause them to rethink entering the country in this area."

"Now the enemy is spread out around an old abandoned airfield which is located at 33 degrees 21 minutes north / 40 degrees 36 minutes east. From our position they are one hundred and ninety-kilometers northwest of our position. Once we level off at one hundred feet AGL we will proceed in a bounding over watch formation for all but the last five clicks. With five clicks remaining we will drop down to fifty feet AGL then fly nap-of-the earth in trail formation. GPS is our primary mode of navigation whereas terrain charts is our secondary."

"We will utilize six birds on this mission. Two birds identified as Chock One and Chock Two will inflict major pain to the rag heads. The two birds identified as Chock Three and Chock Four will sit down one click short of our objective as backup in case one of our birds is dealt a fatal hit. Crew Chiefs, make sure you have the demo charges in place in case we must scuttle one of our birds. We don't want to leave a shred of technology they can use after we pull out."

He continues his brief, "You back up crews will sit at full RPM and will be prepared to be on station in sixty seconds, finish the down bird's mission then pick up survivors. The last two fuel birds will remain fifty miles short of the objective with throttles at flat idle. Remain there in radio silence until we return. While you are sitting there, deploy your ground forces to secure your perimeter so no bad guys can sneak up on you in the darkness."

"The wind is forecast to be out of the east at 10 knots so we will arrive on the west side of the field. Coming in from the downwind side will lessen our noise signature. Our goal is to spread out with two ships, then attack at once. The first ship to take fire will call out contact. That will be the command for both ships to land to the ground then deploy our forces."

"Once the guys are out, lift up then move east into the wind about one hundred fifty feet on the east side of your hornets' nest. You crew chief man the two fifty caliber machine guns for cover fire for our men returning. As soon as they are all on board call Go, Go, Go and we will get out of there. In just a few minutes POW will brief the ground operation."

"On our egress we will depart directly east into the wind. On our way out, we will call Go Home, Go Home in the clear on our VHF radio. That is the command for the two standby ships to pull anchor then follow us out to our rally point."

Cajun points to his sketch of the air field objective. "The rally point is marked here on the chart. It is exactly two clicks east. Once we count all the chicks onboard, we will turn south toward the Forward Area Refueling Point. By the time we arrive at the FARP, the lead birds should be down close to BINGO fuel. If any bird reaches BINGO FUEL before that point, call BINGO over the VHF radio. The lead aircraft, will assess our position and remaining fuel. If we must set it down the Fuel Birds can come to us. At this time, I'm gonna turn it over to POW for the ground operation brief." At that point Cajun turns and backs away from center stage so that his ground leader can take over.

Wyatt Madison stands up in front of the group with that gleam in his eyes they have all seen many times before. Here they are in the middle of the desert in Iraq. POW is dressed tight with the brim of his hat low on his head. He just looks like a fighting machine. The mission will not take place for several more hours yet he already has his signature camouflage face paint on. They all wonder what exactly it is that he has painted on his face. What is it? A tiger? A crocodile? Whatever it is, it is Wyatt all the way

Wyatt begins his portion of the mission brief, "OK, on our bird are the Rangers. On the second bird are the Seals. Mr. Clayborne will be with Cajun. I want to limit our squads to ten men per bird. That will give us ten guns attacking from each flank. In each group of five we will have one 40mm grenade launcher. Should a bird go down and we must be picked up, there will be a limit of twenty-five of us on the backup bird. In that number will be one or two rag heads for the return trip. I want each of you to remember our training. We are lean clean fighting machines. Stay low, move fast, and use continuous fire. By the time we grab a couple rag heads then move back to the bird, you should be down to twenty percent ammo. Use that ammo, boys. Uncle Sam did not send us all this way to pop a couple caps in their asses, he sent us here to kill as many of these bastards we see." With that, Wyatt turns around to sit back down.

Cajun stands in front of the group again. "It's time to grab some shuteye. The crew rosters are posted here on the chart. Crew Chiefs begin your preflight on the birds at 0030 hours. Crews plan on engine starts at 0140 hours. You have ten minutes for power and system checks. Pilots, plan on forming up in clean air one hundred yards to the east with a departure time of 0200 hours. Planned flight time is two hours and twenty-five minutes plus ten minutes on station at flight idle. That flight time includes creep time to the objective and fuel to reach our fuelers. Our fuelers will top off our tanks when we reach them. Are there any questions?"

"Ok guys let's get a time hack @ 1720 in ten seconds." Cajun and the other guys hold their watches to the light. They each make small adjustments while the seconds tick away. Cajun counts down, "Five, four, three, two, one, hack. "Alright guys, let's put our plan into action." Cajun turns then walks out from under the camouflage netting in the direction of his aircraft.

Before missions Cajun always prepares himself the same way each time. Before he lies in his hammock dangling inside his aircraft, he will go ahead and pre-position all his flying charts, night vision goggle equipment, checklist, and mission brief sheets, on his cockpit seat. The next thing he does is to check each of his weapons to have them pre-positioned to strap onto his body within seconds of his awakening. His ammo clips are there ready to stuff into the deep pockets of his flight suit. With one more check he looks to see that his 12-gauge, sawed-off pump shotgun is still in position, strapped to the side of his cockpit chair. Everything is ready so it is time to lie in his hammock. It is time to let his mind drift off to sleep.

Just after midnight Cajun awakes to the Crew Chiefs moving around during their preflight of the aircraft. Raider has joined in just so that he can go behind them to make sure all the panel openings have been closed. He wants to see with his own eyes that the fasteners are tight.

Cajun walks out into the darkness to relieve himself. Out there in the darkness he looks back at all the activity taking place on each aircraft. The only light the men use is red lens reduced lighting flashlights. Their illumination signature is so limited that bad guys would have to be within five hundred yards to see them at all. God he is proud of the professionalism of these men.

Cajun's mind snaps back into the moment. The time is getting late. He wants to be in his cockpit seat, strapped in, ready to perform the checklist items that Raider will call off at exactly 0115 hours. On this morning he will have his copilot Jack fly the leg all the way to the objective. Then his plan is to take over the controls during the actual mission. In this way his eyes and mind will be more rested when the real shooting starts. This is a common procedure but it is more important for Cajun as he will be directing the mission all the way to its completion. He is the Air Mission Commander.

Raider is the last one to drop into his chair to lock in his shoulder harness. Once in position with his personal clipboard strapped to his knee, he looks at Cajun then says, "Standing by with the Before Start Checklist."

"OK Raider, let's complete the checklist."

"Shoulder Harness."

"Shoulder Harness On and Locked."

"Night Vision Goggles."

"Night Vision Goggles On and Operational."

"Anti-Torque Pedals."

"Anti-Torque Pedals Centered and Free."

"Cockpit Windows."

"Cockpit Windows Closed and Locked."

"Battery Switch."

"Battery Switch On."

On and on they perform the checklist items one after another, with the precision of a German watchmaker. Finally, they get to the last item in the Before Start Checklist.

Raider calls out, "Standing by with the ENGINE START CHECKLIST."

Cajun hold up his hand with a "stop sign" gesture, "Let's hold off for few more minutes, it's only 0138 hours."

Cajun calls over the intercom to the men in back, "Are you guys ready for engine start?"

One at a time both men reply. "Station one is ready, Sir." "Station two is ready, Sir, with the fire extinguisher in place."

Cajun waits for another forty-five seconds. At 0139 and fifty seconds he calls out, "Engine start in ten seconds, five, four, three, two, one, starting engine one." And so, the mission begins.

Raider and Cajun continue through the checklist item for item, making sure that the engine start is done by the book. After the Before Takeoff Checklist is completed, Cajun slowly pulls pitch into the blades, which lifts the helicopter smoothly into the air. They continue with their systems check. Finally Cajun pulls in enough power to where they are hovering out of ground effect at a fifty-foot hover. Raider speaks over the intercom, "Ok Cajun, the predicted value for our Out of Ground Effect hover power, at this weight and temperature, is 32 pounds of torque. I am reading 31.5 pounds of torque. It looks like we have slightly stronger than average engines."

Cajun calls out over the intercom, "Ok Raider, let's move out slowly to the east to form up the gaggle." Slowly each aircraft forms up in position. Standard operational procedure is to maintain radio silence. As each aircraft hovers into position, they land their aircraft back on the ground at flight idle to save fuel. Then by Chock Order number, they each turn their rotating beacons off. At 0159 hours and fifty seconds per SOP, Cajun turns his rotating beacon back on. Each aircraft in sequence turns on their beacons as well, meaning liftoff in ten seconds. At exactly 0200 hours Cajun turns off his beacon then says to Raider, "Lift off, it's time to kill some ragheads."

In complete darkness, using night vision goggles aided by GPS navigation, the sortie moves to the North West to the coordinates where the fuel tanker aircraft land to the ground. They remain there at flat idle with ground troops guarding their perimeter.

The other four birds move toward the objective. When the pro fighting force arrives to within five clicks the entire flight of helicopters drops down to within a few feet of the ground, proceeding with Nap of the Earth tactical movement. As the airfield comes into view, the two backup birds land to the ground but remain at full throttle, ready to move forward if necessary.

Cajun and the second attack aircraft move in fast toward the airfield. Raider, who is at the controls, breaks left while Chock Two breaks right. Immediately they see movement of men on the ground. They start to take fire from one gunman. Raider calls out over the radio, "Contact, we are landing to the ground!" The tail ramp is already down so POW and his other nine men jump out of the aircraft in seconds. Cajun calls out over the intercom, "I have the flight controls." Raider releases the flight controls to Cajun.

As POW and his men exit the bird they turn in the direction of the tents on the left side. By this time more of the enemy has awakened and are running out of their makeshift tents.

Cajun pulls up on the collective flight control pulling power into his rotor blades. At this point they have burned off much of their fuel and lost the weight of the Rangers in back. Even though his Chinook is a massive machine, at this point he has lots of available power. Cajun calls out, "We're climbing up and sliding right. Clear us right."

The crew chief manning the 50-caliber machine gun on the right side, calls back immediately, "Clear up and right."

As briefed, Cajun moves the aircraft to the windward side of the action. He flies it to the ground about one hundred fifty feet from the firefight. "All right guys, stay at the ready to provide cover fire for our men."

Unfortunately for the bad guys they are no match for POW and his men. The Rangers have the element of surprise, Night Vision Goggles for the darkness, plus overwhelming fire power. In all the mayhem, the unrelenting rapid fire of Wyatt's men sounds like big firecrackers. In addition, approximately every three seconds they fire a 40mm grenade into the enemy positions. Bodies are flying left and right. POW moves right into the tent area. He and his guys grab two Al Qaeda fighters. Both are dazed. One of them is already wounded. He has taken two bullets, one through his arm and the other through his chest in the vicinity of his left shoulder.

Out of the darkness comes all ten of the Rangers plus two rag heads. One of the Rangers has been seriously wounded by AK-47 fire. He is being carried over the shoulder of one of his fellow Rangers. As they climb onboard, the crew chiefs continue firing into the night with the 50-Cals as other enemy fighters, which are located about three hundred yards away, are desperately trying to bring down one of the helicopters. They even manage to fire off two rocket propelled grenades. One explodes in the dirt about twenty yards short. The other rocket narrowly misses the fuselage.

The door gunner on the left side calls over the intercom, "All aboard, Sir."

Cajun calls out over the radio, "Go, Go, Go." He pulls in a big handful of power to lift off. They are getting the hell out of Dodge.

Just at that moment over the radio comes a call for help from the second attack bird. "This is Chock Two, we're hit! We are down!" the pilot shouts over the radio.

Just as Cajun lifts-up he can see where the fighting is taking place. Chock Two is on its side with the rotors flailing to a stop. Cajun shouts back over the radio, "Ok, Chock Three, come in to pick up these guys."

Chock Three replies immediately, "We're already off the ground. We will be on station in 30 seconds. Set the charges and get your men out."

As Chock Three moves into position to rescue the downed crewmen, Cajun maneuvers his bird to the rear of the fallen helicopter as well. He can see all the guys running and limping away from the bird in their direction. Two men are being carried over the shoulders of their Navy Seal buddies. Both door gunners spray continuous 50-Cal rounds in the direction of the enemy fighters.

POW jumps on the ground while the other soldiers are loading on Chock Three. He pops out five 40mm grenades in the direction of the Al Qaeda fighters. The return fire lessens substantially but is still incoming.

Several small arm rounds hit just above the cockpit window next to Cajun's head. It shatters the Plexiglas sending several shards at his head and neck area. Fortunately for Cajun all that hits him in the head area is defected by his helmet and face shield. However, some of the shards hit him hard in the neck area.

Cajun calls out to Raider, "You take the controls! I'm hit in the neck."

At the same time one of the crew chiefs calls out, "All aboard, Sir."

Raider calls out "Go Home, Go Home!" He pulls power into the flight controls. The aircraft lifts into the night. Raider heads east to the rally point. Chock Three also lifts off. They are formed up on Raider's tail in trail formation. As they fly away the demolition charges explode on the fallen aircraft. It creates a large fireball, which illuminates the whole sky for several seconds.

Within a few seconds the flight reaches the rally point. The flight is joined by Chock Four, which had been held back in reserve. They all turn south to meet up with the fuel aircraft. The fifty-mile trip gives them a little time to assess their casualties. One of the pilots has donned a headset in the back and says, "I'm glad you grabbed a couple ragheads, because our ground guys waded into a large opposing force. We got shot up bad and lost one of our men. Our other seriously injured man is our crew chief. He got banged around hard when the aircraft turned over on its side."

"Alright you guys just relax. Take it easy until we get back to the FARP in a few minutes."

Raider, who is flying the helicopter while Cajun pulls plastic out of his shoulder, comes up over the intercom. "Boss, we're heavier than expected. We have burned off too much fuel. We're about to go BINGO on our fuel."

"OK, I tell you what let's do. Fly straight ahead towards our FARP fuelers for another ten minutes then land to the ground. Go ahead and establish radio contact with out fuel birds, then give them our coordinates. In the meantime, they can mount up and be flying in our direction."

"OK, Boss, I'll get on it."

After they meet up with the fuel birds, the attack birds are refueled then they all fly back to their forward base of operations. The aircraft land to the ground then are immediately covered with camouflage netting. Medics attend to the wounded including the wounded Al Qaeda fighter. Cajun issues an order that they should take this time to have maintenance done. Everybody will stand down to rest before their flight back to Baghdad under the cover of darkness after 2000 hours. With any luck they will be back in the Green Zone eating hot chow by 2230 hours.

The next morning Cajun reports to headquarters to report the details of the successes and shortcomings of his mission. Ryan assisted by his other CIA buddies, take control of the two Al Qaeda bad guys. They start putting the screws to them to gain valuable information. Cajun's mission is complete.

Cajun flies in Iraq a few more months then reaches the end of his second tour commitment. He can easily stay in the Army, but he figures he has had enough and retires back to Louisiana.

CHAPTER EIGHT...
HELLO FRENCH RIVIERA

Lake Charles, Louisiana

A few weeks into retirement, turns into six months. Cajun takes it easy back in the neighborhood. He has an application in with several airlines but none have called back. In the meantime, he has been flying small charters in twin engine airplanes.

Since Savannah is no longer in his life, Cajun's old stopping grounds do not feel as much like home as he thought they might. Of course, it is wonderful that his mother is still alive and kicking, but even she has better things to do than sit around chewing the fat with him.

Heck, that woman plays more forty-two dominos than anyone he knows. A very easy way to get on her bad side is to plan something in the house on the day she plays forty-two with her friends. They bring over Gumbo or Shrimp Etouffee. As you might expect, someone always brings a big ole Southern dessert. His mother Grace does not mind Ethan hanging around while they play so that he can get in on the great food. She just wants him to do like he did when he was a small boy. What was it his Dad used to say about children? "Kids are to be seen not heard."

Ethan tries doing the ole honky-tonk tour around southern Louisiana like he did in his youth. In fact, some of the old dance halls are still hopping after all the years have passed. His favorite is the Bam Boo Club, which featured GG Shin and the Boogie Kings back in the old days. Lord help us all; they are still the main attraction. Ethan remembers back in the day when Fats Domino played at the Bam Boo. He performed his big hit "Blueberry Hill" and the place went wild.

But nothing is the same. He does not have it in him to become a womanizing drunk roaming from club to club. The music is too loud.

One night, Ethan sits in one of his favorite watering holes, called Prejeans, having a quiet beer. In walks a man that looks vaguely familiar. Can it possibly be who he thinks it is? The fellow sits at the bar a couple of seats down. Finally, he takes a long look in Ethan's direction. Ethan looks directly in the face of the man. "Well, kiss my go to hell, is that you, John?"

"It sure as hell is. What in the world are you doing back in Louisiana Ethan? It's good to see you."

"It is so good to finally run into someone I know from my old neighborhood John," Ethan reveals gleefully.

John says, "The last time I heard anything about you was that you were in Iraq flying helicopters. You all done with that?"

"Well, I was in Iraq, but I finally put in enough years to earn a retirement. Now I am kind of bumming around trying to find something useful to do" ,replies Ethan.

Ethan ask of John, "You are looking good. It looks like you have been keeping yourself in fairly good shape. "How about you, what are you up to these days?"

John replies, "I don't think you would believe me if I told you. I started off studying biology and ended up getting a PhD. I started a company, where we specialize in the cultivation of germs."

Ethan laughs and says, "Get out of here. You are lying to me. Let me see if I got this right. You are telling me you make money growing germs?"

"That's right, good buddy, I grow germs. I have done well at it too," John says clearly proud of himself.

Ethan inquires, "Well, I couldn't be happier for you. Good for you. Tell me, what kind of germs do you grow that would make you money?"

"In fact, there are many requirements for germs. One of the uses you would be most familiar with is germs for certain types of septic tanks for people who live out in the boondocks that are still not on the city sewer system. If you have a healthier, more robust bacterium, they consume more stuff in the tank" ,John replies.

Ethan says with respect, "John, here I thought I was something, but I don't hold a candle to you."

Both men share some laughs reminiscing about the old neighborhood. When they finally say their goodbyes, Ethan knows in his heart that it is time for him to leave Louisiana. If there is no more Savannah, there is no more reason to be hanging around.

After several months, a big break comes for Ethan Breaux. His good friend Jon, who had flown with him during his commercial airline days, calls from England. "Ethan Breaux, is that you young man? This is Jon Haden."

Ethan ask, "Is that really you, Jon?"

Jon shot back quickly, "Of course it's me. Who else would call you all the way from Bristol, England to offer you a job?"

Ethan ask inquisitively, "You are offering me a job? I have not seen you since you retired back in 1998. I thought you would be fishing everyday by now. What kind of job do you have for me, Jon?"

"Well, once I retired I moved over here to England so my wife could be closer to her family. I became bored with doing nothing, so I started an air charter business here just to stay active. One thing led to another, then one day a wealthy fellow walked in to ask if I would watch over his airplane when not in use" ,Jon replied.

Ethan inquires further with even more obvious interest, "What kind of airplane was it, Jon?"

"Well, that's the kicker to this story. It was a Boeing 737. The next thing you know he wants me to be his pilot, so I did that a couple years. That was almost six years ago. Since then, a few of his friends have placed their planes here with me. I have had to hire several pilots."

"Why are you calling me Jon? Frankly it sounds like you are doing extremely well?, Ethan ask directly.

"Ethan, the reason I am calling you is that I have cancer and won't be around much longer. In addition, there are several of these rich guys who want to lease out their helicopters to us. I know you have flown just about every helicopter ever made. I thought you might consider taking over this operation", Jon says hoping he has peaked Ethan's interest.

"Dang Jon, I am very sorry for your bout with cancer. It all sounds pretty good, but I don't have the kind of money you would need for me to buy into your business."

"Well Ethan, it's like this. First, although I have built the business up fairly well, I have a fair amount of debt as well. We are making money, do not get me wrong, it is just at my age and in my condition, I don't have the strength to do what is necessary to make it all work. All I really would want is for you to take over the business. There are many opportunities for expanding and making money. All I ask is that as you grow, you take care of my wife and family. Does that sound like something you would be interested in Ethan?"

"Well of course that is something I would be interested in doing. It is just that you have caught me with my pants down. I don't know exactly what to say" ,Ethan replies.

"I tell you what you do Ethan. Give me your address and I will send you a first-class ticket for you to fly over here. Come over to look at the operation. It will be good to see you again. If you don't like the business, the ticket will be round trip."

"Jon, give me a few seconds to check my calendar. Hells, bells there is nothing on my calendar but fishing appointments. Send me a ticket so I can see what you are up to over there in England" ,Ethan says with humor in his tone.

Two weeks later Ethan is sitting in Jon's office in Bristol, England. "I have to say that it is good to see you again. I don't know what kind of cancer you have, but you look good to me."

"Ah it's that prostate cancer. Sooner or later all men get it. If you live to be ninety years old you will probably get it too. However, if you are smart you will go down to get screened early. That way it won't sneak up on you and kill you like it is doing to me" ,Jon lamented.

Ethan says, "All this is new to me, Jon. You just tell me how I can fit in and help."

"Ethan, had I known I could have done this over here earlier in my life, I would never have flown all those years in the airline business. After all, what did I get out of it in the long run? The airline went out of business causing my retirement pension to all but disappear. Here, opportunities to make money seem to walk through the door every other month," Jon replies.

Jon gazes through the office windows at the aircraft ramp, "Look out there on the ramp and tell me what you see?"

Ethan looks at the flightline and ponders his answer, "I see a 737-200, a Lear jet, a Cessna Citation, and a Bell Huey helicopter."

"Each of those aircraft is owned by a wealthy businessman, but they don't travel all the time. The owners just want the aircraft maintained. When they need to go somewhere, they want a crew to fly them where they want to go. When they are ready to leave they want to have a crew fly them home. At the same time, they want me to find other clients to utilize the aircraft when they are not using them. That is why wealthy people are wealthy. Spreading the cost around is their primary goal" , Jon explains.

Ethan speaks up, "Dang Jon, that sounds simple enough. You need to find more people to spread out the operating cost of the aircraft."

"Well, that is it Ethan, as much as I would love to have the energy to do all these things, I just don't have it anymore. But a young man like you could do very well developing this business. I just hate to see the whole thing go to waste."

Ethan asks, "What is the story on that Bell Huey helicopter?"

"Funny you should ask Ethan; a fellow came in here to ask if we would maintain it. Fortunately, I have a mechanic with helicopter experience, so I agreed to maintain it. But nobody other than the owner knows how to fly it, let alone lease out flight time," Jon answers showing his honest disappointment.

Jon continues, "Ethan this is it in a nut shell. The business pays for the ramp space, which of course is leased along with this small building and maintenance hangar. So far most of the pilots work directly for the aircraft owners. I have four mechanics and a nice English lady working in the front office."

"The original agreements I have with the aircraft owners can be renegotiated if we present them with some options. I recommend that the business charge a certain amount per flying hour, regardless of the number of hours flown per month. That figure will include monies for everything from fuel and oil to cleaning services to maintenance hours."

"Once it has been determined the approximate time each owner will be utilizing his own aircraft, a model can be created which represents days it is available for additional utilization. We, the business, charge a percentage of the additional revenue created. The aircraft owner keeps the remaining revenues minus the hourly operating cost. As the utilization goes up the requirement for full time pilots exist. Once that happens, each aircraft owner's expense will go down as a result of shared flight crew expenses."

"Jon, I see what you mean in general terms of this being a substantial opportunity. The business is growing while the largest expense of the business is financed by someone else, namely the aircraft owner. Our cost is stable and known in advance. In addition, our cost go down with more utilization of each aircraft as we are covering cost plus making a profit on charges of hourly operating cost. For me, the most glaring opportunity is the control we will have over such a diverse variety in type and size of aircraft. And Jon, you have no idea what I can do in the way of helicopter utilization" ,Ethan speaks with enthusiasm.

"Well, I am thrilled you see the overall concept that I have envisioned", Jon replies.

Ethan makes a grand statement, "I tell you something else I see Jon, that you have never thought of in your conceptual planning. There is a niche for security related transportation. Sometimes it involves operating in a war zone like Blackwater in Iraq. When the higher ups in the government need to fly across country to meet at a mosque, it is a civilian contractor who flies them.

Another example is when a business leader needs to be protected as he or she moves from one country to the next. Transportation is needed on both the ground and in the air. Jon, that is what I and my buddies did for years in Iraq. Would you mind if I devoted a small percentage of the business resources toward creating such a service?"

"Ethan, as long as you are willing to sign a contractual agreement to take over as the CEO of this business and agree to faithfully pay my family in the years to come a fair percentage of your success, I would agree" ,Jon agrees.

Ethan states with reassuring posture and tone, "Jon, you have yourself a partner. I give you my word I will live up to my end of the bargain or die trying."

"I know you will, Ethan. Come on, let's go inform my wife. She will be so happy that I will not have to work here anymore."

And so it happened that Ethan finds himself at the crossroads to a successful life as an air charter CEO operating throughout Europe. It really is easy to find other interested parties who want to share in the utilization of jet aircraft. Within the first year Ethan triples the dollar revenue for the business, plus he positions the business to take on some security type of operations. He hires several of his old mates from his Special Operations unit in Iraq. Jack Garrity, Wyatt Madison, Booker, and Cotton are all there working for Cajun in England. Cajun jokes about the fact that he has finally made his way back to live in the South. It just happens to be in south England. Oh well!

Chapter Nine...
Downtown London

London, England

Ethan Breaux arrives at the front gate to the American Embassy in London, England. The guards examines him and his two rough looking passengers, Jake Garrity and Wyatt Madison. Everything seems to be in order so Cajun is waived through. He drives his black Hummer through the gate. The Hummer is almost too large to fit into the skinny little parking stall in the back of the building.

Wyatt speaks first. "Cajun, all that I ask is that in the course of our negotiations, if they change the parameters of what we have already planned, that you say that we will take their changes under advisement, but we will need time to recalculate the whole gig."

Jack added, "Yea, this mission is several times larger than anything we have done since our days in Iraq, so let's don't be too quick to change our plan or reduce our price. Don't make any snap, on the spot agreements to change things."

Cajun reassures his men, "Ok boys, we're all on the same sheet of music, let's roll on in and complete this deal."

The three men get out of the car carrying with them all the digital materials for the presentation. They stride in uniformed steps up to the building entrance. Again, the guards examine the identification documents of each man then allow him to enter. The building is the American Embassy in London not known as CIA Headquarters, but there to meet them is none other than Ryan Clayborne. Pigeon says, "Welcome gentlemen, it's good to see you again, and I use the term gentlemen loosely."

Cajun jibes back, "Thank the Lord, I was worried you might think of us as having become too refined. How is Snooky?"

"She is doing quite well, thank you. She told me that if you would come to visit us in Virginia, you could even bring these two with you" ,replies Ryan.

They exited the main entrance then entered an elevator, which dropped down what seemed like ten floors. Cajun says, "Pigeon, when are you going to get these elevators replaced with some American elevators? I think I could take the stairs and beat this old relic."

"I do agree and will pass your request on to management." Ryan turns to look Cajun, "Boy you sure are in a reflective mood today, aren't you?"

The elevator door opens into a room of desk, computers, monitors, and personnel scurrying from point to point doing their jobs. They are doing CIA work. The men leave all the activity behind them then enter a presentation room with theater type seating. The room has a large screen in the front, which lowers from the ceiling. As they walk in, there are two other CIA operatives. Each holds out his hand to greet Ethan, Jack, and Wyatt.

Cajun lays his fat briefcase on a table, opens it, then takes out a computer, which he plugs in and turns on. While it boots up he connects his computer to a very expensive, state-of-the-art, digital projector. While Cajun goes about his business of setting up for the presentation, all the men in the room sit in various places leaving a little distance between them and the other guys.

Cajun begins, "Gentlemen, this is going to be a lengthy briefing for one of the largest, some would argue, one of the most important missions of a privately funded special operations unit ever undertaken. We had better get right to business." With that statement Cajun begins going through the slides in his presentation. He has pictures of countries, equipment, aircraft, etc.

"We have been tasked with retrieving a crate containing a nuclear weapon built by North Korea, captured by pirates off Somalia being transported to Iran. Our understanding is that it is presently being guarded in a walled-in complex in Mogadishu. We could execute this rescue within a week of getting all our equipment and personnel needs met, then garnered in Ethiopia. Obviously we will need multiple false identifications for everyone involved. Make us into anything but Americans."

He goes on to say that he and his men would begin with a two-pronged entry into Ethiopia. The first entry with his ground forces would arrive at the Port of Djibouti on the Red Sea in the Gulf of Aden. As Cajun speaks he flashes a color photo of the Port of Djibouti on the screen.

The mission would require one Humvee and four, duce and a half, trucks all painted up with the Ethiopian National Defense Force (ENDF) paint scheme and flag. His men would travel in the Humvee and trucks in a westward direction out of Djibouti in the general direction of Addis Abeba. They are to avoid contact with all Somali forces around the town of Dire Dawa as much as possible, as they are the dominate force in that part of Ethiopia.

After passing through Gode they are to turn south westerly to coordinates four degrees seven minutes north / forty-three degrees, twenty minutes east. The position was clearly marked on Cajun's slide along with the coordinates. That position would place them on the border of Ethiopia and Somalia where the group would eventually rendezvous with Cajun in the helicopters. The additional trucks would carry fuel to be able to make the trip across country to the rally point. As they use all the fuel on a truck, it would be left off to the side of the road. Each abandoned truck would be destroyed so no one could examine it.

Cajun will fly his company Combo 737 directly into the City of Awasa, Ethiopia. The runway is long enough at 3,851 meters, yet only fifty feet wide. The aircraft would carry equipment in the back of the plane on pallets, yet there would be passenger seats in front. They would bring in all their weapons, equipment, and some of the personnel.

U.S. Special Forces would deliver a Cobra AH-1 Attack helicopter along with weapon stores and spare parts. The CIA would also deliver an unmarked, black Chinook helicopter complete with six fuel bladders. Three bladders would be carried inside, while three of the bladders would be slung underneath. After a couple days to prepare they would fly out to meet Wyatt on the border of Somalia at the rally point.

From there they would fly into Somalia to the town of Baidoa about one hundred sixty miles from Mogadishu. Cajun flashes a map of the area as well as the coordinates. Even though Baidoa is in Somalia, the Ethiopians control the town. The mission to recover the nuke will be staged then launched from there.

Cajun declares that they would need one more refueling with the help of the Ethiopian military. After that, they would be on their own as they enter the outskirts of Mogadishu to complete the mission. Cajun would fly the Cobra with his copilot Jimmy while Raider would pilot the Chinook with Morley, his copilot. Cajun and his team would have the exact coordinates plus satellite photos of the compound where the crate is being heavily guarded. He would escort Raider all the way.

Their plan is a simple direct night attack. They would bypass Mogadishu to fly out to sea a few miles then circle back to about two miles off shore where they would deploy two men with underwater equipment and weapons. Their objective is to come ashore on the ocean side of the Mogadishu Airport.

Once they are given the word that the battle to retrieve the crate has begun, they would take control of one of the refueling trucks. One man would drive the truck and help with the actual refueling of the Chinook while the other set up a defensive position with a fifty-caliber machine gun and a couple of shoulder fired grenades.

The plan would be to abandon then destroy the Cobra, all board the Chinook, then head out to sea. They would have fuel enough to fly out to sea for approximately two hundred and fifty miles to find then land on a U.S. Carrier. They would need frequencies and encryption equipment to contact the carrier to obtain their coordinates.

After dropping off their men, Cajun and Jack would circle back around to fly directly to the location of the crate. At that point Jack would deploy a squad of Special Forces on two sides of the compound. Once in position, Cajun would lead the attack with the Cobra. They would be flying and firing at night with night vision goggles. His job is to fire up the whole compound, destroying everything and everyone he could, yet avoiding the part of the compound that contains the nuke weapon. Cajun flashes up two pictures on the screen. One picture is a satellite photo while the other is a picture taken by their informant in the area.

After softening up the compound, his men would fight their way in to secure the weapon. Cajun would fly around the objective in the Cobra while Raider lands in the compound. The job then would be to get that big heavy crate aboard the Chinook and get the hell out of Dodge.

Cajun goes on to provide a list of the personnel they will need to carry out the mission.

They would need three dual qualified pilots in addition to Cajun and Raider. That would give them one extra pilot in case one of the other pilots is wounded or killed. He adds they would need two squads of seven men for a total of fifteen Special Forces fighters. They would need two nuclear weapons experts, two dual qualified mechanic crew chiefs, and two dual qualified medical/ communications personnel. Cajun adds they would obviously need portable equipment to lift that crate.

Cajun asks that the lights be brought up in the room. He says in a firm positive manner, "Gentlemen if you will provide this equipment at the appropriate times and places, plus pay for the personnel I have requested, we will pull this off for you. The cost for this operation is $20,000,000. Much of that money will go to expenses, however the balance will be divided with all my men. Are there any questions?"

One of the CIA operatives brought in by Ryan half way raises his hand directing attention in his direction. "Assuming our guys can preposition the assets you have requested, how quickly could you bring in your people to put this plan into action?"

Cajun answers, "Sir, we have already contacted all of the people we need to implement the plan. Obviously no details were given, but all have agreed to participate in the mission as soon as I give the word. We could be in Ethiopia in a week, but as you know it is going to take a couple weeks to get a cargo ship from the Persian Gulf, through the Gulf of Oman and the Arabian Sea to the Port of Djibouti on the Red Sea in the Gulf of Aden."

"Even if the Navy starts tomorrow and paints the trucks while at sea, it will take them a couple weeks. It will take my guys a couple weeks to drive the equipment from Djibouti to our rally point on the border of Somalia. Figure another week to mount our attack from Baidoa. We're talking about mission complete in approximately four to five weeks."

"Are there any further questions?"

Ryan looks at his fellow CIA operatives. As they make eye contact, everyone can see that the plan is a go. The United States must get that nuclear weapon away from the terrorist and into safe hands no matter what the cost. Ryan speaks up, "We have to make some telephone calls to get a final GO on the mission. I will contact you personally with the code word BENJI, which means the mission is a go. You will find half of your fee, ten million deposited in your Swiss account. If you hear the code words BENJI IS DEAD, then the mission is off."

With that, Ethan, Jack, and Wyatt all shake hands with Ryan and his operatives, grab up their materials then walk out of the room back to the Humvee. On their way out of the compound, the guards at the gate stand tall, salute, and say, "Good day, Sir."

Chapter Ten...
A Puppy Named Benjii

Bristol, England

Two days after the infamous meeting with Ryan and his CIA buddies in London, Cajun sits in his big functional office looking out his window. Out on the ramp his employees are busy servicing the various aircraft. His phone rings with that funny little English jingle. He lifts the receiver to his ear. "Yes, Mrs. Buckingham?"

Mrs. Buckingham says, "Mr. Breaux, there is a Mr. Clayborne on the line, shall I patch him through?"

Cajun hesitates for a few moments then asks that she patch the call through. He thinks to himself that this is going to be the moment of truth. If the answer is yes to the operation in Somalia, then his life will surely change forever. If the answer is no, then in two hours he will be having an egg salad sandwich for lunch, while flight planning for his next air charter within Europe.

Cajun ask, "Hello, Pigeon, what is the latest in Virginia?"

Ryan makes a wisecrack, "Well, I can tell you this much, Snooky is all over me about when you are coming over for dinner. She asked me this very morning if you somehow did not like her or perhaps you loved it so much in England that you were too good for us back in the States now. Well, is it true? Are you too good for us back in the States, Mr. Breaux?"

"You tell Snooky that I am definitely not too good for old friends. For sure I am not too good for her. In fact, tell her I have been afraid to show up for dinner without my Louisiana spices, that's all" ,Cajun retorts.

Their banter goes on for a few more minutes. It is just meaningless conversation really, until Ryan tells him about their new puppy. "You will not believe this new little puppy I was talked into buying for my kids. That is all I heard for two weeks, so we went down and picked out a little Basenji named Benjii. He pees on my shoes, bites my friends then runs from me. But you know the best part, Cajun, he does not bark. As it turns out his is the only breed of dog in the world that cannot bark."

Cajun jokes with Ryan, "How can you trust a dog that doesn't bark? What is he going to do when a burglar sneaks in your house, mime him into submission?"

Cajun says to Pigeon that he would love to swap more dog stories with him, but he must get back to his real job of flying airplanes and that he would come by for dinner the next time he is in the Washington area. As he hangs up the telephone, he sits back in his chair folding his hands behind his head. He realizes that after these next few moments of reflection, that he has a lot to do in preparation for the mission.

Cajun picks up the telephone to call Mrs. Buckingham to come into his office. He gives her a list of names with telephone numbers. "Mrs. Buckingham, would you please get in touch with each of these gentlemen. Tell them to fly here immediately because we are all going hunting."

Mrs. Buckingham looks at Mr. Breaux with a tinge of skepticism in her face. "Yes, Sir, I will do that as soon as I finish ordering the parts you asked me about earlier."

Cajun is concerned that she does not understand the urgency of the situation. "No, Mrs. Buckingham, I think that you should put this task at the top of your list." Mrs. Buckingham replies that she will get right on it, then returns to her office.

After Mrs. Buckingham leaves his office, Cajun picks up the telephone and touches the page button. Once he gets the page tone he holds the telephone to his mouth. "Jack Garrity and Wyatt Madison, would you come to the office at your earliest convenience?" As he slowly places the phone back in the cradle, Cajun can feel the wheels of the operation slowly begin to turn. He sits back down in his leather L.S.U chair to wait for his men.

After about five minutes Jack and Wyatt stroll through the door with smiles on their faces. They know when the boss pages them up to his office they are about to do something special. It could be as simple as flying a charter flight around Europe for some rich family to rescuing a drug sniffing Greek rich kid from a basement in Morocco. Jack was the senior of the two and asks Cajun, "What's up, Boss?"

Cajun leans forward in his desk and ask both men to take their seats in his other leather chairs. "Gentlemen, we have been given the Benjii code word. We need to start this moment preparing for the mission to Somalia." The smiles slowly disappear from the faces of both men as they know full well there is a serious and dangerous time ahead.

"I have already given Mrs. Buckingham the list of our boys to call. She will have them fly here immediately. Wyatt, I would like you to start your preparation for their arrival. It will take a few days for us to get our gear together and finalize our plans. I want you to get them the best accommodations at the Marriott International. Try to book an entire floor of their deluxe suites. Do not, and I repeat, do not give out any information on where we are going or what our mission will be. I do not want there to be the slightest chance any of the details will get out before we are airborne to Africa."

Wyatt answers in a military fashion and says, "Aye, Aye, Sir, I will get on it immediately."

"It is already three in the afternoon, after you take care of the men go home to get some rest. We will meet in the morning to start our preparations for the mission at 0800 hours having had." Wyatt just gives a half-hearted salute as he leaves to drive down to the Marriott. "Having had" is an old military way of saying that when you show up for work you will already have had breakfast.

Jack Garrity looks at Cajun in anticipation of his marching orders. Cajun says, "Jack, I want you to call in our part-time pilots. Check in with Charter Flights International to see if they can supply a couple more part-timers. I want you to personally check their flight records to make sure they are current and qualified on both the Lear Jet and the Grumman Gulfstream. Get us another helicopter pilot for the Bell 412 to fill in for a month or so. Pay them for at least two months no matter if they fly or not. Get started and meet us here in the morning to begin the finalization of our plans."

Cajun walks out of his office into the front office where Mrs. Buckingham is already at work contacting all the men on his list. He waits for her to finish the call she has going then hang up the phone. "Mrs. Buckingham, we will be preparing for a fairly substantial job requiring the use of the company Boeing 737. Jack, Wyatt, and I will be gone for about five or six weeks. Once we drop equipment at our destination I will have our spare crew fly it back here, so it will only be out of service for about two weeks from today. Please do not take any reservations or bookings requiring our 737 for the next couple weeks. Once the spare crew returns you may continue to book it, however keep in mind that there will be more crew rest required since Jack and I will be off the pilot schedule."

Mrs. Buckingham listens intently without taking notes then replies she will make allowances in the schedule. She never asks where they are going or what they will be doing.

Cajun returns to his office to begin the arduous task of placing his plan of attack for this mission in motion. The first thing he does is to put on some fresh Louisiana Community coffee. After all, he is going to put in some late hours this night. He might as well get the tools for staying alert assembled.

The next requirement is for him to get out the necessary aviation and oceanic charts for all the areas in which they will be operating. He will get the ones for the combat zones laminated. Cajun knows that when the charts are laminated it is easy to use felt marking pens to mark up their areas of entry and exit for each zone. When necessary old flight planned routes could easily be wiped clean and new routes drawn in a hurry.

"All right", Cajun says out loud, "This Air Mission Commander stuff is coming back to me in a hurry." Once all the important positions have been marked on the charts he writes down all the latitude and longitude coordinates. By morning he will have a complete list, with coordinates, typed out to be given later to each member of the team. Minutes turn into hours, then before long it is midnight. It is time for Cajun to call it a night so he can go home to get some sleep

When Cajun arrives home he reheats some Jambalaya he had prepared the night before. He pops the top on a Bud longneck then sits down to listen to some Wynton Marsalis trumpet. He cannot get Savannah out of his mind. Cajun thinks there should be something he can do while in Ethiopia to locate Savannah, just to make sure she is alright. In fact, Cajun is still a little in shock that she is not married, let alone the rumor she is in Ethiopia.

Cajun thinks out loud, "Hey, Ethan, who do you think you are kidding? If Savannah wanted to contact you, she would have already. Whether or not she is working in Africa is none of your business. She is a big girl and so far has not chosen to talk with you at all, therefore she is not interested." Cajun went to bed to get some sleep.

Bright and early the next morning Cajun walks through the office door. Mrs. Buckingham, Jack, and Wyatt are already in the office. He glances at his watch then back at his crew and says, "I tried to do the right thing to be here ten minutes early, but wow, look at all of you."

Mrs. Buckingham replies, "Never you mind, Mr. Breaux, I knew you had your hands full and would need me all day. I already told my husband that I may be home a little late tonight. He will drop by our corner fish & chips restaurant so he will have some dinner."

Wyatt adds, "Yea, Boss, I was so wired-up last night thinking of all I have to do today that I woke up at 0500 hours."

"Well, I do appreciate your dedication so let's get things done first things first. The first thing I need is some coffee and I recommend each of you do the same. Mrs. Buckingham, we are going to be meeting in my office much of the morning, so as soon as you have completed the call up of everyone on the list, please give us a status report" ,says Cajun.

Cajun continues, "Jack, I know you still have a good deal of contact and records checks to complete. Please spend another hour or so on that, then meet us in my office for an update. Wyatt, I know we already have many of the details of the ground mission completed however, there is work to be done. Remove the plans from the safe, review them then meet us in my office in about an hour."

As he turns toward his office Cajun says, "As for me, I will be working with Pigeon for clearances into our various zones and check the progress of the movement of equipment out of the Middle East toward the Gulf of Aden." He knows that there will have to be plenty diplomatic arm twisting to get the Humvee and the four trucks painted up in the Ethiopian National Defense Force (ENDF) paint scheme and flag.

Only the Lord knows what it will take for the Ethiopian military to give them cover and fuel once they make it to Baidoa, Somalia. In fact, Cajun figures he will have to fly to London later in the day, after his staff meeting, to get some of these details ironed out.

"Ah, to heck with it," Cajun says to himself as he picks up his cellphone to call Pigeon. Maybe it will be just as cost effective to have him flown to Bristol. At least the CIA has secure communication gear whereas he does not.

"Hello, this is Ryan Clayborne."

Cajun speaks trying to be as coy as he can. "Ryan, I need for you to fly over to meet me in London or maybe send one of your guys here to meet with me on that new airplane."

"I've already got you covered, Mr. Breaux, I am at the Heathrow Airport. I will be at your place in approximately four hours. Perhaps we could have one of those lovely Budweisers at your local pub after work," answers Ryan.

Even though Cajun is relieved that Pigeon is on his way he pulls his chain a little. "I don't know if I should waste a Bud on you. Perhaps you better count on the happy hour special." Cajun hangs up the phone then waits for his men to come in so they can begin their final phase of the mission planning.

Wyatt is the first to enter the office preceded by a polite knock at the door. Under his arms are several terrain charts along with his mission briefing cards, standard issue in their old Army unit. Cajun tells Wyatt, "Grab yourself some coffee or whatever you want out of the fridge. Jack will come along in a few minutes then we'll get started."

Wyatt does as he is asked. He walks over to the fridge and takes out a long neck Bud.

Cajun whoops and hollers. "Now there's a man who appreciates the finer things in life. Grab a Diet Coke for me will you, for now that will have to do." Just then Jack came into the office, preceded by a polite knock, as the door is already half open. "Hey Jack, grab yourself some coffee or something cool to drink and let's get started". Jack grabs a cold bottle of water out of the fridge then sits down in one of Cajun's leather L.S.U chairs.

Cajun begins, "OK I have some good news. Pigeon is on his way here now to interface with us directly. That will save all of us much needed time. Jack, before we get into the mission itself, give us an update on our pilot situation."

Jack speaks confidently, "The news is good. Fortunately, like us, things have been a little slow for the last couple months so there are several pilots that need more work. I have not reviewed their flight records yet, however, several of them are coming in to meet with me tomorrow. After meeting with them I will let you know if we have any serious coverage problems on our flight schedule."

"Good, I thought as much, I just wasn't sure. Just as an added note I have taken our 737 off schedule for two weeks and provided minimum staffing for another three to four weeks after that" ,Cajun adds.

Cajun holds up several color-coded bound documents. "In just a little bit we are going to be focusing on the minute details of our mission into Africa. Of course, we will also be in and out of a couple countries in the Middle East. I have these briefs that I would like each of you to review, which spell out in detail current relations between the United States government and each of these countries. In addition, there is some up-to-date information on relations between Ethiopia and Somalia, which is clearly the most important dynamic that will affect our operation."

"However, for the time being, I would just like to state the highlights contained within these documents so as to provide context for our mission details. For example, it is important to know that the United

States has a reasonable and cooperative relationship with Ethiopia, Oman, and Djibouti."

Cajun begins by discussing relations with Oman. "The United States has maintained relations with Oman since the early years of American Independence. Relations were improved in 1980 by the conclusion of two important agreements. One provided access to Omani military facilities by U.S. forces. The other agreement established a Joint Commission for Economic and Technical Cooperation, located in Muscat, to provide U.S. economic assistance to Oman. Cutting to the bottom line, we can fly our 737 in and land at the Seeb International Airport, drop off our men without much fanfare, get refueled then be on our way to Ethiopia."

"France provides significant amounts of aid and financial support to Djibouti so therefore maintains a good relationship. French troops remain stationed in Djibouti under agreements signed with the government. The United States of America has one thousand, five-hundred Army troops in Djibouti. It is the headquarters of the U.S. led Combined Joint Task Force Horn of Africa. The CJTF-HOA supports counter terrorism activities in the region. The bottom line is that we will have no problems unloading our trucks at the Port of Djibouti."

"In recent years there was a revolution in Ethiopia, which caused the downfall of the regime. After that U.S. / Ethiopian relations improved dramatically. Diplomatic relations were upgraded in 1992. Total U.S. Government assistance, including food aid, between 1991 and 2003, was $2.3 billion. In fiscal year 2008 the United States provided $455 million in assistance."

"Ethiopia is a partner of the United States in the Global War on Terrorism. Our development assistance to Ethiopia is focused on reducing famine and poverty. Military training funds are provided. In short, our friend Pigeon and his CIA boys will be able to easily secure at a minimum, placid cooperation between us and the Ethiopian National Defense Forces."

Cajun continues briefing his men. "The most important relationship between countries that affects us is the lack of a relationship between Ethiopia and Somalia. Our guys will use these hostilities to execute our mission. Reports in January 2002 indicated that around three hundred Ethiopian soldiers were deployed in Garowe. In addition, other Ethiopian troops reportedly moved into the neighboring region around Baidoa.

Somalia's interim government was then resisting advances to the last unoccupied city of Baidoa. So bottom line, we have Ethiopian military occupying territory in Somalia as close as one hundred sixty miles from our objective in Mogadishu. I ask you gentlemen, could I get you any closer?"

"Gentlemen, that ends the briefing on the United States relations with countries that affect our mission. There are more details contained within these documents, so review them as time permits." Cajun concludes that portion of the mission brief.

Cajun enhances his message, "OK guys, this mission is no different than any of the missions we carried out in Iraq. The only difference is that it will unfold on a much larger land mass grid than we are normally used to. Let us just execute the way we have done many times before then leave it up to Pigeon and Uncle Sam to take care of the logistics. If they get us what we need, where we need it, we will succeed. If they let us down anywhere along the way, we will fail."

Wyatt follows with, "You're right, Boss. Assuming Mr. Clayborne comes through for us, I will be ready with my men. In fact, if we get the help we need from the ENDF, we will move across Ethiopia fast and furiously. My concern is the security of the details of our presence in dealing with the Ethiopian military. If they know we are driving across

Ethiopia moving into Somalia, so will everybody else in the region. How do you intend to deal with that aspect, Boss?"

Cajun thinks for a while before answering. "You're right. That has been lingering in the back of my mind too. Obviously it will be up to Pigeon and his CIA Agency to take care of the secrecy of our mission, however, I will be on him like white on rice the entire time to make all that happen properly. I'll keep you posted on progress in that area."

"Let me just add this requirement for the three of us. We prepare our men without giving out the details or the mission brief papers until after we are wheels up in the 737. I do not want the slightest chance there could be a slip of the tongue with any of our guys. Gentlemen, all mission planning information will we left here at night locked up in the safe." Both men agree whole heartedly and nod in approval at Cajun's directive.

Cajun begins by saying the plan is subject to working out all the logistics with Ryan Clayborne and his compatriots. They will begin by flying from their base of operations in Bristol, England to Luxor, Egypt. After refueling, they will fly to Masqat, Oman landing at the Seeb International Airport. Wyatt and fourteen of his men will be dressed in tourist wardrobe. They will hire transport to the Port in Masqat.

Once at the port, they will hire a tourist vessel to take them out to sea approximately fifteen miles to meet then board the U.S. Navy transport ship heading to the Port at Djibouti. "Hardly anyone on the entire coast will be aware that one of our ships is that close offshore. From there the ship will continue in the Arabian Sea, past Yemen into the Gulf of Aden, then into the Red Sea."

"Wyatt, I would like you to have your ground operation mission complete with all details within forty-eight hours. There is no question in my mind that you can get that done because I know you have most of the plan complete already" ,Cajun encourages Wyatt.

"Once you and your caravan depart the Port of Djibouti on your trek across country to the border of Somalia, I recommend you head in a more westerly direction to stay as far away from the northern Somali border as you can. In particular, stay away from the towns of Dire Dawa and Harar."

Wyatt responds, "Roger, Boss, I will have a complete wrap up on the details within that time restraint and will report back when completed."

Cajun continues, "We will allow seven days for you to complete your drive across country to the rally point. With any luck you and your men will be able to complete that part of your mission in half that time, but we should allow for problems such as mechanical setbacks and even hostile fire on occasion."

"Jack and I will refuel at the Seeb International Airport then fly on to the City of Awasa, Ethiopia. After unloading all our men and cargo, the 737 will refuel then return to base in Bristol. We will be met by Pigeon then be given final clearance. If final clearance is given, Pigeon will turn over two helicopters along with spare parts, weapons, and ammo drums."

They would need one AH-1W Super Cobra Attack helicopter configured with a 20mm Gatling gun, a 40mm grenade launcher, and a pod of nineteen rockets on each wing.

It has two engines in case one engine is hit by enemy fire. With the extra gross weight allowance up to 14,750 pounds, it will be configured with one extra external fuel pod under each wing. They will need two ammo drums, one mounted on the aircraft and the other carried as cargo in the Chinook.

The other aircraft they would need would be a Model-D Chinook Heavy Lift Helicopter. It would need to be painted black or in camouflage like the Cobra. Cajun wanted the aircraft full of fuel, with three, three-hundred-gallon fuel bladders strapped down internally and three,

three-hundred-gallon fuel bladders slung under the belly. With the one thousand twenty-eight-gallon internal tank, they would take off with 18,382 pounds of fuel @ 6.5 pounds per gallon. With this amount of fuel, the Chinook will be able to make it all the way to Mogadishu.

The total distance will be three hundred and fifty-eight nautical miles. However, the sortie will have to land on the border at the rally point with the trucks to refuel the Cobra. Once they land on the outskirts of Baidoa, Somalia they will have to refuel the Cobra one more time from the Chinook's external bladder tanks. After that point the bladders will be abandoned.

The internal bladder fuel will be pumped into the Chinook's main tanks, giving it a range of another four hundred nautical miles. Those internal bladders will also be discarded. All they will need to steal is approximately five hundred gallons from the airport fuel trucks in Mogadishu. With that amount of fuel, they will be able to easily reach the aircraft carrier. Should they fail to top off the tanks, they will still be able to fly out about two hundred miles before running out of fuel. The Cobra will be destroyed in place then abandoned.

At the rally point outside Baidoa, the two remaining duce and a half trucks will be abandoned then turned over to the Ethiopian National Defense Forces. Now that the Chinook will have removed all the weight from the extra internal and external fuel bladders, they would now be able to load all their men, weapons, and equipment onboard then complete the mission.

Cajun concludes, "Well that's it for now, gentlemen. Pigeon will be here soon. I will begin to work out all the logistics with him to get all the things we need. As soon as I have made our case and made some progress I will call you back in here to review the information together. In the meantime, are there any questions I can answer for you to help you in your planning?"

Jack replies, "No questions for now. I still have much to do in getting all our pilots and their records in order to keep our operation running smoothly in our absence."

Wyatt replies, "No, Boss, I don't have any questions right now. I will just continue refining our plan for trekking across Ethiopia to the Somali border."

"Gentlemen, let us break for lunch, then you guys continue with your planning. I will be meeting with Pigeon this afternoon and will make sure we get everything we need" ,says Cajun.

With that Jack and Wyatt get up with their paperwork in tow plus each of them takes a couple of the color-coded binders that contain the briefs on the various countries in which they will be operating. Cajun remains in his L.S.U chair while spinning around to look out his office window at the flight line.

While observing maintenance operations on the flight line for a few minutes, Cajun decides to skip going out to lunch. He walks over to his office refrigerator. Mrs. Buckingham always kept him stocked with a few pre-wrapped sandwiches. On this day she did not disappoint him. "Way to go Millie." She had one of each, ham, turkey, and tuna. She had even remembered to buy them without tomatoes already in the sandwich. He hates mushy sandwiches, so he always keeps a couple of tomatoes in his fridge. Cajun went about cutting a couple slices for his sandwich. He thinks, "Heck I had better take the ham sandwich, as I may not get another for several weeks since I will be in Muslim countries."

He is about half way through his sandwich and Budweiser, when Pigeon sticks his head in the office door. Cajun says, "Hey, welcome to Bristol. Grab yourself a sandwich and a beer then take a load off."

Ryan answers, "Don't mind if I do. Can I have a couple slices of your tomatoes too?"

Cajun says, "Of course, you can have some of my tomatoes. It is my Bud I am having second thoughts about. Ah go ahead, have a sandwich, some tomatoes, and take a Bud too." After cutting a couple slices of tomatoes for his sandwich, he grabs a beer then sits down in the front of Cajun's desk.

They talk about everything but the mission. Both men eat their sandwiches while jousting back and forth.

Pigeon seems to be interested in the commercial side of Cajun's aviation business. He inquires as to the types of customers he has, the aircraft he uses most, and other seemingly insignificant details of the business. Cajun answers his questions. He feels flattered that by asking his questions, Ryan is acknowledging how successful Cajun has become. They eventually finish lunch. Together they clean up around the little kitchen counter by the refrigerator.

As they sit down once more on both sides of the desk, Cajun begins the discussions. "We have covered plenty of ground here in the last twenty-four hours. I expect we will be one hundred percent finished with the mission planning in another forty-eight hours. I would expect we could launch out of here to drop Wyatt and his guys off in Oman in three days, four at the most."

Ryan seems pleased with his statement. "That's good news. My guys further up the food chain are very anxious to get this show on the road. The thought of leaving that bomb in the hands of those maniacs is making everybody very nervous. That is why I am here so early. I couldn't say so on the phone the first time we talked, but when you called me, I was already in London with my ticket in hand to fly here."

"What, no company aircraft to fly you down here" ,Cajun retorts.

Pigeon responds sheepishly, "Well they knew I was ahead of schedule and that you had only begun your final preparations. In addition, my boss is using the aircraft we have in England to travel to Germany."

Cajun lets Pigeon off the hook. "Forget it, Pigeon, I am just pulling your chain. I tell you what I'm gonna do. When we are done, I am going to fly you back to London. Now don't get the idea I'm doing this because I like you, it's just that I want you to get back there and get on that encrypted communication gear to get me what we need to complete our mission. Plus, the fact, there is no way I want to face Snooky in a couple months with the knowledge that I left you to walk back." Both men laugh, but each know it is time to quit futzing around. It is time to get down to some very serious business.

Ryan starts by saying, "We have already begun putting together the equipment list you gave us while in London. We have a cargo ship departing tomorrow out of Kuwait in the Persian Gulf. We are loaded with one Humvee and four duce and a half trucks. So far we have been unable to locate the external fuel bladders you asked for. We were able to locate a large one-thousand-gallon bladder, but I knew from our missions in Iraq that it was too big."

Cajun affirms Ryan's decision to reject the larger bladder. "What we need are three, three-hundred-gallon bladders that we will lock down internally and three, three-hundred-gallon bladders that we will sling underneath the aircraft. Basically, we will hang one bladder from each of the three hooks then have the ground handling guys secure them together. If we do it that way, they will streamline in the wind with very little oscillation. We will be able to travel fast till we use up that fuel."

Ryan says, "OK, I have a call out to the units in Iraq and Afghanistan to locate the assets we need. They will have them flown in to Awasa to meet up with our aircraft."

"Alright, it looks like you have a handle on it. Just keep me informed when those bladders are located. Otherwise, we can order bladders from a civilian company I know in North Carolina then have them flown over here. Let us continue because I have an extensive to do list here for you" ,says Cajun.

Cajun goes down his list with Ryan one item at a time. He needs the cargo ship to stop offshore at Masqat, Oman, where his men will board. When the men board, they will all need to be fitted with two complete sets of desert camouflaged uniforms without any markings. They will also need to have several handheld GPS units issued. He needs Omani currency for his men to spend on transportation and food once they land at the Seeb International Airport. They would likely need about two hundred dollars each, and as of now it looks like approximately fifteen men would be dropped off. Once his men are aboard the cargo ship they will need an assortment of small arms including M-16s, handguns, shoulder fired grenade launchers and plenty of ammunition for each weapon.

When the ship arrives in the Port of Djibouti, they will need plenty of Ethiopian birr, which is the currency in that country. Cajun feels that they will need about five thousand dollars just to be on the safe side. Who knows, they may have to make some payments to some corrupt members of the Ethiopian National Defense Forces or pay for vehicle repairs. Of course, when they drive off the ship, arrangements will already have been made for them to top off each vehicle and fuel bladders. After the initial refueling they will not make any more refueling stops until they reach Baidoa, Somalia.

Cajun goes on to cover the equipment and nuclear weapon personnel that he will need once he lands in Awasa. The Chinook and Cobra helicopters configured the way Cajun wants is of course at the top of his list. They will need to have the aircraft fueled to the top including all the internal and external bladders, which had been discussed earlier.

Cajun leans forward in his desk toward Pigeon. "Now let's talk about the most important things you can do for us to ensure our success."

Ryan leans forward preparing himself for the seriousness of their conversation. "What do you need?"

"All of the planning we are doing, plus all of the monies being expended by the U.S. Government, will all be in vain if everybody and their cousins know we are trekking across Ethiopia headed for Somalia. Our footprint in Oman is small. Oman is no problem. However, when we drive our trucks off the ship in Djibouti, we need a cover story."

"The vehicles will already be painted in the colors and flag of the Ethiopian National Defense Forces. We will need a few of their troops to drive the vehicles off the vessel to the point where they are topped off with fuel. Our cover story will be intended for the ENDF troops as no one else will even know we are around. I will leave it up to you, but perhaps a story that we are going to be involved in a joint food distribution effort originating in Addis Abeba. We will be departing in a westward direction out of Djibouti in the general direction of Addis Abeba, so that seems like the most plausible story."

Ryan assures Cajun, "Ok, I will take care of the cover story, what else you need?"

Cajun intensifies their discussion, "When we land our 737 in Awasa to unload our supplies, we are really going to need another cover story. First of all, you and your men should pick us up in trucks then drive us out of town to a secluded area where you will have the helicopters pre-positioned."

"I will take care of that. We will have a cover story with the officials in the Ethiopian government that we want to beef up our participation in the efforts against Al Qaeda within their borders" ,says Ryan.

"That's good, I like that" ,agrees Cajun.

Cajun continues with seriousness in his voice that Ryan has not heard until this moment, "Pigeon, we have to interact a little with the Ethiopian Commander of the troops occupying Baidoa, Somalia. I have been eating my brain alive worrying about those guys blowing our cover when we will be so close to carrying out our mission one hundred and sixty miles away in Mogadishu. What I know for sure is that because of mission planning parameters involving fuel and weight, we will have a final refueling at Baidoa. When we meet up with Wyatt and his group, there will be a substantial gaggle of men and equipment."

"What we need is a set of coordinates, not too far off the main road before getting too close to Baidoa. Wyatt can meet up with us and our two helicopters" ,Cajun continues.

"I can see where you are going with this. I had some thoughts along these lines as well" ,Ryan replies.

Cajun says, "We will need to perform some maintenance procedures on our aircraft in addition to refueling with the balance of our external bladders. Our entire sortie will have to remain covered by camouflage nets until the early morning when we strike. No matter what we do, we are bound to attract some attention by someone. All we need is for our presence to be known by the wrong person and it will be all over. What do you think? Do you have any ideas, Pigeon?"

Pigeon thinks for a while looking off in the distance out the office windows. Cajun can tell that some very serious wheels are turning between Pigeon's ears. He decides not to interrupt his thought so as not to disturb a professional planner at work. Several minutes go by with not so much as a word spoken between them.

Finally, Pigeon speaks, "I agree with you that this is the most critical point in the entire mission. We cannot allow the mission to suffer because of interaction with Ethiopian troops or any civilians for that matter. The only way to assure that we are not discovered is to not interact with them at all." Both men stop talking to search their minds for an answer.

"Here is our dilemma. The reason I have extra fuel bladders and the reason I have our main ground troops coming across Ethiopia in trucks, is that I do not have enough lift capacity. To refuel a Chinook plus a

Cobra flying all the way from Awasa to Mogadishu then out to sea requires carrying the fuel I have called for. I cannot do that plus carry fifteen Rangers, plus portable steel lifting equipment to handle the weapon. I need those last two trucks to drive from the northern Somali border down to the Baidoa region. If they drive on a main road they will surely be seen by someone."

Pigeon thinks long and hard before answering Cajun. "Consider this scenario. First, we were originally thinking that we would have Ethiopian Government officials in contact with the Commander in the field around Baidoa then notify him to assist our request. We both agree that allowing anyone in that region to know of our intentions is tantamount to running it on television. Our plan is to get permission from the Ethiopian government to allow us to paint their colors and flag on the vehicles, with the ruse that American forces want to move around the country fighting Al Qaeda forces without an American stamp on the operation. Tell the government officials our successes against Al Qaeda will be credited to them."

"Why don't we go with that plan but do not inform anyone in Ethiopia, not even our operatives, that we have a secondary plan in affect? If we stick with that plan plus have real American troops chasing Al Qaeda around Ethiopia, our men will not be noticed."

Cajun says, "When my two remaining trucks drive across the border in the direction of Baidoa, they will not be stopped. In fact, we should get a flag on the lead vehicle which indicates an Ethiopian General is aboard. When it is convenient, our drivers will pull off the main road. We will fly directly to their coordinate location. What do you think, Pigeon? Does it sound like an executable plan?"

Before Cajun finishes what he is saying, Pigeon is already shaking his head in the affirmative and replies with enthusiasm, "Cajun, you have done it again. You have created a logical plan, which will get that nuclear weapon out of the hands of those madmen. You pull this off and your country will be very grateful even though the general public will likely never hear your name."

Cajun looks directly in Pigeon's eyes. "Don't tell anybody. Do not let anyone hear the words I am about to say to you. I would do this for free to get my hands on another Cobra Attack helicopter plus have a chance to find Savannah again."

"Come on, Pigeon, I'll fly you back to London" ,says Cajun as he taps Ryan on his shoulder.

As they stand up to walk toward the door Ryan says, "Cajun, stop calling me Pigeon."

The following morning Cajun walks through the front office door at precisely 0800 hours. Even when he makes a conscious effort not to be on time in his life's activities, because of his training he seems to always find himself right on time. In fact, walking through the door at precisely 0800 hours gives him great satisfaction.

When you think about it, by the time one regulates their wake-up time, breakfast, dressing, and commute time, one usually arrives a little early or a little late. Not Cajun, he knows instinctively how to adjust these activities that have pronounced influences on his schedule. No matter what happens, he is always exactly on time.

"Good morning, Mr. Breaux" ,says Mrs. Buckingham.

"Well, a very good morning to you as well, Mrs. Buckingham," Cajun says in a cheerful voice. He continues straight into his office in anticipation of further meetings with Jack and Wyatt. As soon as he walks in, the aroma of Community coffee fills his senses. It is always at this precise moment, when he smells that wonderful down-home coffee, that he most appreciates Millie. Cajun always wants to address Mrs. Buckingham by her first name, but he always fights the urge as she is what she is. She is an old school English lady.

Cajun pours a cup into his favorite L.S.U mug and sits down in his office chair. He slowly swirls around in his chair so that he can observe the activity out on the flight line. Jack is already working with Mr. Cornwell, their Chief of Maintenance on the Boeing 737 in preparation for the mission.

Their 737 is a unique aircraft known as a Combi. That means it can carry passengers and cargo at the same time. On the left side of the plane, just behind the passenger entry door, is a very large cargo door. The door will lift hydraulically straight up and out of the way so cargo can be loaded. Once the door is opened, a large pallet loader will pull up to the aircraft level with the floor. Cargo that has been loaded onto special pallets will be lifted by the loader on a hydraulic lift then pushed manually into the plane via small rollers on the floor.

Cajun watches as Mr. Cornwell supervises his men while they load a couple pallets that have been assembled by Jack. Weapons, ammunition, and MREs are all part of the cargo, although everything has already been packed in cardboard boxes. Lying on the ground waiting its turn to be loaded is a portable, steel framework device intended to lift then move the nuclear weapon. Cajun just watches with pride at the professionalism of all his men.

As Cajun continues his observation of the activities on the flight line, Wyatt appears in the doorway of his office. He knocks lightly on the door then continues into the office to stand in front of Cajun's desk. "Good morning, Boss. I have completed the details of the drive across Ethiopia all the way into Baidoa."

Cajun replies, "Good morning to you, Wyatt. That is great that you have finished it a little early. We will get Jack in here so we can cover the details together and finalize our mission planning brief."

Just then Mrs. Buckingham appears in the doorway and steps into the office a few feet. "Mr. Breaux, I finished reaching all the gentlemen on the list you gave me. All of them told me they would be here in forty-eight hours at the most. I expect that a few may begin showing up today. The last of the contacts should be here no later than day after tomorrow."

"Thank you so much for the update Mrs. Buckingham, I appreciate your dropping the other things I had asked you to do in order to call all our men" ,Cajun says with a small salute to her.

Mrs. Buckingham ask, "You're welcome, Mr. Breaux. Might I ask a favor of you Mr. Breaux?"

Cajun answers, "Of course, what can I do for you?"

"Will you call me Millie? The older I become the more I dislike being addressed as Mrs. Buckingham. It makes me feel so old. You understand don't you, Mr. Breaux?"

"Millie it is from now on, but only if you will do something for me" , replies Cajun.

"What is that, Sir?"

Cajun answers, "Please call me Cajun or Ethan, whichever you prefer. Whenever people call me Mr. Breaux I always have a tendency to look around for my Dad."

Mrs. Buckingham says, "Very well Sir, I mean, Ethan." With that she turns around and returns to her office.

Wyatt looks at Cajun as if to say, "Wow, what was that all about?"

Cajun reassures Wyatt, "Well there you go, Wyatt, your men will be arriving real soon. When they contact you, why don't you just have them go straight to the hotel? No need them hanging around here, they will just get in the way until we brief them as a group. Besides, they need to hang out in the hot tub and order room service for a few days, because things are going to get much worse for them real soon."

Wyatt replies with a thumbs up gesture, "Sure enough, Boss. I'll tell them to go down to the Marriott."

"Why don't you go find Raider? When he is ready, you guys fall back in up here in an hour so we can continue with our planning" ,adds Cajun.

Wyatt makes a half-hearted salute and says, "Aye, Aye, Boss, we'll be back soon."

Cajun begins removing the sensitive documents from the safe. He wants to review the charts and information he discussed with Ryan before his guys return. While at his desk Cajun becomes heavily focused in the material, so much so that he loses track of time. It seems like just minutes since Wyatt left to retrieve Jack. However, as they both enter his office he glances at the clock on the wall. Two hours have passed.

Jack asks, "Cajun, are you ready to continue with Wyatt and I on our mission planning now or should we give you a little more time?"

Cajun answers, "No, come on in and let's finish this son-of-a-bitch." Both Jack and Wyatt take their seats in front of Cajun's desk. Cajun clears everything off his desk in anticipation of their getting down to some serious business. The only things on the desk in front of them are the documents and charts, which are all part of the mission planning.

"Gentlemen this is one of the biggest, most complicated operations I have ever seen. Yet, at the same time as I see the details gel into an organized plan, it is without a doubt one of the most beautiful operations ever conceived. We have been working as a team for many years and have been involved in all kinds of missions big and small, important and unimportant, but this beauty is the best of all time."

Wyatt replies, "Boss, I have seen you put together some very good missions over the years."

Jack says, "Cajun. You're just doing what you do best."

Cajun replies in a very serious manner. "I would love to take all the credit guys, but no, it's not just me. Everything coming together as though it was meant to be. My planning, Ryan's strategy, Wyatt's incredible ground operational capabilities, and the countries involved, have me convinced that this one is special. The magnitude of the importance of this mission has me convinced it was ordained by the universe itself."

Wyatt blurts, "Whoa Boss, you're getting too heavy for me."

Cajun draws their attention to the material on the desk. "Ok, but let's just review the plan as it stands and see if you don't start to see something else at work in this entire operation. Here we are in England, a commercial aviation company flying fat Europeans to sun bathe topless on the Rivera. We are going to move some of the best, well trained fighters, and equipment all the way to the Middle East then to Africa.

Our forces will split up into two groups to cross Ethiopia all the way into Somalia to within one hundred and sixty miles of our objective. We will attack in the middle of the night to kill as many Hezbollah terrorist skinnies as we can to make up for the loss of our Black Hawk and nineteen American soldiers in 1993. Then we will rescue a stolen nuclear weapon and fly off into the night. Not only will we fly off into the night, but we will fly off into the Indian Ocean where we will attempt to find a Navy carrier then land. Now have you ever conceived that such a plan could work, let alone the fact that it is we who have developed and will carry out this mission?"

All three men slowly ease back in their leather chairs with L.S.U engraved into the headrest. It is at this precise moment that they collectively realize the gravity of the situation.

Jack says, "I see what you mean Cajun. When you get involved with all the details, you have a tendency to overlook the big picture."

Wyatt adds, "I am starting to agree with you, Boss. This is a very large operation being pulled off by relatively few men with limited equipment, civilians no less. However, if we all just perform our jobs individually the way we always have in the past, it will work."

Cajun asks Jack for an update on the pilot situation. He replies that he has interviewed six pilots and reviewed their records in the last twenty-four hours. Four of the pilots have everything in order and will be able to fill in while they are gone. One of the pilots he has hired is dual qualified in helicopters and aircraft as is Cajun and Jack. Jack continues bringing Cajun and Wyatt up to date. He shares that he already has their 737 loaded with supplies, weapons, and ammunition. In addition, he has produced a phony manifest of cargo indicating everything on board is aircraft parts and medical supplies destined for Oman and Ethiopia.

When Jack finishes with his brief, Wyatt picks up on his part of the briefing. He hands Jack and Cajun a folder of information. He goes on to point out the document is broken down into personnel, listed with only their combat call signs and their responsibilities within the group. Wyatt points out that he will have two seven men squads with him as the fifteenth man. That will make one group referred to as the heavy squad and the other as the light squad. In the document, each man has a full description of his training and specialties.

Of course, Cajun and Jack already knew most of these men as they had served together in Iraq. However, it is good to review each man and his strengths as some of them have expanded their training since the last time they all served together in the military.

In the list of combined specialties are weapons experts, explosive demolition experts, paratroopers, snipers, load masters, mechanics, and communication specialist.

In another section of his document are smaller versions of the larger charts they have all been working on previously. The first group of charts is for trekking across Ethiopia all the way to Baidoa, Somalia along with latitude and longitude coordinates for the entire trip. It includes references to expected locations where they will have to head out into the bush long enough to refuel the trucks. When one truck is completely emptied of fuel, it will be abandoned. The second group of papers is comprised of satellite and ground level photos of the compound on the outskirts of Mogadishu where the weapon is being kept.

Another major section of his document contains a battle plan for defeating the enemy and the taking of the nuclear weapon. The battle plan includes positions for each member of the heavy and light squads so that their specialties can best be exploited. Snipers on each squad will remain in the rear approximately one hundred yards in an elevated position. They will have the XM-25 Sniper Weapon used by Army and Navy Seal snipers.

At least one man per squad will have his M-16 fitted with a M203 40mm grenade launcher for knocking holes in the compound rock walls. They will also have a few rounds each of tear gas, which will be lobbed over the wall in the initial stages of the conflict. Each squad will also have a man designated as their explosive demolition expert. They will blow holes in the walls with C-4 should the 40-mm rounds prove to be ineffective.

Wyatt has a whole section on how to quickly erect the portable steel framework for lifting then maneuvering the nuclear weapon. Finally, he has a complete section dedicated to return fire from the helicopter on their egress from the compound.

Wyatt has done his homework. There is no question it is as good a plan as Cajun has ever seen. Cajun looks up from the pages in the document. "You see what I mean, Jack, this plan is going to work. Do you see now why I keep this guy on the payroll?" Cajun puts his arm around Wyatt's head in a playful manner then rubs his head back and forth with his knuckles.

Cajun sits back down in his chair. "Here is what I have worked out with Pigeon." Stated in simple terms, when Wyatt and his boys reach the Port of Djibouti, there will be several troops from the Ethiopian military to drive the trucks off the ship onto the wharf. That will keep your guys low profile. Once the trucks are on the ground and the attention of the stevedores has turned to other cargo, you will walk off the ship a couple guys at a time then jump in the rear of the trucks. After that the trucks will be driven away from the port to a refueling location. That's where you will be taking over from the Ethiopian troops with the understanding that you guys will be on a food distribution mission in Ethiopia. From there you will drive west on your planned route."

"When we take over the helicopters in Awasa, the Ethiopian government will be under the assumption that we are part of a larger effort to root out Al Qaeda fighters within their borders. Our operation will seem to be part of an on-going joint operation between real U.S. Army soldiers and the Ethiopian National Defense Forces. Once we leave Awasa no one will be the wiser as to where we are going or what we are up to."

"Once we all get back together on the northern border of Somalia at the rally point, we will refuel the Cobra then narrow the vehicles down to two duce and a half trucks."

"No one in the Ethiopian government will know we are heading to Baidoa, Somalia, even though the ENDF is the occupying force in that area. We will place a flag on each front fender of the lead truck to indicate an Ethiopian general is aboard. It is unlikely anyone in their forces would try to stop one of their own vehicles. It is even more unlikely they will mess with a General. No matter what, do not stop."

"I give you these orders now. In the unlikely event that Ethiopian guards at a check point challenge you, you will have no choice but to eliminate them then destroy their communication equipment. Remove the guards then leave the gates in the open position as though the guard station has been abandoned. At all cost, we cannot have anyone in that area, friend, or foe, know that we are there. We just need to buy ourselves a few hours until the early hours of the morning when we will stage our attack."

"Once we stage the attack, Wyatt, we need for you to select two of your best Navy Seal men to go into the water offshore then swim into the airport from one mile out. They must secure a fuel truck then defend the area until we refuel after having rescued the weapon."

Cajun looks at his men straight in the eyes. "Gentleman, what do you think? Can we execute this plan? Do either of you have any reservations?" Both men lean back in their chairs after having been glued to the documents on the desk.

Jack speaks first, "Guys, this plan is executable."

Wyatt adds with the enthusiasm of a trained combat veteran, "Cajun, Jack, we will complete this mission to a favorable outcome."

Cajun asks both men to compile both phases of the mission into one document, make twenty-five copies then put them in the safe until they brief their men. At the complete assembly of their men, the mission documents will be distributed to each man on the team.

As both men gather up the papers from the desk Cajun says, "Here is the way I see all this coming together. If all the men are here in the next forty-eight hours and Ryan gives us the word that the Navy cargo ship is on schedule to meet us offshore of Oman, we will execute plan Back to Somalia three days from now. Today is Wednesday. I expect that if things stay on track, we will be wheels up on Saturday morning, Sunday morning at the latest." Each man studies the reaction of the other two, and for a moment share in their solidarity.

Chapter Eleven...
737 Take Us To Heaven

Bristol, England

On Saturday morning all the men have assembled on the flight line. They are all dressed in casual clothes standing around waiting to board the 737. Cajun, Jack, and Wyatt are standing in the office looking out the window as final preparations are made to launch.

The tug to tow the jet out to the taxiway is being hooked up by the ground crew. Jack and Wyatt are each carrying half of the mission brief documents, which had been previously prepared for each man on the team. Cajun turns and faces the two men. "Well, it's time to get this show on the road. Our flight plan calls for us to be airborne enroute to Egypt in approximately thirty minutes."

"Jack, once we are airborne and have reached our cruising altitude, you go back to give each pilot a copy of our mission brief. Tell them you will verbally brief them once we get on the ground in Oman. We will have about an hour turnaround time while we are taking on fuel and having our papers checked."

"I'll take care of it" ,Jack replies.

Cajun continues, "Wyatt, once we level off, assemble your men, distribute the mission brief documents then give them an hour or so to study the details. After that, when all of them are ready, you personally cover every detail of our mission. Once you have finished, retrieve the documents then keep them in your safe keeping while on the ground in Oman. I don't want any stray copies lying around when we are boarded by government officials."

Wyatt answers immediately, "Ok, Boss, I will make sure to pick up all the copies of the mission brief."

"Once you are safely aboard our Navy cargo ship, distribute the documents again so they can memorize the details" ,adds Cajun.

"Will do Boss, once we get away from the Port of Djibouti, we will burn all the documents in the desert just in case something happens enroute which gets out of our control. We will only keep one copy of our latitude and longitude coordinates. We can always claim they are coordinates for rally points related to our food distribution efforts in Ethiopia."

"OK let's go get this show on the road," says Cajun as he walks with a positive, quick stride for the door. Jack and Wyatt follow Cajun to the 737 on the flight line.

Cajun climbs up a couple steps on the air stair leading to the aircraft entry door. He turns to face all the men on the tarmac. "Gentlemen, this mission will be the most rewarding of your lives. Once we get aboard and enroute to our first stopover on our trip, you will be thoroughly briefed on our mission. That's all I have to say for now, let's go." Cajun turns to walk up the remaining steps then enters the 737.

As everybody else boards the plane, Cajun and Jack settle into the pilot seats then fasten their safety harnesses. As soon as they are settled with their personal seats and rudder pedals adjusted, Cajun turns into

Captain Ethan Breaux. He turns to Jack and says, "As soon as you are ready Jack, let's begin with the Before Start Checklist."

Jack replies with standard cockpit protocol language. "I'm ready Captain."

"Shoulder Harness."

"Shoulder Harness On."

"Rudder Pedals."

"Rudder Pedals Centered and Free."

"Circuit Breakers."

"Circuit Breakers Checked In."

"Overhead Switches."

"Overhead Switches On, No Fault Lights."

Captain Breaux and First Officer Jack Garrity, methodically continue through the checklist getting the 737 prepared for takeoff. After approximately ten minutes the jet is on the center line of the runway cleared for takeoff. Jack is handling the radio communication with the control tower.

The controller issues a clearance to takeoff, "Roger, Bristol Charters 100, cleared for takeoff.

Jack replies to the tower and then to Ethan, "OK, Captain, we are cleared for takeoff."

"Roger cleared for takeoff." As Cajun says those words he advances the thrust levers approximately twenty-five percent of their travel range. As the engines spool up to approximately forty percent, he presses the TOGA button on the side of the trust levers. He commands the word TOGA which stands for the Take Off/Go Around. When that button is pressed, the flight control system automatically advances the thrust levers to the programmed takeoff setting, which had been entered into the computer earlier.

First Officer Garrity places his left hand behind the thrust levers to guard against any backward creep then calls out airspeeds as they roar down the runway. Garrity calls out, "Sixty knots, one hundred knots, V1, rotate, V2."

Captain Breaux smoothly pulls back on the yoke to twenty degrees pitch attitude. The jet rises smoothly into the air. Captain Breaux commands, "Gear up." At one thousand feet and one hundred seventy knots, Captain Breaux commands "Flaps one," then allows the jet to accelerate to an airspeed of two hundred ten knots. When the airspeed reaches the mark, Captain Breaux commands, "Flaps up. Let's complete the After Takeoff Checklist."

First Officer replies, "Roger, the engines are set at continuous climb setting. The landing gear is up with three green lights out. Pressurization is climbing normally in the AUTO Mode. The After Takeoff Checklist is complete."

After they clear the Bristol International Airport airspace they are turned over to Bristol Air Traffic Control. F/O Garrity checks in with their position by radio. "Bristol ATC, this is Bristol Charters 100 climbing through ten thousand five hundred feet IFR to Oman.

Bristol ATC responds, "Roger your position Bristol Air Charters 100, cleared on flight planned route."

With those instructions Captain Breaux is authorized to reach up to press the LNav and VNav buttons on the flight control panel. That means the state-of-the art Boeing 737 will now automatically turn on then fly their flight planned route and control the speeds enroute.

Once the aircraft levels off at their cruising altitude of 39,000 feet, Jack gets up and moves into the cabin of the airplane. He issues three of the mission brief documents to the three pilots who would be flying in the co-pilot positions in both the Cobra Attack helicopter and the Chinook. One of them would always be in a standby position to jump in either aircraft.

Jack says to the extra pilots, "Have a look at the information on these mission brief cards then return them to me once we land in Egypt. Once we have a little more time on the ground in Egypt and Oman, I will go over the details with you." The pilots each begin to look through the information. Jack goes to the galley to pour a couple cups of coffee for himself and Cajun, then returns to the cockpit.

As Jack reemerges through the cockpit door, Cajun looks up to see that he has two cups of coffee. "Captain Breaux, I've got something for you." He slowly hands Cajun his cup of coffee so as not to spill a drop on the radio pedestal.

Cajun replies with glee, "Great, I was hoping you would grab us a couple cups. You are truly an officer and a gentleman."

"You know, the best part, is I am getting to where I like this Community coffee" ,Jack exclaims.

"Jack Garrity, I will make a Louisiana boy out of you yet" says Cajun.

Cajun appreciates what Jack said about his Louisiana coffee. It made him think of the times when they were in the Army way out in the boondocks. Mostly they ate MREs and drank the instant coffee provided in the little packets which required adding hot water. Cajun asks, "Hey Jack, remember when we had to drink that horrible coffee in the little packets with the MREs?"

Jack says, "Yea, that was the worse coffee on the face of the earth. Remember on the rare occasion when the cooks would fix us a hot breakfast? We would have to walk the length of a football field to the mess tent to get sunny side up eggs and that half cooked barely warm bacon. Then we would grab a cup of their coffee in those Styrofoam cups."

"Under normal circumstances we would probably throw all of it in the trash, but it had been so long since we had hot chow it tasted like gourmet food. The coffee somehow tasted like a dark roasted blend in the cold air" ,added Cajun.

Jack suddenly remembers and says, "Wait a minute. That reminds me of the best breakfast story ever told. The best story was the time when you placed the French toast, wrapped in aluminum foil, along with the syrup on the air cleaner of your Corvette."

Cajun replies, "Yea, that was when we were stationed in Ft. Rucker. We had to be in formation by six in the morning. The best part was the strawberries I had precut the night before. I never will forget the look on Colonel Reed's face when he walked in our ready room to see me whacking hot French toast with hot syrup and cold strawberries. I think it was on that day he realized that Warrant Officers would eventually rule the world." Both men laugh while they fly along in the direction of Egypt, drinking Community coffee.

Meanwhile in the cabin of the aircraft, Wyatt has all his men studying their individual copies of the mission brief. Wyatt is moving from man to man pointing out various sections in the document. He occasionally becomes animated while explaining a particular aspect of the planned firefights. Every one of these men had accepted many years before, that they could in fact become a casualty. However, all of them are indeed such professional fighting men, that they only think of success in achieving the mission goals.

The jet has progressed into Egyptian airspace and has over flown Cairo. They are about an hour out of Luxor, their first stopover. The aircraft flight computer calculates their position to be at the top of descent point, then slowly reduces the thrust levers to flat idle. The nose pitches down slowly about five degrees, which starts the aircraft decent.

Jack gets on the radio to report to Egyptian ATC that they have departed flight level 390 for flight level 210. The Egyptian Air Traffic Control responds with, "Roger Bristol Charters 100, continue your descent now to one five thousand on flight planned route."

"Roger, Bristol Airways 100 cleared to one five thousand" ,replies Jack.

While Jack is busy communicating with ATC, Cajun tunes up the weather frequency for the Luxor International Airport. When Jack finishes his communication with ATC, he enters the new altitude limit of fifteen thousand feet in the altitude clearance window. Cajun gives him the weather information.

As Jack reviews the information, Cajun says, "Doesn't look like there is anything unusual going on in the way of weather. As expected it is severe clear with the wind out of the northeast at 10 knots. It looks like we will get setup for the ILS into runway 02. So, whenever you get ready let's get the Descent and Approach checklist out of the way."

After F/O Garrity reviews the weather information, he looks in his flight bag to remove the approach plate for the ILS to runway 02 at the Luxor International Airport.

"Captain I am ready for the approach brief into Luxor."

Captain Breaux says, "OK, let's complete the checklist."

"Anti-Ice."

"Anti-Ice Off."

"Air-Conditioning & Pressurization."

"Air-Conditioning & Pressurization Set and Crosschecked."

"Altimeter Setting."

"Altimeter 29.94 Set & Crosschecked."

"N1 and Airspeed Bugs."

"Weight 125,000 LBS., N1 Set, Speed Bug Set 132 Knots."

"Approach Brief."

Ethan continues, "We are expecting Radar Vectors to land to the northeast on runway 02. The ILS frequency is 109.5 with an inbound course of 02 degrees. If we must stay on the approach we will continue to position Pharaoh as shown on the chart. Once we are cleared for the approach we will be cleared to descend to a decision height of 501 feet. The airport elevation is 301 feet. If we must go around for any reason, I will call GO AROUND. We will then fly the missed approach procedure as published on the approach plate. The initial heading on the missed approach is a right turn east to 097 degrees climbing to an altitude of three thousand feet. Are there any questions on the approach brief?"

Jack replies, "Negative, I have no questions on the approach brief." "DESCENT & APPROACH BRIEF complete."

"We're coming up on our next checkpoint in ten miles. Go ahead and give them a call to see if we can get cleared for a lower altitude," commanded Captain Breaux.

F/O Garrity and Captain Ethan Breaux continue their back-and-forth cockpit dialogue until they are three miles out for landing. Jack rings the overhead chime in the cabin then speaks to the men in back over the public address. "Ok men, we are landing at Luxor, please make sure your seatbelts are fastened. Once we get on the ground, the Ground Controller will direct us over to the International Cargo ramp. The authorities may or may not come aboard to inspect us and our manifest, so be prepared to be boarded. Make sure all the mission documents are put away."

Once Cajun brings the aircraft to a complete stop, he shuts down the engines then notices a government vehicle approaching them from the terminal. Cajun makes an announcement on the PA. "Let's get the doors open and the air stair lowered. I need Booker to hop off to chock the wheels then supervise our refueling. Cotton needs to meet the officials at the bottom of the stairs. Allow them on the aircraft. OK, everybody, look relaxed and remember we are on a mission to deliver aircraft parts and medical supplies to Oman."

Booker and Cotton are Cajun's crew chiefs who have been with him since the Iraq days. They were trained on every helicopter Cajun had ever flown, not to mention the fact that they were both very efficient with a 50-caliber machine gun.

Captain Breaux and F/O Garrity complete the aircraft shut-down procedure and walk out of the cockpit just as the government officials come up the steps. Captain Breaux says, "Welcome gentlemen, how can we help you today?"

The heavier of the two men seems to be in charge but as expected is fairly-weak when it came to the English language. Fatman says, "What do you carry onboard?"

"Sir, we have cargo that we are delivering to Oman. "Our cargo is made up of aircraft parts and medical supplies." Cajun answers then motions with his hand to Jack. "Why don't you walk these gentlemen back to the cargo, First Officer Garrity, and show them?"

As the inspector walks slowly toward the rear of the aircraft with Jack, he is looking intently at Wyatt and the other fourteen men. Although Wyatt and his men are all dressed in tourist clothing, the official is nervous of the presence of so many rough looking guys.

As they reach the cargo pallets, all the cargo is wrapped and taped in cardboard boxes. The boxes are labeled as aircraft parts originating from Boeing Aircraft and medical supplies originating from Pfizer Pharmaceuticals. It obvious that to really inspect the cargo will require dismantling the pallets to cut the boxes open.

Fatman looks nervously back to Wyatt and his men, then back to Jack standing in front of the first cargo pallet. "Ok, your papers in order." With that statement, he and his partner walk back past all the men onboard at a brisk pace. As they reach the front, Fatman hands a clearance document to Captain Breaux then departs the airplane down the steps.

Within twenty minutes the aircraft is refueled. Cotton is using a closed fist hand signal to communicate with Captain Breaux to set the brakes in anticipation of engine start. F/O Garrity and Captain Breaux go through the engine start, taxi out, and takeoff procedures without a hitch. Within another twenty minutes they were leveling off at Flight Level 390 enroute to Oman. Cajun comes up on the PA, "Ok guys we have close to four hours before we reach Oman. Do some studying or get some sleep. We'll let you know when it's time to land."

While enroute Cajun and Jack tell old war stories of missions that had gone by. They laugh at the humorous memories then fall silent for periods as they remember fallen men in their care. While telling stories, Jack recalls the order Cajun had given Wyatt about encountering Ethiopian military guards at a checkpoint entering the Baidoa, Somalia area. "Ethan, I wanted to ask you about your specific order to Wyatt to eliminate the ENDF guards at a checkpoint if they are challenged to stop and be inspected. Don't get me wrong, I am not questioning your order, I am just wondering what your reasoning was for that position?"

Ethan replied with a sober demeanor, "I have to be honest with you, it was not a decision I reached lightly. It is troubling. However, keeping in mind how much all of us will have to go through to reach that checkpoint without having already been discovered, it is the only decision that could be made. First-of-all, we will be in trucks with the markings and flag of the Ethiopian National Defense Forces. In addition, we will be displaying the flag of an Infantry General. If those guards stop our vehicles, it is because they are already suspicious. We will be within one hundred and sixty miles of our objective and cannot, under any set of circumstances, be discovered."

Jack continued with his questioning, "Yes, but the ENDF is on our side. What if it is discovered that Americans were responsible for attacking their troops?"

Ethan responds, "It is true those troops are on our side, at least you hope they are. We cannot take a chance that one or more of those guards are not in contact with some of their brethren in Mogadishu? If we allow ourselves to be discovered we will have to check in with the ENDF Commander of the Baidoa area. If that happens, at least two thousand of their troops will know we are inside Somalia. We might as well forget it and go home because the Hezbollah in Mogadishu will know we are coming. They will likely move the weapon. There are millions of people who would not fare well if we fail. We must not take any chances. The guard's fate is in their own hands. They either wave our guys through, or perish."

"Well, that is kind of what I thought the reasoning was. I just wanted to get the full skinny. I never doubted you for a minute Boss" ,says Jack.

Ethan replies, "I know you never questioned my decision, but if you don't ask, you never learn. Besides, I would expect you to question me, that is why we call you Raider. The Oakland Raiders are known to be some real tough football players, but they are not known for being misinformed." Jack just laughs out loud. As he sits and ponders Cajun's explanation, he fully agrees. It was the right decision.

After a long flight down the Red Sea then the Gulf of Oman abeam Yemen, they contact Oman Air Traffic Control. It is time to prepare the cabin for their descent into the Seeb International Airport in Masqat, Oman. Wyatt comes up into the cockpit and sits down in the jump seat. Ethan says, "Wyatt, we are going to land then will be directed to the passenger terminal. Once we get up to the terminal, you and your guys depart the aircraft in groups of three or four. Do not walk off in a steady stream of fifteen. Then each group needs to hail a taxi and have the driver take you to the Mina Qaboos Port."

"No problem, Boss, we know what to do. We'll be on that Navy cargo ship within a couple hours" ,replies Wyatt.

Cajun chuckles at his own nitpicking. "I know, I know, I can be a nag like an old den mother. We will meet you on the border of Somalia and Ethiopia at the rally point in about two weeks. If you get there first, just wait for us under your camo nets until we arrive. One more thing before you go; turn your satellite phone on once a day at eight in the evening in case our plans change and we have to reach you."

Wyatt gets up to leave the cockpit to take his seat. "Aye, Aye, Boss, we will be there waiting for you."

Captain Breaux and First Officer Garrity begin a decent to the Seeb International Airport. Upon arrival, just as Cajun had predicted they are being directed to the passenger terminal. As they approach the gate, Omani ground personnel guide them in just like a professional ramp crew somewhere in the western world. After chocking the wheels, one of the ground guys comes out from underneath the nose gear area and clinches his fist, which is the universal hand signal for affirmation that the nose wheel has indeed been chocked.

Captain Breaux acknowledges his signal, releases the brakes, and makes a comment to Jack, "Can you believe the first-class treatment we are getting?"

Jack says, "Yea, it's just like they see us every day."

"Well, I don't know what I expected, this is Oman and they do have people arriving from all over the world. It is just that I have a basic mistrust of any of the countries in the Middle East" ,replies Ethan.

Ethan says to Jack as he swings his legs around the Captain's seat to leave the cockpit, "Jack, before you get up to stretch your legs would you get us an ATC clearance out of here? Also have the ground controller send a fuel truck over to fill up our tanks. I'm going to say goodbye to our men."

Jack ask, "Ok, Boss, I'll get err done. What is your estimate of our departure time?"

"Well, it is almost 1800 hours. My guess is that we can be refueled and underway by 1900 hours" ,answers Ethan.

Ethan walks through the cockpit door. Wyatt is directing his men to disembark the aircraft looking like tourist in groups of three and four. He is about to walk off the plane with the last of the men when Ethan stops him. He grips Wyatt's hand in a prolonged handshake. "Good luck. We will see you at the rally point. If you run into any major problems you know how to reach us."

Wyatt says, "OK, Boss, keep the sunny side up crossing Ethiopia to meet up with us." Wyatt leaves the aircraft carrying his civilian duffle bag over his shoulder.

After what seems like hours, Jack says to Ethan, "It looks like the fuelers are departing. I will go down to make sure all the panels are closed and locked down. Other than that, I already have secured our clearance so we are ready to depart."

Ethan replies, "Ok, you give the exterior a quick walk around. I will get strapped in and double check our flight plan in the computer."

Captain Breaux and F/O Garrity start the engines, taxi to the active runway 08 then depart to the southwest enroute to Awasa, Ethiopia. They climb to FL 38 for a trip that would normally be just a little over 1,300 nautical miles, however the normal flight path will take them over Somalia and that is a No, No. They do the next best thing, which is to turn into the Red Sea until abeam the Port of Djibouti then turn left to Awasa.

The entire trip will take about three and a half hours. Since Wyatt and his men had left, Ethan is down to ten men. There is Booker and Cotton the two crew chiefs, Morley, Brian, Jimmy plus the three dual qualified pilots. Of course, for the time being, Jason and Javen, the two reserve pilots who will be returning the company 737 to England, are also aboard.

Also onboard are Robert and John the two dual-qualified communications / medical technicians. Pigeon will have the two nuclear weapons experts, likely Air Force personnel, waiting in Awasa. Ethan did a few calculations while enroute to Ethiopia. Once they reunite with Wyatt and his men, there will be twenty-two personnel onboard the Chinook when they commence the attack in Mogadishu. Cajun and Jimmy will fly the Cobra on the attack. Everything is falling into place.

Captain Breaux and First officer Garrity have been flying since Saturday morning. It is almost midnight when the top of descent point to make an approach into Awasa, Ethiopia is fast approaching. Jack says, "The control tower is closed in Awasa. The only navigational aid is an Automatic Direction-finding beacon. To make matters worse, the automatic weather frequency isn't transmitting anything."

Captain Breaux says, "Now you know why we pay the extra lease payment money for this 737-300. Tonight, we will let the computer and flight control system fly the entire approach right down to the minimum descent altitude, which according to the approach plate should be 5,649 feet. That is five hundred feet above the landing field altitude. We are coming up on the descent point. Go ahead and give ATC a call to get us a clearance to a lower altitude."

Jack answers, "Roger, I'll give them a call now."

"Ziway Center, this is Bristol Charters 100 requesting clearance to a lower altitude?"

The controller responds, "Roger Bristol Charters 100, this is Ziway Center, you are cleared to cruise to Awasa Airport. The last reported weather showed a broken layer at seven thousand feet, visibility ten miles, with an altimeter setting of 29.93."

"Roger, Ziway Center, understand we are cleared to cruise to the Awasa Airport, altimeter 29.93" ,responds Jack Garrity.

Jack informs Ethan, "Captain, we have been given a clearance to cruise to the Awasa, Airport."

Ethan says with enthusiasm, "Can you believe we would get that kind of clearance in the middle of the night all the way over here in the middle of Africa? Maybe they know what they are doing after all, because the last time I checked, that means we are cleared to any altitude we want all the way to the airport then cleared for the approach at our discretion. Is that the way you understand the clearance, Jack?"

"You got it, Boss. I'm setting 5,700 feet in the altitude window. That is rounded up to the next whole number above 5,649 feet" ,Jack affirms.

The flight control computer reaches the pre-programmed top of descent point. The thrust levers slowly retard to flat idle, then the nose pitches over about five degrees. This starts the descent of the 737, which finally stabilizes at three thousand feet per minute descent rate. Ethan says, "Jack, let's get the Descent and Approach check out of the way early, I am very tired and don't want to get behind on this approach at all. We've got some high terrain out in front of us."

Jack replies, "I find myself very tired too. Just think, if were flying for an airline right now, they would have grounded us a long time ago for lack of crew rest."

"Anti-Ice."

"Anti-Ice Off."

"Air-Conditioning & Pressurization."

"Air-Conditioning & Pressurization Set and Crosschecked."

"Altimeter Setting."

"Altimeter 29.93 Set & Crosschecked."

"N1 and Airspeed Bugs."

"Weight 124,000 LBS., N1 Set, Landing Speed Bug Set 129 Knots."

"Approach Brief."

Captain Breaux begins his brief, "This is a non-precision approach to runway 27. I have the ADF Approach plate to runway 27 out and identified. The frequency is 285 hertz. The inboard course to final will be 270 degrees from the intersection identified as Jadesee. Our minimum descent altitude is 5,700 feet. I doubt that the weather will be down to minimums, but if it is we will execute the missed approach procedure as published. If we execute a missed approach, we will not mess around at all. We will immediately request a clearance from ATC to fly to our alternate, which is the Bole International Airport. The Bole Airport is 91 nautical miles on a 286-degree bearing from Awasa. One more thing Jack, we are both fighting our circadian rhythm. This jet lag is falling over me like a lead balloon, so help me fly it all the way to the ground. Don't let up till we shut down the engines."

"I'm feeling it big-time too. I am glad you are flying this leg because I can barely keep my eyes open" ,says Jack.

F/O Garrity says, "Descent and Approach Brief complete."

Before the aircraft reaches the turn onto final, while slowing to 210 knots, Captain Breaux calls for Flaps 1 then slows to 190 knots. He calls for Flaps 5 then slows to 170 knots. A couple miles from Jadesee intersection he calls for Flaps 25, Gear Down, then slows to 135 knots.

As the aircraft intercepts the final inbound approach course, Captain Breaux calls for Flaps 30 then slows to 129 knots. He touches the Level

Change button on the Mode Control Panel. The thrust levers reduce automatically to allow the aircraft to descend out of 8,149 feet for 5,700 feet.

After the descent stabilizes, Captain Breaux touches the Vertical Speed button on the Mode Control Panel then dials in an 800-fpm rate of descent. F/O Garrity calls out altitudes and airspeeds as they descend on the approach.

The visibility is not what Captain Breaux predicted; however, the clouds are starting to thin out. He is flying with his eyes locked on the instruments while F/O Garrity is looking forward out the window trying to pick up the airport visually.

F/O Garrity calls out, "The airport is in sight, straight ahead."

Captain Breaux briefly looks out the window and sure enough the airport comes into view. He calls for all landing lights on then clicks off the autopilot with the thumb button on the yoke. Ethan decides to hand fly the airplane to touchdown. As they come to a slow roll on the runway, Captain Breaux turns onto the taxiway on the far side of the field away from the passenger terminal. He brings the aircraft to a stop then shuts down the engines. "Jack, will you complete the Shutdown Checklist, I am going to work with Booker until we get the wheels chocked?"

Jack responds, "Roger, I will get it all shut down." They turn off all lights then sleep until seven in the morning.

The following morning everyone is awakened by big slaps on the side of the cabin door. An officer from the ENDF accompanied by two soldiers with shoulder slung AK-47s are standing on the top step looking through the porthole window in the door. Ethan gets up to open the door then welcomes them onboard. The officer, a Captain asks, "Are you Captain Ethan Breaux?"

Ethan answers, "Yes, I am Captain Ethan Breaux, hang on and I'll get my passport."

The Captain replies, "That will not be necessary, Captain Breaux, or as I have been instructed to address you, Cajun." Cajun and the other men who have been tense up to this moment, laugh. "A Mr. Ryan Clayborne, one of your U.S. government officials, wants me to pass along his message."

Cajun ask, "And what message is that sir?"

"He said to call him when you wake up and have had your coffee," answers the Captain.

Cajun ask, "Well thank you very much, Captain, for delivering the message. Before I call Mr. Clayborne, could you possibly give a couple of my men a ride in your vehicle to pick up some food for all these guys?"

The Captain replies that he will personally drive the men to get some food then bring it back in his van. In fact, he leaves his two soldiers at each wingtip of the jet as guards.

While Cotton and Robert leave with the Captain to purchase some food and coffee, Cajun and Booker start the auxiliary power unit then turn on the air conditioning. Even though all the men could do with a few more hours of sleep, at least they feel somewhat rested after the six hours of shuteye. One by one, each man walks outside to the rear of the aircraft to stretch his legs and relieve himself. With every moment, each man becomes a little more awake and as hungry as a lion in a sheep shearing pen.

Finally, the Captain returns with Cotton and Robert who carry in two large boxes of food plus two thermoses full of Yiragacheffe coffee. As it turns out good coffee is grown in Ethiopia.

The Captain offers these words as the men line up for their breakfast and coffee, "Our Ethiopian coffee ceremony is unique, and a mark of hospitality for visitors. Ethiopians give it the respect it deserves with this coffee ceremony." With that explanation, he goes through a series of hand gyrations and bows as part of his ceremony.

Each box lunch contains a sandwich with injera flatbread, cheese, and scrambled eggs. The box lunches also have an apple and a big banana. Cajun is very impressed with the fresh strong coffee as are all his men. When Cajun tries to pay for the food, the Captain refuses to take any money. "Please, no money; accept our food with the compliments of the Ethiopian National Defense Forces." After thanking the Captain, Cajun excuses himself so that he can continue with the task at hand.

Cajun finally gets around to calling Pigeon on his satellite phone. "Pigeon, this is Ethan. We have arrived. The Captain was nice enough to fix us up with some chow and some very good coffee."

Pigeon says, "I will be over there with a truck to pick up you and your men in about an hour. We are also arranging for a cargo pallet loader to come over to remove your equipment off the plane. Get your stuff ready to unload."

"Ok, we will be ready" replies Cajun. Just then he can see the cargo loader slowly making its way up the taxiway in their direction.

Cajun issues orders to depart, "Guys, get your stuff ready. Be prepared to load onto a duce and half truck in a few minutes. Everybody be sure to bring your mission brief document with you. Do not leave them on the plane. Later we will burn them when we are with American troops. Cotton, Booker, the loader is almost here so let's get ready to unload these pallets."

They answer in unison. "Yes, Sir, we're on it."

Jack says to Cajun, "I called ground control to have them send over a fuel truck. They said they couldn't get them over here for another two hours."

"That's OK, as it will take almost forty-five minutes to complete unloading these pallets" ,replies Cajun.

Cajun corners Jason and Javen, the two standby 737 pilots who are going to fly the airliner back to Bristol. "Guys, there is a box to the left of the Captain's seat, which contains $20,000 in Egyptian pounds currency. As soon as we have cleared the tarmac and you have been refueled, why don't you get underway back home?"

Jason says, "As soon as we have everything we need onboard, we'll get underway."

Cajun is already shifting his mind back to getting the task of having the pallets unloaded.

Both Jason and Javen look somberly at Cajun and Javen says, "We both want you to know we are pulling for you in the successful completion of your mission. You guys stay safe and God speed."

Cajun and Jack both shake their hands, thanking them in silence. Nothing further must be said, but it is nice to have these men supporting their efforts. From this moment on Cajun considers this moment a shift in the responsibility for their 737 to Jason and Javen.

Chapter Twelve...
Where Is Savannah?

Awasa, Ethiopia

The cargo loader labors up to the aircraft. Both Cotton and Booker are there on the ramp supervising the operation. After all, if you do not watch them closely, non-experienced ground personnel can easily damage the aircraft. If that happens, it could take forever to have the necessary repairs made. That would mean the aircraft could not be flown back to England anytime soon.

The first to come off are three pallets, which have passenger seats permanently affixed to them. Booker and Cotton must position themselves alongside each pallet then pull on the cargo netting draped over the pallets. This will make them roll on the hundreds of ball bearings installed in the flooring of the aircraft. After the first initial grunt to get the roll started, the very heavy pallet rolls with just a little force. When they position the pallet abeam the cargo door, just one big push toward the loader is all that is needed. The loader can grab the pallet then roll it onto the elevator to be lowered to the ground.

As the pallets are lowered to the ground, a fork lift picks them up then positions them all in a row at the rear of the aircraft. As that is taking place, Pigeon rolls up with a Humvee, two duce and a half trucks, plus five soldiers dressed in desert camouflage uniforms. They hurriedly remove the cargo netting over the boxes on each pallet then start loading them on the two trucks. The last to come off the aircraft is the portable steel rig for lifting and maneuvering the weapon. Within thirty minutes the pallets are cleared of cargo then reloaded onto the 737.

Jack and Cajun jump in the Humvee with Pigeon. The other men jump in the back of the two trucks containing the cargo. They start to drive off. Standing at the foot of the air stairs of the 737 are Jason and Javen. At first they wave then each holds his fist in the air with thumbs standing straight up. Cajun and Jack are waving back as they drive off then give them the thumbs up as well. There is a real palpable feeling in the air that danger is coming their way soon. The real mission is about to begin.

As they drive out of the airport area, the convoy turns north towards Lake Awasa. After a thirty-minute drive they arrive at a desolate area two miles inland from the northeast shoreline of the lake.

There is a small American compound surrounded by barbwire, complete with guards and guard dogs at the makeshift gate. At the center of the compound are the two helicopters Pigeon had promised, both painted in a desert camouflage paint scheme. All the vehicles come to a stop near the helicopters. Everyone gets out of their vehicles giving the helicopters a good look.

Cajun walks up slowly to take a real good look at the Cobra while Jack is busy inspecting the Chinook. Both men are having a sense of Deja vu as they run their hands over the skin of the aircraft. They stand for the longest time letting their eyes drink in the beauty of the machines. These helicopters had played such a big role in their days in the Army. Finally, Cajun says to Pigeon. "Well, even though I had asked for flat black, I am very pleased with this camouflage paint scheme."

Pigeon says with pride, "I thought you might be."

After a few short minutes, Pigeon calls Cajun aside. "Cajun I need for you to follow me into my tent over behind the mess hall. I want to review all the details of the mission so far, and I have some information on the whereabouts of Savannah."

Cajun's eyes light up when he hears Savannah's name. He decides there is no time like the present to talk about Savannah. After all, that is one of the main reasons he took on this dangerous mission on behalf of the United States. "OK, let's go talk some business." Cajun is already two strides into his walk toward Pigeon's tent.

Cajun stops short of the tent to allow Pigeon to catch up to open the flap on the tent. As soon as they are inside the small tent, Pigeon offers Cajun a seat on a little portable, folding chair. "First let me bring you up to date on the mission and a few loose ends as of today."

"I was able to locate all six of the three-hundred-gallon fuel bladders you requested. We managed to talk two different Chinook Heavy Lift Battalions, temporarily out of three bladders each, with a promise to replace them ASAP. One outfit was regular Army. The other was your old National Guard unit. I expect the bladders to be here by tomorrow morning. Our guys will have them installed and filled with fuel by tomorrow night."

Cajun responds "That's good, I was worried we might have to have them flown in from North Carolina, which would have delayed us a week."

Pigeon continues, "I have two nuclear weapons experts who should be on the same transport aircraft as the fuel bladders. They are both with the Air Force, however one of them is a prior Marine with combat experience. They will be dressed in unmarked desert style camo uniforms with fake civilian identification. I really had to pull some strings to get these guys, so take care of them. Make sure you get them back in one piece."

"We're glad to have them onboard. There would not be much sense in going any further without them."

Pigeon continues with his update, "Our source in Mogadishu stated as of three days ago, the nuclear weapon is still in the same place. He does not see any evidence that it will be moved in the near term. The sooner we get in position to rescue that weapon, the better all of us will feel."

Cajun tries to bring Pigeon up to speed on his team's progress and says, "Well here is where we stand. Wyatt and his guys are still on the high seas headed for Djibouti. It should take them another three days to reach port. We have given them a week to drive across to our rally point near the Somalia border. Once we are on the border and meet up, it will take one more day to set up camp outside Baidoa. If you add all that up, I would expect we would launch our attack and rescue of the weapon early in the morning nine to thirteen days from now."

"Now I have to give you some bad news that may affect the timing of this whole operation" ,Pigeon says sheepishly.

Cajun ask, "What is the problem?"

"Savannah has run into some difficulty down around Gode. It seems the hospital where she was working was attacked and raided by some Somali gunmen."

Cajun reacts immediately and predictably as he jumps from the small folding chair he is sitting on, to get right up in Pigeon's face. He asks question after question, "What do you mean she was attacked and raided? Is she alright? Where is she now?"

Pigeon holds his hands to Cajun's chest to stop him from advancing any further. "Savannah was kidnapped along with an Ethiopian woman with a young son."

Cajun cannot believe his ears. What is Pigeon saying to him? He is having a difficult time digesting all this information at once. All kinds of scenarios are racing through his mind. As rare a case as it may be, Cajun is speechless.

Pigeon raises his voice a little and says, "Cajun sit down and I will give you as much information as I know about the incident. Maybe we can figure something out." Cajun does as he is told. He slowly retreats to a sitting position on the small folding chair. Cajun has a pronounced blank stare on his face.

"The town of Gode is in the Ogaden region. In fact, the whole area is a territory on a plateau. Long story short, although most of the inhabitants there are Somali and speak the Somali language, Gode is part of Ethiopia." Pigeon says as he continues saying what he knows. As one Somali resident stated to me, "Those Ethiopian dogs are a bunch of killers and rapists. We have nothing in common with Ethiopians. It is a real insult to say Somali residents who live in and around Gode are Ethiopian."

"The Ethiopian Army launched a military crackdown early this year in Ogaden. The main rebel group is the Ogaden National Liberation Front, which is fighting against the Ethiopian government."

Cajun is becoming impatient and wants Pigeon to give him the bottom line. "Ryan, stop with this history lesson already, just tell me what you know about what happened to Savannah."

Pigeon continues, "Occasionally, Somali Muslims stage raids in the area just to let the Ethiopian military know that they are still around. They want them to know they can execute guerrilla tactics anytime they wish. We have an informant in the area. He is doing his best to find the location of where they have taken Savannah. Just give me another day or two and hopefully I will have something for you."

Cajun responds with hope in his voice, "Pigeon, just get me some information. Get me anything at all that we can act on."

Ryan sits down directly in front of Cajun so that he can look him straight in the eyes. "I will get you the information you want but you and I have to have an understanding as to what you are going to do. There are multiple countries and millions of people counting on you doing your job. We cannot jeopardize everything right at this moment to find Savannah."

Cajun looks up from the sand, which makes up the floor of the tent. "No way will I jeopardize our mission, but you can bet there is no way I will leave Savannah to languish in the hands of these Muslim fanatics. Now we have as much as eight to ten days before all our assets have to be gathered at Baidoa to stage our attack in Mogadishu. You get me some information and give me some help so that I can get her back, if she is still alive."

Pigeon responds with haste, "Oh she is alive all right and probably unharmed. She is a nurse. That is why they grabbed her."

Cajun's brain is working at light speed. "OK, by tomorrow afternoon the extra fuel bladders will have been installed. Give me some of your men. We will take the Cobra and Chinook into the area. Once you have the location identified, we'll go in and get her out."

"I cannot give you American forces on a mission like that. You will have to find another way" ,Pigeon responds with authority in his voice.

Cajun knows he must get Pigeon's undivided attention if he is to get any backup to get her out. He speaks in a slow steady voice, "Do not tell me that. There are American forces all over Ethiopia staging raids to root out Al Qaeda. In fact, you and I agreed several days ago that the cover story for our presence in Ethiopia is to assist in that joint task force. What was the name of that force, Pigeon?"

Pigeon rolls his eyes and makes a rolling gesture with his right hand, and says, "It is the Combined Joint Task Force Horn of Africa."

Cajun continues getting more excited as he continues. "As I recall, the U.S. has around fifteen hundred American troops for this CUF HUA outfit."

Pigeon corrects Cajun. "CJTF-HOA, it's called the CJTF-HOA Task Force."

Cajun's mind is already knee deep into his mission planning phase. "Follow me here, Pigeon. I know this is an unexpected request, but it all makes sense. No way in hell does it put you at odds with your bosses or the Ethiopian government. That task force is there to support counter terrorism activities in the region, right? The Ethiopian government would like nothing better than me going in and shooting up a bunch of skinnies after they were just humiliated with the raid on Gode."

He continues, "I just need you to authorize a couple of squads and some refueling. I will get her out then we will get back on station in time to complete our real mission. Now what do you say, Pigeon, just like the old days? We will kick their asses and make them very sorry they ever took an American woman, then be back in time for breakfast." Cajun asks earnestly, "What is it going to be Pigeon, you with me?"

Ryan reels to sit back down on his little chair while the wheels churn in his brain. There is no question that his risk-taking buddy Ethan Breaux is once again placing him in harm's way, but he also knows Cajun has it right. There really will be no explaining to do with the Ethiopian government. He knows he is bending the rules with the State Department, but what the hell. Pigeon gets right up in Cajun's face. "Ok, I will start making some phone calls tonight to see what I can do, but with two conditions."

Cajun looks puzzled, "And what are the conditions Pigeon?"

Ryan looks at Cajun defiantly. "One, you take me with you on this raid. And two, quit calling me Pigeon."

Ryan immediately walks past Cajun out of the tent, but on his way out he says, "You had better start doing some mission planning because we are going to be airborne before you know it."

Cajun is left standing with his mouth open. He has created a college boy, CIA ass kicking machine. Pigeon is tired of standing in the wings. He wants to eliminate some of those skinnies first hand. After all, they have messed with his old girlfriend as well.

The first thing Cajun does is to leave the tent to find his men. He gets their attention then summons them over to the rear of the Chinook. As each man walks in his direction they can already tell the plans have changed. After they gather, Cajun turns to walk into the interior of the helicopter motioning them to follow. He is leading them off the beaten path to have a private strategy briefing. Jack, being the senior man of the group speaks up first. "What's up, Cajun? Have our plans changed?"

Cajun looks back at the men, alternately searching each for their reactions. "Men, something fairly drastic has happened. You all remember my ex, Savannah?" Each of them is familiar with Savannah and they know that she means everything to him.

Cotton speaks up, "Yea, Boss, we all know Savannah. What about her?"

"Well as it happens, she is a nurse working in Ethiopia helping the poor inhabitants. As it turns out she was working in an area controlled by the Ethiopian National Defense Forces. Some Somali skinnies came across the border to stage a raid in Gode. They took her, along with a couple other people. Right now, we don't know where she is, but Pigeon has a couple informants in the area who are trying to find out."

"I have Pigeon trying to get us a couple squads of Special Forces to accompany us in to shoot up the place and get her out of there." Cajun continues with humility in his voice. "Now I know this is way above and beyond what you signed up for, but I am asking, if any or all of you will go with me to get her out. Before any of you answer, I want you to know that if any of you decide not to join me, I will not hold it against you. I will just find another way."

The men are looking back and forth at each other when Jack speaks up. "Cajun, no way are we going to let you go off to get even with those skinnies without us." The other men nod in the affirmative that they are in for the rescue mission.

Cajun feels a great relief, and smiles a grateful smile at his men. "Ok, here's the deal, we must get everything ready for the mission so that we can launch ASAP. Get the Cobra armed. As soon as the fuel bladders show up, strap them down in the Chinook then get them filled with JP-5. Cotton and Booker, get those 50-Cals mounted in the doors. Let's all get our personal weapons and night vision goggle equipment checked out ready to go. Make sure the hoisting equipment is checked out operationally as we may be forced to lift some personnel up with the hoist rather than land."

Everybody scatters taking care of the multitude of details necessary to carry out a mission over one hundred miles away.

CHAPTER THIRTEEN...
RESCUE MY WOMAN

Awasa, Ethiopia

Cajun opens his personal bag to remove all the terrain mission planning charts. He is searching for his box of multi-colored felt pens. Already drawn in black with great accuracy are the routes from Awasa to the border, to Baidoa, then to Mogadishu. Searching for a different color marker to trace out his route on the chart for the Ogaden region, he instinctively grabs the red marker. Cajun thinks, "Yea this red route is the color I want because it denotes this mission is an emergency and it denotes the blood that will be shed by the skinnies for grabbing my woman." As Cajun begins to plan the mission, he has severe malice in his heart. Somebody is going to pay dearly if they lay so much as a hand on Savannah.

It seems like a lifetime before Pigeon comes along to check on Cajun's mission planning progress. Pigeon knows there simply is not a better man alive who can take certain conditions, equipment, personnel, enemy position, enemy strengths, weather, and overall mission objective, to produce an executable plan in a short amount of time.

Pigeon walks up the rear loading ramp onto the Chinook to find Cajun listing positions on the chart. He is logging distances, bearings, fuel loads, plus flying times onto pre-made mission briefing cards they had developed in their days in Iraq. Pigeon shakes Cajun back into the present and says, "Let's take a break to go eat some chow and talk about our progress."

Cajun looks up from his planning as if he does not want to take his mind off his work then thinks better of the suggestion. "Ok, maybe I should take a break. Do you have any more information on Savannah's whereabouts?"

Pigeon has been expecting his question. "Come on, let's get some food, then I'll bring you up to date."

The two men walk down the ramp of the helicopter in the direction of the outdoor chow hall area. It is just an area where a couple cooks have placed their outdoor kitchen equipment. Other soldiers within the compound are starting to filter through as well. Pigeon and Cajun grab their paper plates then go through the line. Within twenty seconds they come out on the other side with rice covered in beef stew. There is neither salad nor vegetables. After grabbing bottled waters, the two men sit on the tailgate of a duce and a half duce and a half truck.

Pigeon begins providing what information he has because he knows if two seconds of silence should go by, Cajun will be bugging him for news. "I have been in contact with headquarters back in Djibouti. They have agreed to send us two squads of ten men each and seem very glad to be involved. Anytime they can get in on events that are hot, they are Johnny on the spot. The Special Forces will be flown out in the morning in a Chinook, then meet us at a specific rally point. They will sling extra fuel bladders to top off each helicopter in the field. I will give you the coordinates when we get back to your office."

Cajun asks with a sense of urgency, "What about Savannah? Has she been located?"

Pigeon has just shoveled a mouthful of that questionable beef stew and cannot answer for several seconds. Cajun is squirming in anticipation, while Pigeon chews his beef stew. He swallows hard then answers, "My informant on the ground knows where the Somali base is located. It is no secret; even the Ethiopian military knows where it is. What my informant does not know is where within the base camp she is located."

Tomorrow morning, our agency will have one of our intelligence satellites being redirected over the area to get some high-altitude photos of the camp. It will be taking pictures for about five minutes at a time, every time it passes over this part of the world. Pigeon looks directly at Cajun and says, "Go ahead, don't be shy, ask me how I was able to get the big boys to redirect one of our spy satellites?"

Cajun responds with his question, "I am proud of you. How did you get them to place our situation at the top of their priority list then redirect the satellite?"

"Well as you know, there is a fairly big operation underway with the CJTF-HOA Task Force. This recent attack by the Ogaden National Liberation Front in Gode is the most aggressive action in months. In fact, I was given an attaboy for my offensive stance. Can you believe that? Here we are going to rescue your girlfriend, who was my old girlfriend. I am not only given troops and equipment but they offer to redirect a billion-dollar spy satellite."

Cajun cannot restrain his impatience. "Well, what are the chances we are going to get some actionable intelligence as to where Savannah is located? She may not even be in that camp. Maybe it was a rogue group that raided Gode?"

Pigeon tries to calm Cajun down. "Cajun, tomorrow morning we will have multiple high-quality photos of the entire camp every couple of hours. For that matter, we might even see her being moved from tent to tent. If nothing else we can identify all the tents where soldiers are housed. Then all we must do is to locate a headquarters or medical tent. Plus, my informant has ways of getting near the encampment even though he is an Ethiopian. So just relax, we will come up with something tomorrow."

"This is my recommendation. The C-130 transport will be in early in the morning around 0300 hours. My men will meet the aircraft then grab the fuel bladders along with the nuclear experts. We will have the bladders installed earlier than my previous prediction. I will expect that we could launch by noon tomorrow then fly in the direction of Gode. Our men will fly up from Djibouti to meet us half way. After that, we will form up in the desert to bed down so that everyone can get a few hours of sleep. While all that is happening, we will compare all the photos with updated information we'll get from our informant. Once we have that information in front of us, we will complete our mission planning. We should launch around 0300 hours. What do you say to that, Cajun?"

After thinking for a few minutes in silence, Cajun answers, "Ok, that plan sounds good enough to me. I am going to check with all my guys to make sure we are taking all the steps necessary to be able to fire up the engines and go with five minutes' notice somewhere between ten am and noon tomorrow. My goal tomorrow is to get this gaggle moved across Ethiopia then south down into the area of Gode as soon as we can. That way, when we get there, our guys can refuel then perform some maintenance on the birds before settling down for some rest."

Pigeon says, "All right, we have the assets and a plan. Let my guys get those fuel bladders installed then we'll go."

Cajun feels good about the way things have progressed. He gets up to head over to his Chinook to bed down. As he walks away, he turns to add one more request. "For now, we are going to bring the Air Force nuclear guys with us, but when we launch against the encampment, I want them left behind. We cannot afford to get those guys injured."

Pigeon laughs and replies, "Can you imagine taking our Air Force personnel into a fire fight? I would never hear the end of it. My guess is that those two guys already expect they are going to be housed in air-conditioned tents."

As Cajun walks over to where the helicopters are located, his guys see him coming. They know instinctively they need to check in with him as often as possible. For all they know, the plans may have changed again. They could be airlifted to South Africa to eat mussels and drink beer with the Prime Minister for all they know. With Cajun, you just never know. Jack speaks up and says, "What's up, Boss?"

Booker adds, "Boss, are we still on track to locate Savannah?"

Cajun reports, "Guys, everything is on track to get her back. We hope to pull pitch somewhere between 1000 hours and noon tomorrow. So let me know if there is any reason why the Cobra, the Chinook, or any of you are not ready to go. Tomorrow night we will be studying satellite photos of the area as well as obtaining some ground intelligence. After we bed down tomorrow night, we will get up and kick some skinny ass around 0400 hours."

Cotton interjects his two cents. "Cajun, everything is looking good here. All the maintenance on both birds has been performed. We are pretty much ready to go. All we must do is collect our fuel samples early in the morning. Just say the word and we will be ready to pull pitch in five minutes."

"Ok guys, get some sleep tonight while you have the chance because you won't get much tomorrow night."

Early the following morning, Cajun is awakened by the movement of a duce and a half truck starting up then departing the compound. He falls back to sleep with the knowledge that Pigeon has sent some of his men to pick up the bladders and Air Force nuke specialist.

Just before dawn, Cajun can hear the duce and a half returning with the cargo. Sure, enough the truck pulls right up to the Chinook. All who are sleeping wake up grudgingly. They dismount from their hammocks hanging all over the inside of the Chinook.

It is amazing how quickly these men are standing with their hammocks in hand after having unhooked them from their mooring hinges. Within five minutes from the time the truck arrives, the aircraft is completely empty and ready to have the fuel bladders strapped down. Cajun puts his hammock away in his bag then leaves the area for the compound latrine.

When Cajun returns, he brushes his teeth with water out of his canteen. Pigeon walks over to him with two men in tow. "Ethan Breaux, I would like you to meet our two brainiacs representing the United States Air Force."

Cajun spits out his toothpaste then wipes his mouth with the back of his hand. He wipes the excess moisture on the side of his flight suit then reaches out to shake hands with both men. "Hello, please call me Cajun, everybody else does. He asks the man on the left as he shook his hand, "And what is your name?"

"My name is Master Sergeant Nathan Truman."

The other man steps forward. "My name is Senior Master Sergeant Paul Bell."

Cajun ask, "One of you is prior Marine Corp."

"Sgt. Truman speaks up and says, "That would be me, Sir."

Cajun looks at Sgt. Bell and ask, "You have more stripes, I take it you are the senior, most experienced of the two. Is that correct?"

Sgt. Bell answers swiftly, "That would be correct, Sir, however, when it all boils down, our knowledge of nuclear weapons is pretty much equal. You can count on either of us."

Cajun wants to put them at ease. "First of all, gentlemen, did you know that although I was once in the Army, today I am a civilian under contract with the United States government?"

Sgt. Bell replies. "Yes, Sir, we have been thoroughly briefed on your civilian status and your military record. I might add that both of us are proud to be working with you on this mission."

Cajun replies, "Well I do appreciate your kind words, but you must understand something. When I was on active duty I was a Chief Warrant Officer. My men referred to me as Chief or Cajun. Please call me Chief or Cajun, whichever you prefer. I plan on referring to you as Nathan and Paul. Is that ok with you?" Both men nod in the affirmative.

Pigeon breaks in on the conversation and says to Cajun, "Well for now we will leave you to take care of your personal business. You guys can talk again when you're ready." They turn and walk away. Before long, Pigeon is introducing them to all the men. They all sit down to share some war stories like who was where, when, and who knew who back in the day. The new guys fit right in as part of the team.

After a while, Cotton and Booker walk the two new guys through their positions and responsibilities when the attack to rescue the nuclear weapon takes place. They are briefed on emergency exits, ammunition boxes, night vision goggle equipment, plus everything else they could think of to prepare them for action.

Cajun walks onto the rear ramp of the Chinook to ask the four of them to take seats on the fold down chairs. After everyone is seated, Cajun ask them, "I believe it is safe to say that between me and my guys we don't know enough about nuclear weapons to fill a thimble. Just what is it you guys will be doing when we get our hands on the weapon?"

Sgt. Bell answers, "Our job is to immediately check the condition of the weapon. Has it been armed? Has it been damaged? Is it really a nuclear weapon?"

Sgt Truman adds, "Once we have a general sense of the condition of the weapon, then we'll be there making sure it is not damaged when it is moved and loaded onto the helicopter."

After thinking about their answers for a few seconds, Cajun asks another question. "Tell me, what happens if during the time you guys are making the checks that you just described, you determine that the weapon has been armed or is in some way a threat of detonating?"

Nathan answers, "If it has been armed, we will disarm it. We all must remember this weapon is crude as compared to weapons made in the U.S. Arming and disarming is relatively simple."

Cajun thinks then answers after several seconds of silence. "I won't ask for an answer now, but think about what I am going to ask you and perhaps give us an answer in an hour or so. If for some reason neither one of you can be involved with the weapon, could you advise us on disarming the weapon?" To lighten the mood, Cajun adds, "You never know around here, you could both come down with Montezuma's revenge by eating this Army chow."

Everybody laughs aloud for several seconds. Sgt. Bell finally quits chuckling and motions with his fingers to those listening to come a little closer, as though he is going to pass along some words of wisdom. "If the bomb has been armed and we cannot get to the weapon to disarm it, run like the wind."

Everybody laughs just as hard as before. Cajun was hoping there could have been a more satisfactory answer. Ah what the hell, either he will be able to get them in to handle the weapon or he will not.

One of the regular army troops walks by where Cajun is jawing back and forth with the men. "I have been told to tell you guys that this morning will be your last chance to grab some hot chow. Breakfast is being served over in the dining room." All the guys more-or-less drop what they were doing to start walking toward the chow truck.

When Cajun arrives at the makeshift chow hall, Pigeon is already in line. In fact, he has made it all the way to the coffee thermos. Cajun stares at Pigeon's plate as he walks past. "MMMMmmmm scrambled eggs, rice, plus mystery meat." Cajun takes his place in line, which at this point is only five deep.

Cajun has his paper plate filled with food then retrieves some coffee. He sits down next to Pigeon on one of the small folding chairs. "Here we are again Pigeon, getting ready to ride off into battle once more. I thought we had better sense than to get involved in this stuff again."

Pigeon takes a sip of his coffee. "It seems to be our fate in this life alright." Both men eat their chow in silence.

After Pigeon finishes his breakfast, he walks over to throw his trash in a big plastic bag. He turns to the group still sitting around eating breakfast. "Alright, listen up everybody. The installation of the fuel bladders is going much faster than we thought it might. I expect they will be finished and full of fuel in another hour or so. My recommendation is that you get your gear together then check in with Cajun.

He looks at Cajun still sitting on the little folding chair. "Cajun, all we want you to do today is lead us across country to our rally point so we can meet up with our Special Forces by nightfall." Pigeon reaches down to hand Cajun a piece of paper then continues, "Those are the coordinates of our rally point."

Cajun stands up to address the group. "We will have a mission brief at ten hundred hours by the Chinook."

At ten hundred hours sharp all the men who are participating in the movement of the gaggle of helicopters across Ethiopia to the rally point near Gode are gathered around. Cajun begins, "Well it looks like we have everybody who is going with us today." He hands out mission brief cards to the pilots then continues speaking. "I will be flying in the Chock One position in the Cobra along with Jimmy. Jack will be in the Chock Two position flying the Chinook with Morley as his Co-Pilot. Brian, you will fly in the jump seat position on the Chinook and back up any of us whose asses get too sore in the seat." Pigeon will be riding with you guys, so if you want to switch out of the jump seat with him, feel free."

The briefing continues covering all the standard items such as checkpoints along their route utilizing GPS. Cajun also covers both primary and secondary frequencies for radio communication. After the complete brief, Cajun says, "OK, engine start in fifteen minutes, ten minutes for systems and engine power checks, then we will be underway." All the pilots started putting on their gear then dropping into their individual pilot seats.

As Cajun and Jimmy lower themselves in the Cobra pilot seats, the crew chiefs are there aiding them with their shoulder harnesses. Once they are settled in, Booker helps Cajun attach the long rail on the top of the canopy to the attachment fixture on his helmet. The rail is part of the armament aiming system. As the pilot selects then activates a particular weapon system, the rail aiming system controls the turret in the nose of the helicopter. As the pilot moves his head from side to side or up and down while peering through an aiming eyepiece on his helmet, the turret will follow his head movement.

Cajun feels the excitement of having a Cobra Attack helicopter strapped to his back like the old days. He speaks to Jimmy over the aircraft intercom. "OK, Jimmy, here we are again. It has been a while since we both flew one of these machines so let's take it slow. Let's take our time going through the checklist so that we can familiarize ourselves with all the switch locations."

Jimmy begins with item one on the checklist. Cajun replies to each call out on the checklist.

"Shoulder Harness."

"Shoulder Harness On and Locked."

"Night Vision Goggles."

"Night Vision Goggles Not Required."

"Anti-Torque Pedals."

"Anti-Torque Pedals Centered and Free."

"Cockpit Windows."

"Cockpit Windows Closed and Locked."

"Battery Switch."

"Battery Switch On."

Jimmy and Cajun continue through the checklist item for item, making sure that the engine start is done by the book. After the engines are started, Cajun slowly pulls pitch into the blades, which lifts the helicopter smoothly into the air. Cajun hovers the Cobra out into a clear area away from the compound so as not to blow all the regular Army troops off their feet. They continue with their systems check. Finally Cajun pulls in enough power to where they are hovering in out of ground effect at a fifty-foot hover. Jimmy speaks over the intercom, "Ok the predicted value for our Out of Ground Effect hover power, at this weight and temperature, is 32 pounds of torque. I am reading 31.5

pounds of torque. It looks like we have slightly stronger than average engines."

When Jack and Morley go through and complete their engine start, they immediately hover out near Cajun. Jack calls over the radio to Cajun, "I thought we had better move out here otherwise we would likely have turned over some equipment if we stayed to do our Out of Ground Effect power checks." Cajun and Jimmy lower the Cobra back on the ground. They reduce their power to flat idle to conserve fuel.

After a few minutes Jack and Morley are back on the ground at flat idle. Cajun sees this and turns his rotating beacon off then back on as a signal that both flight crews have thirty seconds to bring their engines back up to takeoff power. They are going to pull pitch to depart. After thirty seconds, Cajun turns his rotating beacon off then pulls in takeoff power. Jack follows close behind and to the right in an Echelon Right formation. Both flight crews hack the time at 10:44 hours then write their fuel on board onto the flight plan.

During the flight toward Gode area Cajun and Jimmy take turns finding and identifying every switch and circuit breaker in the cockpit. They take turns finding the weapons control switch. At first the idea is to find it by feel without looking at the switch. Then they practice selecting each weapon system by rotating the switch in a counter clockwise direction.

"AAAaaaaahhh, this air conditioner is just as good today as it was during the hot days back in Iraq" ,says Cajun.

"Yea Boss, I have it turned up high here in the front too. You know when they switched us out of these Cobras then transferred us into the Chinooks, this air conditioning is what I missed the most. Wow, I can feel that cold air being ducted under my legs and along my back" ,adds Jimmy.

Cajun says with admiration, "I know what you mean, Jimbo. Don't get me wrong, I love the Chinook for all the things that it will do, but I never let the fact that it doesn't have air con go unnoticed."

As the gaggle moves away from the Awasa area and gets closer to Gode, Cajun slows to approximately one hundred knots forward airspeed, then drops down to low level flight. Being lower will reduce the chances of them being seen. Jack follows him down then slows as well.

Cajun is going to run low on fuel before they reach Gode since the total distance to their rally point of three hundred and six nautical miles is a little beyond the Cobra's range. Cajun picks a point way out in the boonies then slows to a hover. He lands the Cobra helicopter to the ground stirring up massive amounts of dust. Jack is right behind him. As soon as the Chinook is on the ground, Cotton and Booker refuel Cajun's Cobra out of the internal fuel bladders. Not a word is said to maintain radio silence.

Within fifteen minutes, Cajun is refueled and the crew chiefs are back onboard the Chinook. Cajun turns off his rotating beacon then turns it on again, signaling they will be pulling pitch to depart in thirty seconds. In thirty-seconds his rotating beacon is turned off again. The two pilots aggressively pull pitch into the rotors so the helicopters lift off quickly. This technique helps reduce the amount of dust stirred up on takeoff. Within a couple minutes the flight is level at one hundred feet AGL cruising at one hundred thirty knots.

As the gaggle gets closer and closer to their rally point, Cajun slows the flight down to fifty knots so they will not over fly the rally point. As they reach the GPS coordinates, Cajun can see why it had been selected by the Army unit flying up from Djibouti. Those crews have hundreds of hours of experience flying all around Ethiopia and have used this spot before.

The rally point is on the Ethiopian side of Gode. It is ten miles short of Gode, across the Shebelle River. The spot has protection of trees behind them and is an excellent location. The gaggle lands with the nose of the Cobra pointed in the direction of the only ground approach access to their location.

These men are all professionals. Within thirty minutes of their landing the aircraft, they already have them covered in camouflaged nets. Immediately, maintenance procedures are already being performed on both aircraft. The weapons bay on the Cobra has been opened checking the condition of the 20mm Gatling gun as well as the 40mm grenade launcher. Rockets in the two tandem rocket launchers are being removed and reinstalled in the tubes. This Cobra is certified to go to war at any time. Now all they must do is to wait for the two squads of Special Forces to arrive from Djibouti.

It is almost 1500 hours in the afternoon when the two Army Chinooks arrive. The pilots hover into the rally point. As soon as they land, the maintenance guys already cover them with camo nets. They can be seen performing all the maintenance required for their birds. The aircraft are topped off with fuel. The internal fuel bladders are removed from Jack's Chinook. They do not want that extra weight onboard while maneuvering during the attack on the Somali encampment. The fuel bladders are certified to be selfsealing tanks, but who knows for sure what will happen if an incendiary round goes through the walls of the bladder.

Within a few hours it is dusk. All the maintenance and aircraft preparation has been completed. The flight crews out of Djibouti have brought along fifty high resolution photographs that were taken in the morning hours by the spy satellite. Pigeon walks over to Cajun and Jack who are sitting inside the Chinook, just inside the back ramp. He holds up the photos and says, "We have our pictures. Let's look these over and try to determine what is what. Later, I will be in contact with my informant who is near the encampment area. All he has is a pair of long-range binoculars. If he gets too close and is captured he will be executed on site."

They all settle around Pigeon as each of the photographs is passed around and examined one after another. Just as Pigeon had predicted, the tents for the Somali soldiers are different from the two big tents near the western side of the encampment. Pigeon proposes, "If Savannah is being held captive in this encampment, there is no way they threw her to the dogs, they need her too much. There is no way she is being held in any of these soldier's tents, which make up eighty percent of the encampment."

Jack added, "Fortunately these dummies don't know the first thing about setting up a troop encampment area in a combat zone. Look how they have set up the two main tents on the edge of the encampment. All but two of the soldier's tents are located on the east side of the Headquarters and Medical tents."

Cajun speaks up and says, "Yea, I guess these guys think they did something good when they put the big tents toward the rear. So, what, we can just as easily swing around to the back as we could attack from the front."

Pigeon points at two of the photos that focused on the two big tents. "I do not see anything here, which tells me anything about who is in each tent. We could guess, and probably would be right, but we don't know for sure which one is the medical tent."

Cajun speaks up in a slow, aggressive voice and says, "My plan will be to use the Cobra to wipe out all the tents and soldiers near the two big tents. When I say wipe them out that is exactly what I mean. From the moment we arrive on the scene we will expend all but twenty percent of our ammunition. We will blast them with rockets and 40mm grenades. Within minutes there will not be a tent or a soldier within one hundred yards of the main tents."

"While we are eliminating the bad guys, Jack, you land directly in front of the big tents. Our Special Forces will jump out the back then immediately enter both tents. Their instructions will be to identify then rescue Savannah and any other captive nurses, then bring them out. Other than that, I do not expect there to be anyone else left standing. Again, I want all but twenty percent of their ammo expended. We want the survivors to think long and hard the next time they plan on crossing the boundary into Gode, let alone taking my woman."

While Cajun is voicing his battle plan, Pigeon and the other guys are looking down at the photos. They each lean back from their examination to look at each other. They know from the sound of Cajun's voice that he is out for bloody revenge. This attack will be carried out with extreme malice. Cajun adds, "Hopefully you will glean some information from your informant, Pigeon, but as far as I am concerned I already have enough information to plan out this mission. "Give me two hours and I will have the battle plan drawn out, then we will have our mission brief. I want these guys to get some sleep ASAP because we will be on station at precisely 0400 hours."

As everybody leaves to start taking care of their personal business, Cajun grabs Sgt Bell and Sgt. Truman then leads them aside. "I want you men to stay here in base camp tonight. This mission has nothing to do with you guys and we don't want you getting hurt."

Sgt Truman speaks up and says, "Sir, you do know that I am a former Marine. I would love to go with you to help. You can always use another gun."

"I know you are a former Marine and a Marine is always a Marine. However, you are now too valuable an asset. The whole world needs you to show up to deal with that nuke. Everything else takes a backseat to that obligation. Thank you for your offer, but the answer is no.

"Very well, Sir, but if you change your mind you can count on me," adds Sgt Truman.

At precisely 2000 hours Cajun calls all the men involved with the mission over to the Chinook for a briefing. As each man arrives,

Cajun hands them a mission brief card. On it are the coordinates for the Somali encampment, primary and secondary frequencies, engine start, assemble, and departure times. Also listed are the light beacon communication signals plus alternate return to base coordinates. That is just in case their base camp is discovered and attacked while they are gone.

The distance to the enemy encampment is ninety-eight nautical miles, meaning that with an average flying speed of one hundred thirty knots, the trip would take them approximately forty-five minutes. Cajun figures ten minutes on station at the outside, then a forty-five minute, return flight. The Cobra should land back at base with at least a thirty-minute fuel in reserve.

Cajun then stands in front of the group with ten photos Pigeon had given him earlier. "Pass these pictures around and give them back to me once everyone has had a chance to look at them." Cajun hands the packet of photos to Booker. He immediately examines the photos then passes them to Cotton.

"When you see them you will discover that there are two large tents in the south-western part of the base encampment. All the rest of the tents are surely soldier barracks. Our plan is to attack from the west straight to those two large tents. Jimmy and I will go in first. We will stay at one hundred feet above ground level in a firing hover. Chock One will be firing at and eliminating all the resistance in those tents within one hundred yards of the big tents. Jack and Morley will come in low then land next to the big tents. Jack, as soon as your forces have cleared the back ramp, reposition your aircraft. The rear should be facing the tents at an angle so that at least one of your door gunners can provide cover fire as our men exit the big tents."

Cajun goes on explaining the roll of the Special Forces by saying, "Both squads will exit the aircraft immediately to storm both of the larger tents. Do not fire indiscriminately as there are civilians inside. There are two or three nurses, one white woman and at least one, possibly two black women. Your job is to free them then kill everyone else. Whoever locates the women needs to depart the scene to return them to the Chinook immediately."

After the intense part of the briefing, Cajun lightens his tone just a little. "Ok guys, I want to be on station firing the first round at exactly 0400 hours. We need to lift off by 0315 hours. That means we form up at 0310 hours. I want to start engines at exactly 0300 hours. That will give us ten minutes to do systems and power checks. Once we get away from here, Jimmy and I will perform our weapons check by firing off a few rounds."

"All right gentlemen, now is the time to ask questions." Only one hand rose. It happened to be one of the Special Forces squad leaders

He asks, "Sir, are you the Cajun we heard about who was with the 1294th Aviation Battalion in Iraq?"

Cajun was a little taken aback but answered, "Yes, I was there as were most of the men sitting here tonight."

The squad leader continued with his questioning, "Is it true that you routinely point out that your group never takes prisoners, because GITMO is already full?" Everybody chuckles because they already know the answer.

Cajun answers emphatically, "The only time we ever captured a prisoner as opposed to killing the son-of-a-bitch, was when the CIA specifically asked us not to. They wanted to question a couple of them, so we obliged."

Wyatt walks back up to the front to stand next to Cajun. "It is not all that important what has taken place in the past. What matters is the type of enemy we will be facing when we attack at 0 dark thirty. These Somali fanatics are bottom feeders when it comes to low life human beings. They are products of a civilization which is stuck in the 13th century. They are underfed human beings who have in one way or another been mistreated by one leader or another. Their view of life is cheap and they have no honor."

"When you are dealing with Somali fighters you are dealing with uneducated misfits who would cut your heart out for a plate lunch. So, when we get in the camp do what you must do so we can leave and put as much distance as we can between us and them. Let's break up this briefing and get a little sleep" Wyatt says then turns to walk toward his tent.

All the men turned away from the briefing to seek out their sleeping bags.

It did not take long for Cajun to be awakened by Cotton and Booker as they move about the Chinook in preparation for the mission. Within a few minutes he and Jack are up and had put away their hammocks. Cajun leaves the aircraft then walks into the darkness to relieve himself. This is always the point of his missions that he loves the best. He loves to stand out in the darkness alone looking back to see the professionalism of all his men.

He gazes over to where the Special Forces have been racked out. He feels very proud that he will have the opportunity to watch these guys in action. In a way, he feels a bit of sorrow for the skinnies that will get in their way. Because these men are absolutely, hands down the most bad asses on the face of the earth. Thank God they are on his side.

As Cajun walks back to the aircraft, Cotton has already untied the rotor blades of his Cobra. Jimmy is in the process of lowering himself into the Gunners station. Cotton climbs up to help him strap in. Cajun climbs up into the Pilot in Command station. Cotton walks around and climbs up to help Cajun strap into his shoulder harnesses. He dons his helmet then installs his night vision goggles to the front of his visor. Cotton helps him attach the long rail for the turret aiming system to the attachment fixture on his helmet. Cotton finishes his preparations and holds his thumb up on his right hand. Cajun returns the OK signal by holding up his thumb.

Jimmy comes up on the intercom and says, "I'm up on the intercom and ready when you are to complete the Before Start Checklist."

Cajun replies, "OK Jimmy let's get started with the checklist all the way up to the point of pushing the button to start the engines. My watch shows 0255 hours, so we will complete the checklist and wait till 0300 hours to start the engines."

Jimmy said, "Roger Cajun, the first item on the checklist:

"Shoulder Harness."

"Shoulder Harness On and Locked."

"Night Vision Goggles."

"Night Vision Goggles On and Operational."

"Anti-Torque Pedals."

"Anti-Torque Pedals Centered and Free."

"Cockpit Windows."

"Cockpit Windows Closed and Locked."

"Battery Switch."

"Battery Switch On."

Jimmy and Cajun continue through the checklist item for item, making sure that the Before Engine Start checklist is completed, by the book, until they reach the point of engine start. At exactly 0300 hours Cajun presses the button to start engine number one. After both engines are started, they air taxi away from the compound to complete the systems and power checks. Jimmy fires off a few rounds to make sure the weapons are functioning correctly.

By 0310 hours they are in position to take off with their rotating beacon off. Within thirty seconds Jack and Morley land to Cajun's right rear in an echelon right formation. At 0314 and thirty seconds, Cajun turns on his rotating beacon indicating he will be pulling pitch in thirty seconds. Jack turns on his rotating beacon as well to indicate he was ready to go. At exactly 0315 hours, Cajun pulls pitch and takes off in a southerly direction headed to his first checkpoint. Jack is right behind him in the Chinook off to the right rear of the Cobra.

The aircraft stay at fifty feet above ground level enroute to the last point on the chart before they turn eastbound directly into the Muslim encampment. As they hit the checkpoint and roll left on a heading of zero nine zero degrees, Cajun slows the flight down to seventy knots. It is not long before they are picking up some light out of the darkness with their sensitive night vision goggles. Cajun slows to fifty knots forward airspeed.

As every second ticks by, more and more of the tents within the encampment come into view. Cajun climbs another fifty feet so that he will be in a better position to fire his weapons. Jack will be in a position under Cajun's Cobra, to land straight ahead directly in front of the big tents.

As they come to a hover, Cajun starts firing the 2.75, 70mm folding fin rockets. The rocket system is designed to fire in a direct line with the fuselage of the aircraft. Cajun puts a little pressure of the left anti-torque pedal, turning the nose of the aircraft left. He fires one pair of rockets. Tents blow up as bodies fly into the air. He fires a second pair of rockets with the same results and more. Several nearby tents disappear in balls of flame. The fires are so illuminating that Cajun's night vision goggles start to shut down.

Cajun applies a little pressure to the right anti-torque pedal, turning the nose of the aircraft to the right. He fires another pair of rockets which cause catastrophic devastation. Soldiers are running back and forth with their clothing on fire. The rockets are really intended for small vehicles and trucks. They are absolutely devastating to unprotected troops in the field. Cajun is completely, destroying the area.

Jimmy has his head down in the Gunners gyro stabilized scope. He begins his attack by firing the 40-mm grenade launcher. The "Chunker" is also a weapon designed to take out larger targets. Jimmy has four hundred rounds to fire and rains down absolute hell on the skinnies.

As skinnies escape their tents to grab their AK-47s to return fire, Jimmy switches weapon systems to the 20-mm Gatling gun. Now he has a weapon capable of firing seven hundred fifty rounds per minute. Every seventh round is a red incendiary round. As he fires, visions of Star Wars enter his mind as he turns his head left, right, up, and down while causing the weapon system to do the same. It looks as though he is firing a red laser into the abyss darkness of the soldier's tent area. Jimmy kills at least fifty soldiers.

Meanwhile Jack lands the Chinook straight to the ground in front of the tents. Both squads of Special Forces exit the aircraft then enter each tent within a few seconds.

Cajun fires all but two of his rockets. He saves them in reserve. Jimmy has completely run out of 40-mm grenades. He holds back some of his 20-mm ammo for their egress out of the area. Cajun looks down from his one-hundred-foot position. He keeps his eyes searching for Savannah to be led out at any moment. The seconds tick by and he still does not see her even though he witnesses an intense exchange of gunfire. Cajun thinks frantically to himself. "By God, I can't do anything for Savannah perched here at one hundred feet. We have already expended most of our ammo and did completely, destroy the tent area in excess two-hundred feet". He shouts over the intercom, "Lets land and help with the fight on the ground."

Jimmy shouts back over the intercom, "No need Boss, isn't that Savannah running out of the tent on the left?"

Cajun's heart sinks into the back of his chest. He yells into the intercom as though he is yelling down at Savannah, "Run Savannah! Run! Come on, Savannah, do not look back, just run!"

The Special Forces from both squads emerge to board the Chinook. Jack breaks radio silence and calls out "Go, Go, Go," just as he pulls pitch to climb into the night. At the same time the Chinook is lifting off the ground, it begins taking fire from about two hundred fifty feet away.

Cajun calls over the intercom, "Jimmy, empty your guns on those sombitches." At the same time Jimmy holds the trigger down with a steady burst, Cajun can see the incendiary rounds lighting up the night striking the intended targets. Cajun fires his last two folding fin rockets. As they turn to depart, the enemy return fire is no more.

Cajun pulls in lots of power with the collective increasing the Cobra's airspeed to 145 knots. Within seconds they have caught up with the Chinook. Everything starts to settle down as Jack comes up on the radio for a casualty check. "This is Savannah Chinook 100 calling Cajun, are you there, Cajun?"

"This is Cajun, is Savannah alright? Is she hurt?"

Jack replies with glee, "Why don't you ask her yourself? She's right here."

Savannah presses the microphone on the headset Pigeon has placed on her head in the cabin, "Ethan, Ethan, are you there?" He is so overwhelmed at hearing her voice he literally cannot speak.

Jimmy knows his old buddy is in bad shape. He comes up on the intercom, "Cajun, I have the flight controls, you just relax and talk to Savannah."

"Thanks Jimmy, you have the flight controls."

Savannah calls again over the radio, "Ethan, Ethan, are you there? Are you all right? Are you hurt?"

Cajun musters the strength to answer, "I'm all right Savannah, what about you? Are you hurt?"

"No, I'm not hurt except for my wrist where they had bound us with rope. Ethan, I cannot believe what has happened. What are you and your guys doing here in Africa? I cannot believe this! What are you doing here? I thought you were in England. How did you know where I was? She paused and asked, "Do you love me, Ethan?"

God he loves this woman. Here they are in Africa at five thirty in the morning, flying in the dark with night vision goggles after a fire fight rescue, and all she can do is ask question after question. A funny thought passes through his brain at the speed of light. He should have left her there so that she could ask so many questions to the Somali leader that he would pay money to anyone who would come to pick her up.

Jack speaks up and ask over the radio, "Boss, there are at least five people on headsets waiting for you to answer Savannah. I believe the question was do you love her?"

"Of course, I love Savannah, now let's get off the radio and maintain radio silence." Everybody smiles at the thought of what just happened. Cajun cracks a thin smile then leans back to cruise and ponder the recent events as Jimmy flies them back to base.

Chapter Fourteen...
Back To Base

Gode, Ethiopia

Once back at their temporary base and the rotor blades slowly quit spinning, everyone races over to the Chinook. As the ramp is gradually lowered, all the men on the two Special Forces squads come off first. Cajun is there to meet them. He can see there are some injuries. He recognizes the squad leader of team number one and ask, "Sergeant, what is the casualty report?"

The squad leader answers, "Sir, we have two men who were hit. One was hit in the arm and the other in the leg. We took several rounds in the chest area." The Sergeant pounds on the body armor protecting his chest.

Cajun sighs with relief, "No casualties, that is great news Sergeant. We will forever be in your debt."

Finally, Pigeon walks down the ramp helping Savannah. She starts to run down the ramp then picks up the speed to the point that she jumps off the ramp onto Cajun, nearly knocking him off his feet. They are completely oblivious to everyone else as they hug and kiss as though they will never part. Cajun starts to regain his composure and reality sets in. He starts to examine her body for injuries. "Are you injured anywhere?"

Savannah replies, "My face is bruised where those animals slapped me around. My wrists hurt the most. They bound our wrists very tightly to a tree."

No sooner had the words left her lips, her friend appeared at the top of the ramp. She begins slowly walking down with a small boy in tow. As Cajun looks at her and her son, he has the distinct feeling she is suffering from trauma. In fact, when she reaches the bottom of the ramp and starts to step down to the ground, her knees buckle to the point that Cajun and Pigeon must catch her. Cajun calls out loud and clear, "Medic! Medic!" Cotton picks up the small boy to console him saying that his mother will be all right. Within a few seconds both medics arrive and start to attend to the Ethiopian woman.

Cajun pulls Savannah aside. "What happened while you were there?"

"Ayana and I were taken because we were both nurses in the small clinic where we attended to the people around Gode. Her son always came into work with her because she did not have anywhere else to leave him. When the soldiers attacked, they were going to leave her son behind, but she wrapped both arms around him and would not let go. Even though they hit her in the face several times, she would not let go of him. Because they were in a hurry, they just decided to bring Negasi along too. His name is Negasi" ,Savannah explains.

"Once we got there, they demanded we treat the sick and injured in their camp. However, it was clear Ayana was despised because she is Ethiopian. The first night they separated us. They bound my wrists to a small tree by the medical tent."

"They took Ayana into the other tent. I could hear them shouting at her. She screamed as they began to hit her. Then her screams were in defense as they raped her again and again. Her screams subsided then finally stopped. I did not see her at all the second day."

"I kept Negasi with me in the medical tent. The third day she was brought back to the medical tent. I tended to her facial wounds. The fourth day they came in to demand she get back on her feet and begin treating their soldiers. She did as she was ordered. Finally, I lost track of time."

Savannah finally broke down and started to cry as she pressed her nose into Cajun's chest. The impact of what she had lived through started to come into focus. She wept for several minutes. Cajun did not move. He just held her, waiting for her grief to subside.

Cajun later rigs his hammock inside the Chinook to put her to bed. She falls asleep within a few minutes. After she is asleep, Cajun walks over to where the Special Forces men are about to turn in for the night.

Cajun sits down among them and asks how the rescue inside the camp went down. Only the two squad leaders respond. The first one says, "We took them completely by surprise, plus we were able to see in the dark as they could not. When we entered the tent we were hesitant to open fire until we had the civilians identified."

"We fanned out looking in our own sectors of the tent, when the skinnies started to reach their weapons. We had no choice but to open fire. Even as we opened fire we were all still scanning for any sign of the civilians. As it turned out, it was a sizable tent and there were more skinnies than we thought. It was a hell of a fire fight, but they lost, we won."

The second squad leader speaks up. "Our story is identical. The only difference is that we were able to immediately identify the civilians tied to a metal ammo box lying on the floor. As soon as we identified the situation we shouted for the women and the boy to stay down, then opened fire, and killed everybody in the tent. Many of the skinnies reached their AKs to return fire, but we were the victors. All I have to say, is God bless the son-of-a bitch that invented this body armor!" All the other men yelled, "Hua!"

Cajun lightly pounds his closed fist to his chest and says, "You guys did one hell of a job. We all owe you a debt of gratitude."

Cajun knows that nothing else need be said. He turns and walks away from their area. It is time he started thinking about bedding down himself, as tomorrow will be a big day. Cajun walks back up the ramp of the Chinook to where Savannah is sleeping. He rolls out a sleeping mat on the floor of the helicopter and lies down. As he lies there in the darkness, scenes from Savannah's rescue continue to play in his mind. Thank God none of men under his charge were killed. The last thought he has before he drops off to sleep is how good it is to be back in the Pilot in Command seat of his Cobra. That helicopter absolutely is an ass kicking machine.

"Wake up, wake up, Boss", says Cotton as he gently nudges Cajun with his boot. Cajun opens his eyes and instinctively knows there is a something wrong. Cotton will never wake him unless something needs to be addressed.

"What's the problem, Cotton?" ask Cajun as he slowly sits up to lean on his elbow.

Cotton explains, "Boss, we have a little problem with the Cobra."

Cajun ask, "What kind of problem, Cotton?"

Cotton kneels-down to talk with Cajun so that nobody else can hear. "You took some hits in your main rotor last night. One round went through one of the blades and another round grazed the second blade. You're lucky they only hit you with those two rounds, because any more hits and we would all be in big trouble."

Cajun sighs in relief, "Damn, Cotton, those skinnies almost got me didn't they?"

"Yea, Boss, it could have led to a catastrophic failure of the main rotor. You took three more bullet holes through the skin but they just passed through and kept on going. I can patch the hole in the blade with a temporary patch that will get us through the rest of the mission, but you may feel a slight out of balance oscillation in the cyclic" ,Cotton explains.

Cajun says to Cotton, "Go ahead and patch the hole as soon as possible. Do you think the patch material will be dry enough to fly out of here tonight?"

Cotton reassures Cajun, "No problem, Boss, the patch will be dry and sturdy within a few hours."

As Cotton turns and walks down the ramp, Cajun looks up to Savannah's hammock to see if she was awake yet. Savannah says, "I can feel you staring at me, Ethan Breaux. Why don't you help me get out of this hammock so that I can properly thank you for getting me out of that hell hole last night?"

Cajun stands up to put his arms around Savannah. He hugs her with all his might. Savannah lightly squeals, "Whoa, if you keep on squeezing me so hard I may never walk again."

Cajun slides his left arm under her legs to lift her out of the hammock. As he lowers her to the ground he finally speaks, "Savannah, you sure do feel good. I have so much to talk to you about and so much to ask you, I don't know where to start."

"Ethan, it will take a long time for us to get back up to speed, but for right now you have many other people to tend to before we get out of here. Don't worry about me right now, just show me where the restroom is located"

Cajun laughs and says, "OK follow me and I will take you to the master bathroom." While grabbing his toiletries, he takes the time to pull one of his Berettas from the holster, then walks her down the ramp of the

Chinook. Cajun leads her to the bush outside the landing zone. "Here is a toothbrush, toothpaste, toilet paper plus a little water to take care of your business." He also hands her his Berretta. "There are scary critters out here in the bush, so shoot them with this if any of them bother you."

She reaches to take the pistol with one hand while at the same time gestures for him to go away with the other. "OK, run along, I will be just fine."

Cajun walks back into camp looking for Pigeon. He locates him talking with the pilots of the Army Chinooks. Cajun walks up to join the conversation and says, "We have to start formulating a plan to get the hell out of here."

Pigeon replies, "Yea, we were just talking about that. These gentlemen want to get their men together to start back to Djibouti within a couple hours."

One of the Chinook pilots joins in the conversation. "We are back on the Ethiopian side of Gode, so we don't really have any problem with flying at any altitude we want on our way back to base."

Cajun says, "You guys are good to go. Our problem is that our next stop is the rally point to meet our men on the Somali border. We need to arrive there under the cover of darkness so that our position is not compromised. Our rally point is only ninety-one nautical miles from here. If we will take off at dusk, we will land no more than one hour later just after dark."

It appears the Djibouti based pilots have their plan for returning back to base. Cajun and Pigeon shake hands with them then turn to rejoin their crews. While walking back to the Chinook, Cajun says to Pigeon, "I would consider it a personal favor if you returned with those guys to Djibouti and took Savannah with you. In fact, you'll need to take her friend Ayana with you too."

Pigeon ask, "Is that what Savannah wants to do? Does she want to leave Africa all together?"

Cajun replies immediately with definite determination in his voice. "This is not all about what Savannah wants. At least if she returns with you to Djibouti, she will be in a different country without a passport. Put her under your wing then take her back to the United States. Now I know you can do that. Tell her the passport situation is out of your control and she has no choice but to go back to the U.S. to get her paperwork in order."

"Yea, you want me to take the wrath of Savannah because you want her out of Africa. And besides, Cajun, I am not going straight back home immediately. My plan is to be flown out to the U.S. Ronald Reagan and wait for you to complete the mission. I'm still working here you know."

"Why don't you take her with you to the carrier? After all, she is the responsibility of the U.S. Government now that we rescued her. I would imagine it would be proper protocol to have her debriefed once you get her back to proper facilities."

Pigeon ponders for a minute. "I will never know how you think all these things up, Ethan, but you're right again. It is within my responsibility to debrief her if I think it is necessary. I guess I think it is necessary. I will keep her with me until I get back to the United States. But let's you and I get one thing straight. I am not going to take grief from Savannah if she does not want to leave Africa. She will know you are behind it and will be on me like stink on a baby diaper."

Cajun smiles and reassures Pigeon, "I will take care of it, just leave it to me."

Cajun walks up to his men standing by the back ramp of the Chinook. Cotton is talking with Savannah, who has returned from the bush. Cajun smiles then walks up to Savannah to kiss her on the cheek. "Well, Sweetpea, are you ready for lunch?"

"Don't you Sweetpea me, Ethan Breaux. I saw you talking to Ryan about me. You were asking him to leave me here in Ethiopia, weren't you? Before he could answer she added, "I have had enough of Africa and want to go with you. You said you loved me and I do not want to get separated from you again."

She starts to continue nagging him when Cajun holds his hand to her lips. "Shush, nobody wants you to stay in Africa." He cannot believe his good luck that Savannah already wants to do what he wants her to do and says, "Pigeon and I just thought that you would likely want to continue your nursing work here in Ethiopia." Cajun is thoroughly enjoying this conversation, knowing that for once in his life he is going to influence Savannah to do what he wants her to do.

Savannah intensifies the conversation, "No, I have had enough of Africa. When I was handcuffed to that ammunition box by those animals to sleep on the floor, I said to myself, if I ever get out of here I will never return to this God forsaken country."

Cajun takes Savannah's face in both hands so she will have to look at him straight in the face. "There is something I am counting on you to understand. I was not sent here just to rescue you. My men and I are here on another mission for the U.S. Government. You cannot go with me when we leave this place. You must go with Pigeon. He will get you out of this country. In fact, he will be flying onboard a United States aircraft carrier to meet up with me and my men in about a week. If I can arrange it, would you fly with him to the carrier so we can meet up later?"

She looks back into his eyes wanting to ask a million questions, but decides maybe this time she would go along with the plan. "Can you persuade Ryan to take me with him?"

"I don't know but I will try" ,Cajun fights hard to hold back his smile.

Cajun motions over to Pigeon who was several yards away talking with Paul and Nathan about the nuclear weapon. He calls, "Pigeon, would you come over here for a few minutes?"

Pigeon nods then walks over to where Cajun and Savannah are standing away from everybody else. "Yes, what can I do for you two?"

"Pigeon, Savannah and I agree that she should leave Africa. Is it possible for you to take her with you back to the United States? She knows she will have to go with you on the aircraft carrier until we have finished our mission. And no, I did not tell her about the details of our mission so there is no need to kill her just yet."

Pigeon cannot believe his ears. He thinks to himself that Cajun must be the most silver tongue devil in the world as he can literally talk the stripes off a zebra. He tries to look surprised at the request then visibly ponders before he answers. "Well, I will have to make a few calls when we get back to Djibouti, but I will do my best to take her with me. Are you sure you want to fly aboard an aircraft carrier?"

Savannah immediately answers, "Oh yes, Ryan! Please do not leave me here in Africa. Take me with you to meet up with Ethan on the aircraft carrier."

Cajun winks at Pigeon out of sight of Savannah. "Well, it's settled then. Gather your friend and her son then get aboard one of these Chinooks headed back to Djibouti."

Pigeon looks back at Cajun in disbelief. Cajun had persuaded Savannah to do exactly what he wanted her to do. And what he wanted her to do is what he had convinced Pigeon to do just minutes earlier.

Cajun changes the conversation to another subject. "All right then, let's have lunch". He reaches down to the lower pockets of his flight suit and pulls out two pre-packaged ready to eat meals. Cajun offers them to Savannah. "Take your pick, roast beef or spaghetti with meat sauce."

She reaches with her hand opened and says "I'll have the roast beef please."

Pigeon walks away shaking his head from side to side in disbelief at what he had just witnessed. He walks over to inform the Chinook pilots that Savannah and the Ethiopian nurse would also accompany them back to base.

After lunch Savannah brings food and water to her friend Ayana. Her son Negasi was at her feet. Ayana appears to still be a little groggy from the sedative given to her by the medic in the early morning hours. Savannah opens the meals and helps feed her while Negasi devours his food. Savannah says to Ayana. "After you eat some food and you rest a little more, we are going to be flown out of here to safety." Ayana nods her approval without saying a word. Savannah feels that her silence has more to do with her mental trauma than the remnants of the sedative. She decides it best if she just lie down beside Ayana and Negasi. Savannah soon falls asleep.

Cajun could see the women asleep in the helicopter. So that he would not wake them, he signals his men to assemble under the largest tree on the most western side of their compound. All the guys, including Paul and Nathan, make their way over to the tree.

Once everyone is gathered, Cajun hands out briefing cards to the crewmembers. "Guys, our plan for the rest of the day is to stay out of the sun as much as possible and rest. Cotton, I have not yet examined the aircraft logbooks, but I would guess based on the activity I have seen, that all the maintenance has been completed."

Cotton replies, "That's right, Boss. We did a complete post flight maintenance inspection. All the fluids have been replenished."

Booker added, "Boss, all the machine guns have been cleaned and the ammunition drums refilled. Of course, the Cobra armament was broken down, cleaned, then reinstalled. All of the ammo drums have been reloaded."

"Thanks, guys, I appreciate your professional work. All of us know that if it was not for you two, this whole operation would come to a halt" ,Cajun says to make clear how much he admires their work,

Cajun continues his briefing, "Tonight at around sundown we will light the fires and kick the tires to reposition our group to the rally point on the Somali border. Jack the coordinates are written on your briefing card along with our communication frequencies. Although I have included all new frequencies in case the enemy has learned them, the light signals will remain the same."

Jack nods his affirmation that he has the new frequencies and coordinates.

Cajun says, "Once we land at the rally point, let's take the night off and rest. It may be two or three more days before we see Wyatt and the trucks. Early in the morning, while it is cool, I would like to see as much maintenance accomplished as you can before the heat gets too unbearable. In the late afternoon, you can finish up. Take your time, but continue with the task at hand until we are at a one hundred percent readiness level."

"The reason I say all of this now is just to give you an end of mission outlook on the maintenance and preparation for what is to come. Once Wyatt and his guys show up, we will, under the cover of darkness, proceed to our last rally point. The only difference will be that the last rally point will be within the borders of Somalia on the outskirts of Baidoa.

"On that last night, we will only complete light maintenance and mostly concentrate on refueling the helicopters. We will concern ourselves mostly with the permanent removal of the fuel bladders. That will include both internal and external fuel bladders. For the time being take it easy. Wait till dusk to come. I expect that to happen around 1900 hours", Cajun wraps up his relocation brief.

After another hour, Cajun can hear the auxiliary power unit start up on the two regular Army Chinooks. He knows they will be starting engines to fly off to Djibouti soon. As he looks up into his own Chinook, he can see Savannah sitting up on the blanket where she had fallen asleep. After entering the Chinook, Cajun kneels beside her so that he can speak softly in her ear.

"Savannah, you have to help us get your friend Ayana up and on one of the aircraft headed out to Djibouti."

"Give me a few moments alone with Ayana. I will get her up and on the aircraft. Just tell them not to leave us" ,replies Savannah.

Cajun turns and walks back off the aircraft without saying anything further. As he steps off the rear of the ramp, Pigeon comes walking up. Cajun turns him around and walks back with him toward the Chinooks. "Pigeon, I've given Savannah a few minutes to get Ayana and her son out of our aircraft then onto yours. When you get back, I believe Ayana is going to need some real serious medical attention."

Pigeon reassures Cajun, "I will do my best for her help her when we get back to Djibouti."

"We will see you, my friend, on the U.S. Ronald Regan in about three to five days, depending on when Wyatt shows up with the trucks. Please take Savannah under your wing and do not let her out of your sight until I see you again. If she comes up with any request out of left field, deny them on the grounds that you do not have the authority. Your orders are to bring her back to the States for a debriefing. Do not take no for an answer."

Pigeon answers, "How you ever learned how to get along with that woman I will never know. But you can count on me. She will be waiting for you on the aircraft carrier when you come aboard."

Cajun says, "Ryan, I will forever be in your debt."

Ryan says, "Now you call me by my real name. Which reminds me, I want to talk to you about the mission a bit"

Cajun says, "Man, now is too late to be adding any wrinkles into an otherwise flawless plan."

Pigeon replies, "All I want to say is, if for any reason it becomes too hot and heavy, just destroy the weapon. Do not risk additional lives just so that we have it in our possession. Yes, the CIA boys want to get their hands on one of those crude North Korean nukes, but it is not mandatory. What is most important is that those crazy ass Hezbollah guys do not sail it into an Israeli port."

Cajun answers his suggestion, "Roger, Pigeon, I read you loud and clear."

"See, there you go with that Pigeon stuff again" ,Pigeon complains again.

"Ah, take it easy, Ryan, we'll be all right. We will bring you the nuke or die trying" ,Cajun reassures him.

Pigeon smiles and pats Cajun on the shoulder, "Yea, that's what I am afraid of."

About this time Savannah, Ayana, and Negasi come walking by headed for the Chinooks. Savannah says to Cajun, "Let me get them onboard then I will come back to see you."

Cajun says, "I'm looking forward to it, Sweetpea."

Pigeon gets on the other side of Ayana to help.

After about five minutes Savannah walks back over to Cajun. The auxiliary power units for both aircraft are whining away making a quiet conversation difficult. "Ethan, I just want to say something to you."

Cajun says, "Ah, Savannah, don't get mushy with me, I still have a war to fight."

Savannah says, "I don't have any idea what you are doing on active duty out here in Africa. You are supposed to be flying jet charters in Europe, not fighting bad guys in Ethiopia. I just want you to know that no matter what happens I will never forget your coming to save my life. When it all happened, I thought I was in a dream. How could it be that my Ethan could be here in Africa saving me from these animals?"

"Ah, Savannah, you know there is no way I would ever let Africa consume you" ,Cajun says while blushing just a little.

Savannah continues, "Well just the same, you keep my words on your mind. I want you to go and do whatever you are going to do then fly out to that aircraft carrier. Do not let anything happen to you. Nothing happens to you; do you hear me?"

Cajun says, "I hear you Savannah, and keep these words on your mind. I love you. You are the only woman I have ever loved. Now go get on that helicopter." Cajun pats her on her behind then slightly pushes her towards the Chinooks. He turns and walks back to his Cobra.

The pilots on the Chinooks start their engines then depart toward the northeast. Cajun and all his men wave goodbye even though the doors are all closed-up.

After a few more hours the dark night falls upon Cajun and his men. They start their aircraft engines, do their systems checks then fly the approximately one hundred nautical miles to the next rally point.

Chapter Fifteen...
It's About Time

Somali Border

On the second morning, Wyatt and the two remaining trucks pull into the compound to meet up with Cajun and his helicopters.

The men waste no time concealing the trucks under camouflaged netting. In no more than fifteen minutes, an enemy detail would have to stumble into the compound to find its location. It certainly could not be seen any further way than two hundred yards from the adjacent road.

Wyatt dismounts from his truck. He looks weary. He brushes and smacks himself with both hands and dust flies everywhere. His face has dirt rings around both eyes where his sunglasses had protected him. "Greetings, fly boys."

Cajun says, "Well, Wyatt, it's about time you showed up. We were beginning to think you guys kept on going to South Africa for a vacation.

Wyatt replies, "Well, Boss, it has been slow moving. Many of the roads shown on our charts were much less useable than we thought. It is a good thing we allowed for extra time. Anyway, me and my boys are here now. We just need a little rest then we will be with you to complete the mission."

"Why don't you guys leave everything to us? You guys take a shower and a long rest. We plan on moving to our final rally point inside Somali tonight. The mission will be complete by this time tomorrow" ,Cajun replies as he motions them to walk away.

Wyatt says, "OK, Boss, count us out for the remainder of the day. We'll be ready to go by sundown."

During the hot, down time of the day, Cajun continues to refine his mission planning for the assault on the compound hiding the nuclear weapon. Now he is eliminating the old set of communication frequencies. There is a chance that with so much recent activity on the air, that the enemy may be waiting for additional air crew communication attempts.

Another area of his planning he deems needs some changes is the expectation of the Navy Seals. They are to capture then hold a fuel truck until the Chinook helicopter arrival at the completion of the attack on the compound. Yes, they could capture and hold a fuel truck, however, they should not fight to capture it until minutes before the helicopter's arrival. The reason is that should the Seals lose the fight, or otherwise be discovered before the aircraft arrival, it could prove to be the mission undoing.

Cajun sees Cotton and Booker walking out of the Chinook. "Hey guys, come on over here to join me under my shade tree."

Cotton laughs as he approaches Cajun. "Dang Boss, what are you doing way over here in the boonies? Are you writing a book?"

"I might as well be writing a book. Actually, I am just refining my mission planning" ,Cajun replies.

"Well if anybody can come up with a perfect mission plan, it is you Boss" ,says Cotton as he pats Cajun on the back.

Cajun smiles with his guys obvious respect and says, "Listen, I just called you over here to get ready for our move into the rally point outside Baidoa tonight."

Cotton says, "Whoa, I did not know we were going tonight. I thought tomorrow night would be more likely."

"Well, that is what I thought we might have to do, but since Wyatt made it in early this morning, the options have changed. They took a shower then ate some food. Now they are sleeping all day and will be rested by nightfall. Every day that we are out here increases the chances we will be discovered. There is too much at stake not to take the earliest opportunity to strike" ,Cajun replies.

"That's why I called you guys over here. This evening, when Wyatt and his guys wake up, We will have the manpower necessary to deal with all the fuel bladders on the Chinook. Once we move from here to Baidoa, our biggest task is to get the Cobra and Chinook refueled full to the brim. Then we need all the fuel bladders removed from the Chinook. There will definitely be some bladders with fuel remaining, which means they will be heavy. We don't want to just dump it because there is always a possibility a fire could start and compromise our position."

Cotton chimes in, "We got you, Boss. You want us to lead the way with the refueling and removal of the fuel bladders, using Wyatt and his men to do the heavy lifting."

Cajun holds his thumb up in the air and says, "Exactly."

"No problem Boss, when we get into camp tonight we will get our maintenance iterations completed, then handle the fuel issues once Wyatt and his guys arrive with the trucks."

Cajun speaks with approval in his voice, "Great, guys, I knew I could count on you."

Time goes by very slowly in the afternoon. Cajun knows that is a good thing because it means that all necessary preparation tasks have been completed. Finally, he sees Wyatt come out of the Chinook. He heads to the bush to take care of personal business.

After about fifteen minutes Wyatt strolls over to Cajun's tree. "What do you have going on under this tree, Boss?"

Cajun replies, "Not a thing, brother, just waiting for you to get enough beauty rest so we can move on down the road. How do you feel?"

"I have to say that I feel much better now that I got some sleep. Do not ask me to drive across Ethiopia again, Boss. I would rather take a beating than to do that again" ,Wyatt says while wiping his brow.

Cajun says, All you and your guys need to do is to drive your trucks from here to our next rally point coordinates. I have all the information right here. Just let me know when you are ready to sit down and discuss it."

Wyatt says, "Heck, Boss, it might as well be now. That way, my men and I can take our time doing what we have to do."

"All right, here is a briefing card. You will see two additional set of coordinates on the card. You will drive the trucks from here, join the main highway, then continue down the highway until you get to the first set of coordinates. That drive is the longest leg at eighty-four nautical miles. There will be a road joining the highway. I want you to turn left then drive two point three miles to your next set of coordinates. Turn left off the main road and you will see a large stand of trees" ,says Cajun.

Cajun continues, "Make your way to the other side of those trees because there is a hidden area behind them. It is an open area. If you encounter any local tribesmen avoid any close contact if you can. Remember, to them, because of the way your trucks are painted, you are with the Ethiopian National Defense Forces. They will be afraid of you. We will not leave here until well after dark, so you and your men will arrive first and set up our perimeter."

"I just want to say again out loud how important it is that you do not stop at any ENDF checkpoints to allow yourselves to be inspected. If they will not wave you through you will have no choice but to take out the guards. I know that sounds harsh, but if we are detected, the success of this entire mission will be in question."

Wyatt reassures him, "I understand, Cajun. We will take care of it."

"OK, the brief has been completed. As soon as you guys get something to eat, I would like for you to get started. The drive should take you about an hour and a half to two hours," Cajun completes what he has to say.

Wyatt suggest, "Cajun, I think the best thing for us is to leave within fifteen minutes and eat enroute. That will get us down there way ahead of you. It will give us more time to do what we need to do tonight then get some rest."

Cajun agrees and says, "Good thinking. Go ahead and get started as soon as you and your guys are ready. We will meet you at the next rally point."

Cajun has spent enough time under his shade tree. He and Wyatt walk back up to where his men are gathered around the helicopters. As he approaches the group he stops to address them. "Men, those of you with Wyatt will be departing soon. You guys follow his lead and we will meet you tonight further down the road near Baidoa."

Wyatt continues walking past the helicopters and says with heaps of enthusiasm, "Come on you Special Forces bad asses, let's go to Somalia." He keeps walking in the direction of the trucks so all his men just naturally follow him.

After Wyatt and his men are out of ear shot, Cajun turns to his men. "There is nothing for us to do until dark except eat, rest, and drink plenty of water. Tonight, at dark, we are going to knock down this compound, start our engines, then fly less than one hundred miles and land. Wyatt and his guys will already have the perimeter set by the time we arrive. Tonight is when the real work begins preparing for the execution of our battle plan early tomorrow morning."

Cajun breaks the seriousness of the moment by complaining about his selection of MREs. "I have here in my hands two spaghetti with meat sauce meals. Does anybody have anything else they would trade for these? It seems all I get is spaghetti with meat sauce."

Nathan reaches in his personal bag and pulls out MREs. "Chief Breaux, I will trade you these two meals. One is roast beef and the other is meat loaf. Will these be OK?"

Cajun answers, "I should have known the Air Force guys would have the good selections. Yes I will trade you mine for yours and throw in an extra pack of gum."

Nathan says, "Consider it a done deal, Chief." They exchanged the meals.

Everybody continues doing what they had been doing before Cajun made his announcement. In the meantime, Wyatt and his guys have mounted the trucks and started the engines. Within another five minutes, they pull out of the compound to start their journey into Somalia. Cajun looks at his watch. It is 1700 hours.

The next two hours seem to drag by. Cajun has been able to doze off a little bit in his hammock strung between two shade trees. The sun was setting over the African plain. He thinks to himself how beautiful the landscape is to his eyes. After all, it was in this same land where man climbed down from the trees then learned to walk upright. It was on the very ground he was standing where man's ancestors learned to make weapons and use fire. Sadness floods over him, when he thinks how sad that in the place where mankind arose, the inhabitants still do not have running water or electricity.

He snaps out of his dreamlike state then says aloud to himself, "What the hell is wrong with this picture? You would think by now the people of this land could make a little more progress."

Cajun folds up his hammock nice and neat then walks back over to the helicopters. "OK men let's remove the camo nets to get ready to fire up the engines. Jack, could I talk to you over here for a minute?"

Jack responds in the affirmative immediately, "Sure enough, Boss, I'm listening."

"Here is a briefing card with the coordinates and communication frequencies. However, as per SOP we will maintain radio silence. We will utilize light signals to communicate. There is not much more to cover, other than if we run into some unexpected problems or maintenance issues, we will use this location to return to land. Any questions on what we are going to do, Jack?"

Jack answers, "No, Boss, this is pretty much just a repositioning flight."

Cajun says, "All right, let's help these guys with the camo nets then crank up in about thirty minutes."

"Roger, Boss" ,says Jack".

Within thirty minutes the equipment has all been loaded and strapped down onboard the Chinook. Cajun and Jimmy complete the Before Start Checklist then start their engines. Jack and Morley start the engines on the Chinook. After a few more minutes to complete systems and engine power checks, the helicopters are underway. Cajun takes the lead while Jack follows in an Echelon Right formation.

Cajun makes it a point to stay at least five miles away from the highway headed down into Baidoa. They fly at fifty feet at one hundred knots airspeed. He does not want anyone seeing them other than a few isolated Bushmen tending their herds.

When the flight is within one kilometer from the rally point, Cajun slows down to fifty knots forward airspeed. Finally, Jimmy calls out over the Intercom. "Cajun, I have the tree line in sight at twelve o'clock. The clearing is coming into view and I see our trucks. Wyatt and his guys are just finishing up on covering them with the camo nets."

Cajun responds, "OK, I have the clearing coming into view. I will land facing our weapons south just in case we're approached by vehicles from the road on the other side of the tree line."

"That's good, Cajun, that will leave plenty room for the Chinook in the rear. The trucks will not matter anymore as they will be left behind from this point on. Right, Boss?"

"You got it, Jimbo. We are nearing the completion of this ordeal soon. We should be back in England eating shepherd's pie in a week" ,answers Cajun.

Cajun leads the flight of two Army helicopters to a successful completion. The Cobra is located in the front of the clearing close to the trees with the Chinook safely protected near the back of the clearing.

Jimmy and Cajun shut down the engines then climb out of the Cobra. "Well, Jimbo, we are officially on Somali soil."

"Yea, Boss, this is a first for both of us."

Cotton comes up with a couple of the Special Forces guys carrying a camouflaged net. "Cajun, we will have this Cobra covered in a few minutes then I'll complete the maintenance iterations."

"All right, Cotton, let me know when you and Booker need help lifting the fuel bladders."

Jimmy and Cajun meet up with Jack and Morley as they walk toward the trucks to meet with Wyatt. Wyatt is gathering up his personal gear from one of the trucks and says, "Well, it was certainly nice of you fly boys to join us."

Cajun ask, "You know what I want to know the most, Wyatt. Did you guys have any trouble passing through any of the Ethiopian military checkpoints?"

Wyatt replies, "Boss, if it were any easier I don't know what we would have done. Those guards did what they are supposed to do when they see a General flag on a vehicle. They stood tall and saluted as we drove through. The only barrier at the checkpoint was on the lane leading out of Somalia back into Ethiopia."

"Well gentlemen, we did it. We have made it to within one hundred and sixty nautical miles of Mogadishu without being detected. What we need to do now is help Cotton and Booker handle the fuel bladders once they have the maintenance completed on the aircraft. You can count on that in about one hour from now" ,says Cajun.

Wyatt said, "I'll have my guys standing by to help them in one hour."

Cajun announces, "OK it is 1930 hours now. We will allow two hours to complete the maintenance and refueling. Of course, the steel rig for handling the nuke needs to be transferred to the Chinook then locked down. That means that we need to meet at the Chinook for a mission brief at 2030 hours on the dot." Everybody agrees on the time and gets busy preparing their personal gear.

Chapter Sixteen...
Mission Brief

Baidoa, Somalia

Everyone is gathered around Cajun and Wyatt in the center of the circle. Cajun has passed out mission brief cards to each of the pilots. Wyatt hands out the ground attack mission brief cards. Those men in the front are sitting on the ground, whereas the others are in a kneeling position so they can see over the front row.

Cajun begins the briefing. "Gentlemen, I could begin by saying this is likely to be the most hotly contested fire fight you have ever been in. I could say that this mission is bigger and more important than all other missions we have ever carried out. I could say that the payday for each of us on this mission will be substantial. I could go on to say any number of things. But what I want to say the most is that we are going to carry out this mission the way we have carried out all our other missions in the past. In all other missions where we have fought our enemies, we used the element of surprise, we could see in the night with our NVGs, and we had overwhelming firepower and experience."

"Most of our enemy combatants are asleep when we attack. They can't see in the darkness, they don't have the weapons we have, nor are they experienced, trained professionals like we are." Cajun asks his men,

"Who can tell me the one advantage our enemies have over us every time?"

One of Wyatt's men in the second-row answers. "The enemy out numbers us five to one, Boss."

Cajun says with bravado, "That's right, they always out number us by a substantial margin. But why do we succeed in the face of overwhelming numbers?"

Another ground pounder responds, "Because we limit our fight to those combatants that stand in the way of our completing our objective."

Cajun jumps back in with increasing enthusiasm and says, "That's right, and this mission will be no different. We are not trying to take over Mogadishu to right the wrongs of the 1993 President Clinton failure.. We are not trying to defeat and kill all the skinnies in the city. Our one and only fight will be to neutralize the threat surrounding our objective, load the nuke on the Chinook then depart the area. With those words of wisdom, I am going to turn this mission brief over to POW."

POW stands up to address his men. He holds up satellite photos of the compound. "Pass these surveillance photos around. Each of you study them thoroughly. You can see that the compound is on the outskirts of the northern side of the city. It is on the extreme west side of what looks to be an industrial area. Note the small two and three-story housing areas three hundred yards away.

"The compound is fairly large in terms of land area. Looks to me like the entire area, out to the surrounding walls, is at least an acre. You will see two structures near the center of the compound. We believe the smaller structure is where the weapon if located, but nobody knows that for sure. When Cajun begins the attack, he will be destroying the larger of the structures because that is where we believe most of the soldiers are located. If it turns out that we are wrong, there certainly is the chance that we will damage the nuke.

"After Cajun's initial attack using anti-personal fragmentation 2.75, 70mm folding fin rockets, we will go over or through the exterior rock walls from two directions. I want a man from each squad to lob in a few canisters of tear gas while Cajun is firing up the place. We will not go over or through the walls until Cajun calls a cease fire on the rockets. We will be hurt if we go over the wall while he is still firing those rockets. Wyatt asks his men, "Is that clear to everyone?"

All his men answer in unison, "Hua!"

"Take note of the markings I have made around the compound. Even though we are attacking from opposite directions from walls that are parallel, we will not mistakenly fire on each other because we will attack from the northern sides of the walls firing at a fortyfive-degree angle from each other. No one will fire at a ninety -degree angle, is that clear to everyone?"

All his men again answer in unison, "Hua!"

"Once we are inside the compound and the enemy has been neutralized, I want A Squad to secure the perimeter then direct fire out of the compound at skinnies coming at us from the housing area. I want B Squad to help the nuke guys, Paul, and Nathan, remove the portable rigging from the aircraft. Get in there to haul that weapon out to the Chinook ASAP. Once it is in position on the aircraft, do not worry about locking it down because Cotton and Booker will do that. You pick up your weapons and provide protective fire for A Squad as they return to the bird. Once all are onboard, Jack and Morley will take off in a northerly direction, then circle back around offshore to the airport." Wyatt asks his men, "Are there any questions on any part of this mission?"

One of the men from B Squad asks, "What happens if we lose the Chinook to hostile fire?"

POW answers, "Cajun will be covering that along with rally points in his brief. Are there any other questions?"

Since there seems to be a few moments of silence, Cajun stands up to continue his mission briefing. "That was an excellent question a few moments ago. I would like you to note the rally point on your briefing cards that is blank. It is blank for a reason. In case one of us is captured we do not want these skinnies figuring out where the remainder of the force is located. I am going to give it to you now. I want each of you to write it on your ankle with a black felt marker."

"This rally point is just a mile northwest of the compound. It is in the brush off to the side of a highway intersection. Since we will arrive by helicopter, the skinnies will likely be looking for us to head back to the shoreline to be rescued. We are going to head back inland then slowly make our way back to Baidoa and turn ourselves over to the Ethiopian National Defense Forces."

Cajun continues, "Your instructions are to confiscate vehicles, in groups of two or three, then head to the next town up the highway moving north, which is the town of Afgooye. When you take over a vehicle, be sure to take the vehicle occupants with you. Do not leave them behind to report your actions to authorities. The coordinates are 002.02 / 45.165. Do not write the compass designators."

"There are three important aspects of this mission I want everybody to understand. If at any time we lose control of the nuclear weapon for any reason, fire as many rounds as you can into it. Destroy the weapon. It will not detonate if you fire into it. We have to make sure that it is unusable."

"The next point I want to get across is this. If we get out of the compound with the weapon and the Chinook in good shape, we are going to circle around off shore to enter the airport area where our guys will have the fuel truck secured. If you men securing the fuel truck are discovered and cannot hold the area, fall back into the water then swim off shore.

When you hear us overhead flying toward the shoreline, pop a flare and we will pick you up. If for any reason we cannot refuel, we will still have about an hour of fuel to fly out to sea to search for the aircraft carrier. At the very least, we should be able to contact them to report our position at sea," Cajun continues his brief with increasing bravado.

"OK, I just said the magic words that you have never heard before. Yes, the third goal of this mission is to survive at sea. This will be the first mission we have ever conducted where we escape out over open water. No problem, we came prepared. As soon as each of you gets back onboard the Chinook, reach under your seat, and grab a one-man raft. They have two large Velcro straps on them so strap them to your leg between the knee and your ankle. If we go in the water, we will each pop open our raft then secure all of them together."

"Listen up, these are the times for the mission. We will start engines at exactly 02:40 hours. Have the systems and hover power checks completed by 02:50 hours. We will form up into the wind at 02:55. As you can see presently there is no wind, but when there is a breath of air, it is coming out of the south. Departure time is 03:00 hours on the dot."

"The distance to our objective is one hundred and sixty nautical miles. Flight time to abeam our objective at one hundred-forty knots is one hour and ten minutes as we are basically in a no wind condition at the present time."

"Once we are five miles abeam Mogadishu we will keep our speed up until our turn off shore toward an abeam position to the airport. At the off shore turn point we will slow to seventy knots. The Cobra will come to a one-hundred-foot hover two miles out from the airport. We will wait for the Chinook to drop off the Seals for their swim to the airport. Once the Chinook returns we will fly at one hundred-forty knots retracing our route to abeam Mogadishu. From there we will turn inbound to our objective to commence the attack."

"Gentlemen, that pretty much completes the briefing for our once in a lifetime mission. Are there any more questions?"

A voice comes out of the back row. "Chief Breaux, what's up with these Muslim fanatics? How could they even consider detonating a nuclear weapon to kill millions of people in Israel?"

Cajun responds with, "I would like to say this about the Muslim fanatics. They are sorry, cowardly punks all running around with their little beards. The beards are supposed to represent something of a covenant with their religion. These fanatics are waiting for the twelfth Imam to rise-up out of a well. Can you believe that, rise-up out of a freaking well?"

"They are fighting for the whole world to live under Sharia law. Sharia law allows them to slap around and even kill their woman as routine. When it comes to fighting, they have no honor, as it is frequently their practice to hide behind woman and children."

"The list of things the United States has given the world in the way of freedom and technology would take volumes to write. You could list the accomplishments of Muslims and Islam written on the back of a matchbook. It is true, I say kill as many of the sons of bitches as you can." With that Cajun turns and walks away from the briefing. Hell, he is so jacked up by his own speech, that he will be lucky to fall asleep.

Cotton ask, "I have one more question, Boss. Is it true those Navy swabys eat pretty well at sea?" Everyone laughs out loud.

Cajun answers while laughing, "Yes, it is my understanding that Navy personnel eat well. Ok, men, let's get a couple hours of sleep then go get that nuke back."

All the men respond with a big, "Hua!"

Chapter Seventeen...
Back To Somalia

Baidoa, Somalia

Cajun looks at the illuminated hands on the face of his watch. It is only one in the morning. He thinks to himself that at least he was able to grab a couple hours of sleep.

As he opens his eyes wider and wider, the thought that this day will likely be the most important day in his life is foremost in his mind. Cajun fights the urge to hop out of his hammock and start moving around, as that would wake up everybody else. He wants everybody to get all the sleep they possibly can, knowing that sleep in the last two weeks has been elusive.

While Cajun just lies there, he thinks this will be a good time to just let his mind reflect on the things in his life that had brought him and his men to this point. After agreeing to, then preparing for this dangerous mission, he and his men have traveled all the way from England to Africa. Many hours of planning have gone into this mission.

Finally, Cotton starts moving around the aircraft. Wyatt and his men begin to move around outside as well. Cajun thinks to himself with a certain degree of excitement. "It's time to get up to put this hammock away." At the same time, he feels a bit of foreboding at the thought of what is ahead. He knows he has taken every precaution and made all the right mission planning decisions so that this mission above all others, will go off as planned. Cajun cannot shake the feeling that he has forgotten some small detail that could mean the difference between success and failure.

Cajun finally walks off the aircraft. He approaches the area where Wyatt and all his men are getting their gear together. He knows that the details of running the mission will mean that he will not have another opportunity to speak with them again until it's all over. Cajun slowly approaches Wyatt, "Well POW, here we are again flying off into the night to fight another battle."

POW replies, "Yea, Cajun, this seems to be our plight in life. Uncle Sam trained us to do this. You know the drill by now. If we do not carry out this mission, who else will do it?"

Cajun fires right back, "No one would do it. There is something else I wanted to talk to you about. I just wanted to clarify a couple of the statements I made last night during the mission brief."

POW has an idea of what Cajun is about to say. He tries to let him off the hook by saying, "Boss, you don't have to worry about me and any of the men. All of us know that this time, on this mission, that any of us who make it all the way to the aircraft carrier are going to make enough money to retire."

Cajun tries to clarify his thoughts before POW could get the words out. "Yea, I didn't mean for our men to survive for a big payday."

POW says, "Boss, nobody thinks this is about money. When you stand a good chance of being maimed or killed, it really isn't about the money. Not one of us would hesitate, not even for a second, for the opportunity to participate in this mission, even if we had to do it for free. We all know that it's our job to take that nuclear weapon out of the hands of that bunch of maniacs who are straight out of the 13th Century."

POW also comments on the expected violence of the mission. "Cajun I know you are going to question your speech on what we will have to do to gain the upper hand."

"Yea, I didn't mean to continue killing in cold blood after we have achieved our objective. Sometimes, just for a few seconds, we get so caught up in the moment we kill indiscriminately" ,says Cajun.

POW replies, "Boss, I can assure you, that these animals would kill every one of us, in cold blood if they could. If they happen to capture a prisoner out of this fight, they will cut his head off while they chant Allah is good, and death to the Americans."

By this time most of Wyatt's men are standing fairly-close and listening to Cajun's concerns. One of them spoke up to say, "Boss, don't worry about us. We have the element of surprise, we are equipped with night vision goggle equipment, and we have armored chest protectors. Plus, we hate these sons of bitches. I really hope these guys prayed last night to Allah, because any of them that raise their little skinny heads will be on a fast track to meet him." Everyone laughs out loud.

Cajun raises his voice, "All right then, let's go kick some ass."

Jack came along to hear the last statement Cajun made to the troops. As the group breaks up to start to walk away, Jack says, "Come on, Boss, it's about time to mount up for the engine start."

Cajun says, "Raider, get your game face on. Get ready to rock and roll. Good luck to you, stay safe." With that, Cajun walks toward the Cobra where Jimmy is waiting. Jack walks onto the Chinook to greet Morley.

Jimmy says to Cajun, "Boss, how do you want to handle the stick time this morning?

Cajun instructs Jimmy, "You fly us to Mogadishu, while I run the mission and keep up with our lat/long positions on the computer. Once we bypass the city we will fly out to sea then circle back to cover the Chinook, while they drop off the SEALS swimming into the airport. At that point I will take over the flight controls while you navigate us back to the location of the nuke."

"Once we attack, you alternate as necessary between the 20-mm Gatling gun and the 40-mm Chunker. I will fly the aircraft and fire the rockets. As you know we only have nineteen 2.75 folding fin rockets on each side. I plan to fire the first seven in pairs then I will ripple off the rest. If I fire them in pairs, I will have seven opportunities to cause damage. All my rockets need to be expended over the wall before our guys get in, otherwise they could be injured. Depending on how much damage I cause with the first four or five volleys, I may keep a couple rockets for when we depart to refuel."

Jimmy says, "Ok Cajun, we all got the skinny; I'm ready to saddle up."

Both men climb in their respective positions in the Cobra. Jimmy is in the front manning the Gunners seat while Cajun is in the back seat, which is the primary pilot station.

Cotton is there helping them to get strapped in. He helps to affix the weapons sighting rods atop Cajun's helmet. Both pilots attach their night vision goggles to their helmets to make sure the reserve battery pack is functional. They lay the pack across their chest in case they need it in a hurry. Cajun gives Cotton thumbs up. Cotton moves to the ground then positions himself in the front left of the helicopter with a fire extinguisher. He is standing by until the signal is given that Cajun will be starting engines.

Cajun speaks to Jimmy over the aircraft intercom, "Ok Jimmy, let's get everything completed on the checklist up to the point where we start the engines." Jimmy begins with the first item on the checklist:

"Shoulder Harness."

"Shoulder Harness On and Locked."

"Night Vision Goggles ."

"Night Vision Goggles On and Operational."

"Anti-Torque Pedals."

"Anti-Torque Pedals Centered and Free."

"Cockpit Windows."

"Cockpit Windows Closed and Locked."

"Battery Switch."

"Battery Switch On."

Cajun and Jimmy continue through the checklist item for item, up to the point for the actual engine start. Cajun looks at his watch and speaks to Jimmy over the intercom, "The time is 02:38 hours. "OK Jimbo, we have two minutes until engine start. Do you have everything ready up there?'

Jimmy comes back and says, "Yea, but I wish I had taken a P.D.P. latrine run."

Cajun laughs and replies, "Well I took one, but I could sure use another run to the bushes."

At exactly 02:39 hours plus forty-five seconds, Cajun announces over the intercom, "Starting engine number one in ten seconds. Ten seconds, five seconds, four, three, two, one, I'm starting engine number one."

After the engines are started, Cajun slowly pulls pitch into the blades, which lifts the helicopter slowly into the air. They continue with their systems check. Finally Cajun pulls in enough power to where they are hovering out of ground effect in a fifty-foot hover.

Jimmy speaks over the intercom, "Ok, the predicted value for our Out of Ground Effect hover power, at this weight and temperature, is 32.5 pounds of torque. I am reading 32 pounds of torque."

Cajun hovers the Cobra out into a clear area away from the Chinook. He lands the helicopter to the ground then rolls the throttle down to flat idle and says to Jimmy, "OK Jimbo, you have the flight controls."

Jimmy responds, "Roger, Boss, I have the flight controls."

After a few minutes Jack and Morley are back on the ground at flat idle. Cajun sees this and turns his rotating beacon off then back on as a signal that both flight crews have thirty seconds to bring their engines back up to takeoff power. They are going to pull pitch to leave exactly on time at 03:00 hours. After thirty seconds, Jimmy turns his rotating beacon off then pulls in takeoff power. Jack follows close behind to the right in an Echelon Right formation. Both flight crews hack the time and write down fuel onboard onto the flight plans on their knee clipboards. The battle is on.

The flight down to Mogadishu is easy, because they are basically flying downhill to sea level. They easily maintain one hundred forty knots with relative ease. Their flight plan takes them over countryside brush lands, remaining clear of the highway that leads into the city. As they pass abeam the city they fly NOE then fly off shore three miles so that their rotor blades cannot be heard. Jimmy remains at a hover three miles offshore making sure to remain high enough so as not to give off a water flume signature. Jack flies in closer to drop off the two Navy Seals. They have two mini scooters to power themselves into the shoreline toting a fifty-caliber machine gun in a waterproof bag.

Jack reverses course then flies back out to sea to meet up with the Cobra. Cajun sees them coming, turns and flies a parallel course to the beach. Jack joins up in a trail formation. After flying parallel to the coast for three miles, Cajun turns north and crosses the shoreline. They fly abeam the city all the way to the main roadway that heads into Mogadishu. Cajun slows their forward airspeed to fifty knots as they approach the final checkpoint before reaching the walled in compound. Jimmy comes up on the intercom and reports, "Cajun, I have the compound in sight through my stabilization scope. It's at eleven o'clock, approximately two clicks out."

There is no more need for radio silence so Cajun comes up on the VHF radio to call Chock Two. "Raider, break off here and start to deploy your troops left and right. I am going straight in from here. We will commence firing in thirty seconds."

Jack responds, "Roger, commencing troop deployment."

Cajun closes the gap fast then comes to a hover. He calls over the intercom to Jimmy, "Ok, Jimbo, save your ammo until I soften them up with my rockets." Cajun fires a pair of rockets and hits the main living structure with one of the two rockets.

Jimmy raises his voice and says, "Cajun, good shooting."

He fires a second pair as Somali soldiers run out of the structure firing their AK-47s. Once again, the structure suffers a hit by one of the two rockets. Jimmy shouts over the intercom, "Cajun, you scored another hit!"

By this time at least two dozen soldiers who have escaped the first two rockets run out into the yard. Jimmy calls over the intercom, "Cajun, skinnies in the open to the left of nuke building." Just as he finishes speaking, the entire canopy is sprayed with bullets. Cajun pulls off rapidly down and to the right. By the time he finishes his turn, he has pulled back a good fifty yards. The skinnies no longer have a clear shot at them. Cajun calls over the intercom, "Wow, Jimbo, that was close." Cajun waits for several seconds then calls again, "Jimbo, you alright? Were you hit?" There is still no response from the front seat.

Cajun knows that before he can attend to Jimmy he will have to come up and fire off more pairs of rockets. His very stern warning to POW and his men was that they are not to breach the wall until he has called his cease fire from the rocket attack.

Cajun pulls power into the collective. He adds forward cyclic to pitch the nose down to gain a little forward momentum. He pulls back on the cyclic then relaxes a little of the power he has applied into the collective. The Cobra pops up above the wall. Cajun tries to fire another pair of rockets. Nothing happens when he pulls the trigger for the rockets. He tries firing again but nothing happens.

Again, he dives the Cobra down and to the right to get out of the line of fire. Just as he starts down his Cobra is struck with several more bullets. It sounds as though his mast has been hit. Cajun calls out over the radio, "POW, I can't fire rockets, I can't fire rockets!"

POW yells back, "Roger, your rockets are Winchester. We are going through the wall". The two soldiers with the 40-mm grenade launchers begin firing chunkers at the wall from both sides. The problem is that they can only fire one round at a time then reload.

The snipers from both squads have found higher ground in small trees several yards back from the compound. They are picking off skinnies as they get a good line of fire over the top over the wall.

Cajun reaches over to pull the fore and aft spring-loaded turret switch to deselect the gunner station control and select rear pilot control. Now he has control of the turret weapons. All he needs to do is turn his head, look through the eyepiece on his helmet, then pull the trigger on the cyclic. He selects the 40-mm on his turret selector as he figures he had better start with the chunker as POW has not yet entered the compound.

Cajun pulls power into the collective. He adds forward cyclic to pitch the nose down to gain a little forward momentum. He pulls back on the cyclic then relaxes a little of the power he has applied into the collective. He pops up above the wall. This time he kicks the right anti torque pedal, which turns the Cobra parallel to the wall. As he looks left his turret also turns left. As Cajun pulls the trigger the nose mounted weapon starts firing 40-mm grenades. The difference between this weapon and other 40-mm weapons is that it is accurate. Where he looks he fires up the target. Large explosions throw bodies left and right. Cajun adds forward cyclic and some power into the blades to fly down the wall. He does not want to stay unmasked for more than ten seconds or he will be a sitting duck.

As Cajun flies the length of the compound, he pulls as much power into the blades as he can. He uses that power to gain as much airspeed as possible. When he has enough momentum he pulls back on the cyclic, which brings the nose of the Cobra up into the night sky. For three or four seconds the aircraft climbs steeply. As the Cobra reaches the top of the arc, Cajun can feel the momentum draining off so he kicks in left pedal. The Cobra turns one hundred and eighty degrees. At the same time the nose drops. Cajun is on a roller coaster ride now as his helicopter dives down toward the rock wall. He reduces power into the blades then pulls back on the cyclic. Now he is flying level over the wall with the nose of the Cobra pitched up in the air.

With the nose pitched up the airspeed bleeds off rapidly. Now Cajun looks right and the turret turns right as well. Cajun pulls the trigger and again starts blasting the place with 40-mm grenades. He is careful to avoid hitting the small structure, which likely houses the nuclear weapon. Cajun comes to a stationary hover abeam the entrance to the compound. He can see that POW's A Squad is having limited success blasting down the rock wall with their one shot at a time 40-mm weapon. Cajun pops off about ten 40-mm rounds into the wall and blows it open. The hole is big enough to drive a jeep through now. Cajun shouts at POW over the radio, "A Squad, you are cleared in hot."

Just below him to the left Cajun can hear and feel the impact from explosions. He dives the Cobra down and left just to get another running start. He already knows the explosions are not intended for him. B Squad trying to blast through the western wall. Cajun quickly circles around to the right to come up over POW and his men fighting their way through the hole Cajun had made. He aims the turret system through his eyepiece then pumps ten more chunkers into the western wall. Cajun sees the wall collapse and open-up, so he pulls off down to the right. He calls out to the men waiting outside the wall, "B Squad, you are cleared in hot."

Cajun comes to a hover twenty-five yards in front of the compound then reaches down to reselect his weapons system to the 20-mm Gatling gun. This time since both squads are already fighting their way in along both exterior walls, he will pop up straight over the front gate in the center while giving them cover fire. He knows he will have to fire in short six second burst as his weapon cyclic rate of fire is 750 rounds per minute. His ammo drum only holds 1,000 rounds. He figures he has twelve, maybe thirteen six second burst of seventy-five rounds each. God, he loves the Gatling gun even though it is sometimes temperamental. The six second burst is just about the right amount to stay unmasked yet keep the weapon cool. He knows to stay away from the long bursts because that is usually why the gun jams.

Cajun pulls in a little power then adds forward cyclic to pitch the nose down to gain a little forward momentum. He pulls back on the cyclic then relaxes a little of the power he has applied into the collective. He pops up above the wall. He moves his head a little to the left of the aircraft nose then pulls the trigger. The good thing about the 20-mm rounds is that every seventh round is a red incendiary round. As Cajun fires, it looks like a red laser beam right into the skinnies location. He moves his head to the right then pulls the trigger. Again, even though he fires in short burst, each pull of the trigger means he has sprayed sixty to seventy rounds down range.

It looked as though POW and his men are getting the upper hand as there is less and less return fire. Cajun puts in left cyclic to slide his aircraft left so the Chinook can come in to land in the front of the compound. As he slides to the left, he glances back at the aircraft nose to gauge his progress, and sees a bright flash out of the corner of his eye. It is a shoulder fired rocket, fired by a skinny on the roof of the smaller structure. Cajun has just enough time to brace for impact. Time slows to almost a standstill. He thinks, how ironic that he has finally found Savannah, yet he is about to die from a shoulder fired rocket. The lights go out.

"Cajun, Cajun, are you alright?" shouts POW.

Cajun tries to regain consciousness, "Am I dreaming? Why can't I wake up from this dream? And why is POW whispering to me?"

POW shouts again while slapping Cajun on the cheeks, "Cajun, Cajun, snap out of it, wake up, wake up!"

All of the sudden, Cajun can hear loud noises as he regains consciousness. POW is doing his best to keep the cockpit entry door open, unbuckle Cajun's shoulder harness then lift him out of the Cobra. The Cobra helicopter has rolled over onto its left side. Cajun's faculties are returning to him. He shouts at POW, "Just hold the door up and I will crawl out from under it". POW holds the large Plexiglas cockpit door up while Cajun grabs his shotgun. He rolls out then down to the ground. Cajun immediately looks into the front seat at Jimbo. He shouts, "Jimbo, Jimbo, you all right?"

POW pulls Cajun to the ground as rounds are hitting all around them. "Cajun, we'll have to get him out after we find cover. He's dead, Cajun. Jimmy was hit in the head." Cajun continues to peer into the front seat area at Jimbo in disbelief.

Cajun reopens the entry door to the Cobra. He reaches in the cockpit to grab a metal axe. It is always strapped to the inside wall of the cockpit, near the floor, for just such occasions. It is there for pilots to break their way out should the aircraft be rolled on its side. Cajun begins hacking at the thick Plexiglas window separating him from Jimbo. POW takes the hatchet from Cajun then shouts, "Let me have at it, I'll use the pointed end." POW hacks three or four times into the window until it shatters. Both men start breaking away the pieces by hand. They reach down into the forward cockpit to pull Jimbo from the wreckage.

POW says to Cajun, "Come with me, there are just a few skinnies left. Let's clear the path for the Chinook." Cajun nods and both men grab one of Jimbo's arms to drag him across the yard to the structure. As they move across the yard, the firing ceases. POW's men start to emerge from all sides of the compound. They have five Somali soldiers with their fingers locked together behind their heads.

The skinnies are lined up against the wall with their noses firmly touching the wall. POW takes over then shouts orders to his men. "A Squad, get in position on the walls then fire at anything that moves. B Squad, open-up the door of the nuke structure. Leave one man here on the skinnies. If any of them make a move, waste them."

As Cajun and POW approach the remaining structure, his men place a stick of C-4 on the doors to blow them open. "Fire in the hole!" The doors of the structure are blown into smithereens. Within seconds they have the front section of the crate removed and can see inside. None of them have ever seen a nuclear weapon up close and personal, yet they all know exactly what it is.

Cajun's mind snaps to the task at hand and commands, "POW, call Raider to land the Chinook in the front area of the compound with his nose facing the front gate. You get your men to load the weapon. I will guard the skinnies and relieve your man to guard the exterior with A Squad."

POW calls over the radio, "Raider, Raider, bring it in and face your nose toward the gate, we're ready for you."

Raider replies immediately, "Roger, ETA in thirty seconds."

Cajun walks out into the compound by the wall where his man guards the skinnies. "Ok, you join your team I've got these guys." He places the shotgun barrel to the temple to the man nearest to him. A Squad continues sporadic firing at skinnies coming out of the housing areas. It is clear they are not just upset neighbors they are soldiers. In addition to small arms fire, the skinnies fire a shoulder fired rocket every minute or so. Fortunately, their rockets are no more effective at penetrating the rock wall.

Raider comes to a hover directly over the courtyard then begins his pedal turn one hundred and eighty degrees so that his nose faces the front gate. He reduces power into the rotors and the Chinook descends into the courtyard. Raider does not waste time slowly lowering the aircraft to the ground for a landing smooth enough to write home about. He drops it in hard and fast. The ramp has already been lowered, so as soon as the helicopter hits the ground Paul and Nathan run off the aircraft in the direction of the structure containing the nuke. POW and his men run onto the Chinook. Within seconds they emerge with the portable steel framing, which will be used to lift and move the weapon.

Cajun has taken his eyes off his prisoners while Raider lowers the aircraft into the courtyard. One of the skinnies jumps Cajun while his head is turned. His shotgun discharges a round into the air as it is hit hard out of his hands. The two men exchange blows to the face and body while rolling around on the ground. In a flash, the skinny pulls a knife, which has been hidden in his boot. Cajun catches his forearm as the knife comes down toward his chest. He reaches down then pulls out the snub nosed 357 Revolver strapped to his ankle. He brings it up to the side of the skinny then pumps two rounds into his side. He collapses then rolls off to the side as Cajun jumps to his feet. Cajun's adrenalin is pumping through his body and shouts at the other skinnies that still have their noses touching the wall. "NEVER, NEVER, NEVER, MESS WITH A SNAKE KILLER!" There was so much noise from the helicopter and it was so dark to the naked eye, the skinnies did not even know there was a fight going on ten feet from them. If they had known, Cajun knew he probably would be dead. He says to himself, "Come on, Cajun, no more screw-ups."

Within a few minutes, the entire crate has been torn away from the nuke by POW and his men. Paul and Nathan have determined that the nuclear weapon has not been armed. The nuke is no in danger of detonating. In another five minutes, POW and his men emerge from the structure with the steel framing supporting the nuke. They are rolling it on four small wheels. It takes them five minutes to load then move it across the courtyard to the rear cargo ramp of the Chinook.

Now the hard part begins. POW calls out to his men over his headset microphone, "All right everyone, push on three to get this thing started up the ramp. Ready now, one, two, three, push." They continue for another five minutes pushing the weapon completely into the belly of the Chinook.

As soon as the nuke is onboard, Cotton Bend Booker take over to shackle it down to the large metal rings in the floor designed to hold the load. POW calls out, "Everybody get onboard, we're ready to go; Go, Go, Go." A Squad pulls off the wall and starts running toward the aircraft.

Cajun stands the skinnies up then runs them toward the breached western wall. He shouts, "Run, Run, Run", while he gestures with his hand. They run with their hands up looking back at Cajun, half expecting him to shoot them. Cajun runs toward Jimbo lying in the yard. It takes a great deal of effort, but he pulls Jimbo off the ground. He carries him over his shoulder to the rear cargo ramp. POW is there to help lift both men aboard the aircraft. Cajun shouts into his headset, "Raider, I'm the last one, Go, Go, Go."

Raider replies, "Ok we're out of here, give me cover fire." Cotton and Booker fire out from each door with the mounted 50-caliber machine guns. A couple of POW's men fire out the front doors next to the 50-cals. Everybody else fires out the aircraft to the rear as they fly off into the night. It was like a mad minute.

Cajun makes his way through the fuselage to the cockpit. He has donned his flight helmet and can see the terrain with his NVGs as Raider circles around flying just above the buildings. Raider crosses the shoreline then heads out to sea.

Cajun ask, "Raider, how much fuel do we have?"

Raider answers, "We have just under 1,200 pounds of fuel remaining."

"OK let's circle back around low level into the airport. Hopefully our guys have a fuel truck for us" ,Cajun replies.

Raider circles around then comes in low level approaching the shoreline at one hundred knots. He calls over the radio, "Refueller One, this is Spiderman, do you read me?"

The Navy Seals on shore come right back on the radio and respond with, "Spiderman this is Refueller One, I expect you guys are thirsty. We have a truck waiting for you on the far east end of the ramp to top you off."

Raider answers, "Roger we have you in sight, we will be there in thirty seconds."

Raider is a very skilled Chinook pilot. He drops the collective all the way down then pulls back on the cyclic causing the nose to rise sharply. The airspeed bleeds off dramatically. By the time he lowers the nose again, they are dropping onto the tarmac next to the fuel truck at zero forward airspeed.

As soon as the aircraft touches the ground, Cotton and Booker jump off to begin the refueling process. Cotton hurries to grab the grounding cable on the fuel truck, which unwinds off the spool as he tugs it in the direction of the Chinook. Booker goes straight for the refueling hose then starts to unwind it in the direction of the refueling ports. Refueller One already had the truck started and the fueling pump engaged.

As they are about to begin the fueling operation, several pickup trucks filled with skinnies with roof mounted machine guns race down the taxi way in the direction of the Chinook. The second Navy Seal is stationed at the edge of the ramp where the Chinook is starting to take on fuel. He lies in a prone position then begins to fire his 50-caliber machine gun. At the time he begins firing, the trucks are a little beyond his effective range. He just wants them to know there is going to be a fight. Two of the trucks break off from the group to circle around wide so they can mount an attack from two directions on the machine gun emplacement.

Cajun can see all this happening and knows the skinnies have too much fire power. He realizes if they don't depart immediately they could have the aircraft immobilized. He shouts over the radio, "Abort the fueling, everyone jump onboard immediately, we are pulling out. Gunner, pull the bolt out of the 50-cal and leave the weapon." He repeated his command, "Abort refueling, everyone onboard immediately, we are pulling out."

Booker unhooks the grounding cable from the main frame of the aircraft. It has spring tension on it and begins to wind back on its own. Cotton pulls out the fueling hose then throws it back about ten feet from the aircraft. He quickly replaces the fueling cap. Both jump onboard in their normal gunner's positions manning the machine guns in the front doors. By this time both the Navy Seals have reached the rear cargo ramp then dive onboard. POW shouts over the intercom, "We're all onboard, Go, Go, Go."

The trucks are in range now and are steadily firing. Booker and Cotton are returning steady fire with their fifty-cals. The guys in the rear of the aircraft are not yet in position to fire. Cotton, firing off to the right, scores a direct hit, killing two of the skinnies in the bed of one of the trucks speeding in from the right. At the same time, he places several rounds into the engine area. The truck explodes then swerves out of control. It tumbles over and over. High velocity rounds hit the aircraft and kill one of POW's men on the spot. Another round hits Brian, the co-pilot. He is killed instantly. Only his shoulder harness keeps him from falling over onto the flight controls.

Raider pulls in lots of power then kicks hard on the left pedal to perform an aggressive one-hundred and eighty-degree pedal turn. When he completes the turn he lowers the nose aggressively to gain forward airspeed ASAP. Now POW and his men in back open fire on the trucks as they come to a halt at the shoreline. The trucks are soon out of range as the aircraft disappears into the darkness.

Cotton leaves his gunner door to help Cajun unbuckle Brian's shoulder harness without allowing him to fall forward into the flight controls. They struggle to remove him from his pilot station. After several minutes they are able to remove him then lie him down on the floor in the cabin area. Cajun moves into the pilot station then buckles his shoulder harness. He plugs his helmet into the intercom. Jack looks at Cajun. His eyes appear as wide as saucers.

Cajun says, "Raider, why don't you let me take the controls while you relax a few minutes?"

Raider replies, "Roger, you have the flight controls." He then raises his hands out in front, which is the standard visual signal for releasing the flight controls to another pilot.

Cajun says, "Check yourself out Jack. Make sure you don't have any holes in you. Maybe you were grazed and just do not know it yet. Do you have any pain anywhere?"

"The only pain I have is the pain of having one of my best friends killed in the seat next to me while flying. I cannot believe he is gone" ,Jack laments sadly.

Cajun replies, "Yea I know what you mean. Jimbo bought it when we were shot down in the Cobra. He's in the back too." Both men fly out to sea into the darkness without saying another word.

Chapter Eighteen...
Swim With The Fishes

Indian Ocean

Finally, Cajun speaks over the intercom, "Raider, we have to get it all back together as we are not out of the woods by a long shot.

We only took on a few gallons of fuel. Plus, I have been keeping an eye on the fuel gauge for the right main tank. It seems to be dropping down at a fast pace. My guess is that we took a round in the fuel tank on the right side. I am going to switch the cross valve so we can burn fuel out of the right tank for both engines. It is better to burn it out at a faster rate, because it'll just be lost overboard anyway. Raider, get out the emergency checklist and complete the items for the Loss of Fuel from a Single Tank."

Jack replies, "Roger, I am completing the checklist for Loss of Fuel from a Single Tank."

After flying along for another five minutes, burning as much fuel from the right tank as they can, Cajun says, "Jack we are going to have an asymmetrical weight problem here real soon as we burn the tank dry."

Jack says, "Boss, that seems to be the least of our problems. It is clear to me that we will be lucky to fly another forty-five minutes before we are completely out of fuel. Reaching the aircraft carrier is out of the question."

Cajun answers, "No question about it, we're all going swimming tonight, Jack. I think we need to do two things to get ready to ditch. You talk to the guys in the back. Have each of them locate their one-man raft packs and strap them to their legs. Everybody, including the wounded, go into the water with a raft strapped to their lower leg. I am going to climb up to a higher altitude and try to make radio contact with the carrier. If I can reach a friendly voice I will give them our positions as we move further out to sea."

"OK, Boss, I'll get right on it" ,Jack says while beginning to unstrap to get up out of his pilot seat.

Cajun stops his progress and says, "Jack, before you go off the radios, would you tune our VHF to our contact frequency? I do not want to look down to tune the radios and try to fly at the same time. I may induce some vertigo."

"I've got you, Boss. I have the frequencies right here on my clipboard. Do not forget to remove your night vision goggles if you are going to climb to a higher altitude" ,Jack replies.

"Good idea, Jack" Cajun replies as he flips his NVGs up to the top of his helmet, he starts a climb of five hundred feet per minute. He knows he must be smooth in his applications of power and airspeed to minimize chances of inducing vertigo.

Cajun calls out over the radio hoping to contact their ride, "This is Rescue One calling the United States Carrier Ronald Reagan. Do you copy this transmission?" Several seconds go by with no response, so he repeats the call, "This is Rescue One calling the United States Carrier Ronald Reagan. Do you copy this transmission?" There is no answer.

After speaking to the men in the back, Jack rejoins Cajun on the radios. "Were you able to reach the carrier?"

Cajun answers, "So far I only tried to reach them a couple times. We are just too far out. I have leveled off at five thousand feet, so with any luck we will be able to reach them in another fifteen minutes. Let's just sit tight for now."

Jack says, "OK Boss, I will make a call in the blind in about fifteen minutes."

Cajun addresses Jack over the intercom, "While we have a few minutes I want to talk to you about something we've never done."

"Yea, we're finally ditching a helicopter, not only at sea, but at sea at night" ,says Jack.

Cajun says, "Yes, we are going in the Indian Ocean, no question about it. This is the way I see it. First-of-all, everyone should keep their helmets on with their night vision goggles attached until they hit the water. The helmets will keep us from being knocked unconscious. Without the NVGs, we would be lucky to get out of the aircraft because of the pitch-black darkness."

Jack adds, "Yes, and we need for everyone to keep their flashlights dry in a plastic bag until we get into the rafts."

"Right, keep the flashlights dry at all cost. I will bring the aircraft to a hover then everybody onboard, including you, will jump into the water" ,says Cajun.

"Once everybody is out, I will hover away into the wind another one hundred feet and cut the throttles. What I want to avoid, at all cost, is waiting too late then actually have the engines quit from fuel starvation. That would be disastrous" ,Cajun continues.

Jack replies, "Cajun, that is a perfect plan, however, you should be the one who jumps out with the other guys. I'm younger than you and will be able to roll the helicopter upside down in the water and get out better than you."

Cajun can see the argument coming. He must be forceful right up front otherwise it will turn into an academic debate as to who would fly the aircraft into the sea. Cajun says in a strong yet compassionate voice, "Jack, just because you are a little younger than me, does not mean you are in better condition than I am. I was raised on a river and can swim upside down, sideways, you name it. There is no question about it, when the time comes, I need for you to do as I say, and go out the back with the other guys."

Jack does not reply, as he will surely loose the argument. He thinks it is a good time to try to reach the aircraft carrier on the radio. He keys the microphone. "This is Rescue Chinook One calling the United States Carrier Ronald Reagan. Do you copy this transmission?" Within seconds a reply comes back loud and clear. "Rescue One, this is the U.S. Carrier Ronald Reagan, go ahead."

Jack reports, "We are descending out of five thousand feet and will be ditching at sea due to lack of fuel. We departed the Mogadishu Airport headed out to sea on a one hundred and forty degree bearing. We have the weapon onboard. Our present position at this time is zero zero-one degrees, zero two minutes north / forty-two degrees, one niner minutes east. Do you copy, over?"

The U.S. Carrier Ronald Reagan responds, "Roger, Rescue One, we copy your transmission, squawk emergency transponder 7700. We are much further out to sea, but will immediately launch rescue aircraft. It will be daylight in forty-five minutes. Do you copy, Rescue One?"

Jack answers the instructions, "Roger, we are squawking 7700. We copy rescue operation underway. We will lose communication soon as we descend."

The carrier answers, "Roger, Rescue One, good luck and God's speed."

As they descend at about 700 feet per minute, the Low Fuel light illuminates, indicating they have twenty minutes of fuel remaining.

Cajun clears the yellow caution light. "We will be in position to jump in the water in less than ten minutes. I would much rather go in the water and waste five to ten minutes of fuel than flame out the engines. Have the men in back make sure everyone is ready to go out the back ramp within five minutes then report back to you."

Jack replies, "Roger, Boss, I'll talk to them in the back." He switches to Intercom and calls Cotton to relay the order.

Within minutes the aircraft is within five hundred feet of the water. Cajun flips his NVGs down in front of his eyes and says, "OK, Jack, keep your night vision goggles on as long as possible and stay with me here on the flight controls till I get this thing straight and level at a hover. In this pitch-black darkness I want to make sure no vertigo sets in."

Jack answers, "Yea, this landing at night over open water is tricky." Once they come to a twenty-five-foot hover and the gyro in his brain is stabilized, Cajun shouts over the intercom, "OK, Jack, go ahead and jump out of the back with the other guys. Keep your helmet plugged into the intercom in the back so you can tell me when everybody is clear."

"OK, Boss, I am unplugging here. I will talk to you from the back in a couple minutes" ,Jack answers.

Within a couple minutes Jack comes up on the Intercom, "Cajun, about half of the men are in the water now. Give us another thirty seconds and we will be clear. After another twenty seconds Jack calls Cajun again. "Cajun, they are all in the water. I am going to disconnect in ten seconds and will be clear. Remember when you go in the water, roll the aircraft to the left so you will be on top, then get out. Boss, I want to see your ugly head bobbing in the waves in just a few seconds."

Cajun orders, "Ok Jack, I'll see you in a few minutes, now you have five seconds to jump in the water." Jack jumps off the cargo loading ramp into the Indian Ocean.

After Cajun counts to five he starts hovering the Chinook into the wind until he is approximately one hundred feet away from his men. He brings the aircraft to a zero forward airspeed hover, then looks at his fuel gauge, which indicates zero. Cajun lowers the collective slowly and smoothly until the aircraft settles into the ocean. He knows what most everybody else has forgotten, and that is that Chinooks are designed to land in the water. Of course, they were not designed to land in open ocean water in the middle of the night with large waves hitting the aircraft.

Before he is knocked over, he decides to simultaneously take all lift out of the rotor system then roll the aircraft over onto its left side. He reaches above his head with his left hand and brings the throttle levers to the back, stopped position. The aircraft rolls smoothly until the rotor blades begin striking the water. Cajun is amazed at how violent the whole process is as the blades strike with tremendous force.. The rotor system is massive, so as the blades hit the water the forward transmission actually-torques out of its mount, just behind the copilot seat. The impact is so loud it sounds as though the aircraft has hit a mountain.

Cajun knows to wait until the rotor blades have decelerated to a standstill and the aircraft's violent movements have subsided before he unbuckles his shoulder harness. Because the back ramp is still in lowered in an open position, the aircraft fills up with water amazingly fast. As soon as Cajun's helmet goes under water, the NVGs batteries short out. He loses all vision in the pitch-black dark water. He is not sure which way is up or which way is down. Cajun knows that if he does not get out of the cockpit soon it will be too late. By the time he works his way out of the seat and reaches for the cockpit door, the inside area is already three quarters under water.

The only thing that gives Cajun an edge is that the aircraft slows it's roll as more water fills the fuselage. Cajun takes a deep breath then lunges for the gunner's door, which is normally open. He does not know whether the door is up or down as he pulls his body through the opening. Once outside the fuselage, the first thing he thinks about is that he is glad he is still wearing his helmet. He is quite sure part of the rotor system will strike him as the aircraft rolls over.

Cajun does not have time to speculate on what might happen. He starts swimming up to the right because his senses tell him that is the direction to swim. Somehow or other the aircraft sinks further while he swims for his life toward what he thinks is the ocean's surface. For a brief moment, Cajun thinks maybe he is swimming in the wrong direction. It seems like it is taking forever to reach the surface. Just as Cajun figures he has perhaps two or three more seconds of air before he drowns, he surfaces and takes in a deep breath.. He smiles way down in his soul as somehow he has lived through a tough situation one more time.

After Cajun catches his breath, he knows that he wants to grab the one-man life raft strapped to his lower leg, deploy it, and get inside as soon as possible.

Once he completes that successfully, he will look for the other men, not the other way around. As he finally pulls himself onto the one-man raft, he lies there completely exhausted for several minutes. As he opens his eyes a smile comes across his face, as he begins to see the distant rays of the morning sun.

Within a few more minutes he hears Jack and Wyatt calling his name.

Cajun shouts out, "Hey, guys, I'm over here." Within a few minutes and the addition of more morning rays, he can see all the guys bobbing on the waves. Cajun starts to paddle in their direction with both arms as though he was on top of a surfboard. Finally, after another few minutes, he joins his men who seem to be no worse for wear. They have tethered all their rafts together. Cajun ties on as well..

Wyatt says, "Boss, we were wondering if maybe you just flew back to Mogadishu without us."

Cajun laughs and says, "Believe me, I thought about it."

The men lie on their rafts for an hour or so discussing the very real successes and failures of the mission. Wyatt says, "Cajun, do you think those swabys will ever find us?" As the words make it pass his lips, a large black pole emerges from the ocean about one hundred yards from their location. It seems surreal to all of them. It takes a full thirty seconds before everyone can see. It is a submarine. As it fully emerges out of the water they can see it is a U.S. Navy submarine.

Within minutes, lifeboats emerge to rescue the downed airmen.

As Cajun lowers himself down the ladder from the deck down into the submarine, he comments to Jack who is waiting his turn, "Did I ever tell you that I have claustrophobia?"

Jack laughs and replies, "Don't worry about it, Boss. It beats swimming back."

Once they are all onboard, the top hatch is closed tightly. One of the Navy guys says to the group, "Follow me, Gentlemen." He leads them down a metal staircase to the next level where they come in contact with the Captain.

As Cajun comes to a stop, the entire gaggle of men behind him stops too. The Captain reaches out his hand to Cajun and shakes it with enthusiasm. "Chief Ethan Breaux, I presume? I am Captain Frank Burke."

Cajun answers, "That's correct, Sir, and these are all my men. We lost several men, who went down with our aircraft, along with the nuke."

Captain Burke replies with the greatest degree of humility in his voice. "On behalf of a grateful nation, we all salute you and your men, and mourn the loss of your men as though they were our brothers." Cajun does not reply he just looks down at his feet while they all think of Jimbo, Brian, and the other guys from Wyatt's team. After several seconds of silence, Captain Burke motions to one of his men. "Ensign, take these men below to get them some dry clothes and something to eat. Maybe you can scrounge up some hot coffee for them too."

The Ensign replies, "Aye, Aye, Sir. Gentlemen, please follow me." With that, he walks in front of the men and leads them below.

Once they are below in what appears to be living quarters, there are at least two dozen men standing, waiting for their arrival. As Cajun and his men enter the area, the men begin slowly clapping for them.

The clapping picks up speed until the Navy guys are clapping and whistling for them as well. Cajun, Jack, Wyatt, Booker, Cotton, and all the men on the team do not say anything as they are somewhat taken aback. Finally, all but a few of the Navy personnel leave the area. Those who remain are handing out dry clothes to the soaking wet men. Once they are all dressed, the Ensign says, "Gentlemen, follow me to the chow hall."

After climbing down another deck then walking toward what must have been about the center of the submarine, they enter a chow hall. The Ensign announces, "Gentlemen, eat what you like." The other guys nudge Cajun to go through the line first. Before he even starts through the line, Cajun can see that it is true. Submariners eat the best. He grabs a tray, some silverware already wrapped in white linens then starts through the line. Wyatt is right behind him.

The cook behind the food counter asks Cajun, "Which entrée would you like, Sir?"

Cajun replies in amazement, "Are you kidding me? Which entrée would I like?

"Yes, Sir, this morning for breakfast we have eggs benedict, steak and eggs, or sausage with pancakes."

"I believe I will have the steak and eggs" ,Cajun answered.

The cook came right back, "Sir, how would you like that prepared?"

Again, Cajun cannot believe his ears but replies enthusiastically, "I would like the steak prepared medium well." The cook looks over at one of his helpers and nods at him. Boom, the steak is placed on the grill immediately. Cajun moves on down the line adding grits and fruit to his tray.

The first cook looks at Wyatt and ask, "What entrée would you like, Sir?"

He answers, "I believe I will have the sausage and pancakes, thank you. Then he adds, "Just call me Sergeant. I work for a living." He smiles as it is the first time anyone has addressed him as Sir.

Cajun sets his plate down at one of the tables then walks over to the coffee pot. He pours himself a large black cup of coffee. He goes back over to the table to sit down. Before he does anything else he brings the coffee cup to his lips to take a sip. His eyes nearly roll out of sight. It seems like years since the last time he had a good, hot cup of coffee. He pauses just for a split second then thinks to himself. "My God, just an hour ago I was within a couple seconds of disappearing into the depths of the Indian Ocean. Now look at me. I am eating a steak for breakfast with a good, hot cup of coffee, on a nuclear submarine. There is a God after all."

After about forty-five minutes, the men have been fed and begin to look restlessly around, with the look on their faces saying, "Now What?" Cajun catches the eye of the Ensign. "Could you take me back up to the bridge to see the Captain?"

The Ensign responds, "Certainly, Sir, follow me."

Cajun adds to the conversation, "When you get back, feel free to put these men to work to earn their keep. They get pretty restless doing nothing."

"I'll come back and find something for them to do.", the Ensign replies With that, the Ensign leads Cajun back up one floor to the Bridge.

When Cajun arrives on the Bridge, the Captain says, "Well, Chief Breaux, you look much more comfortable out of those wet clothes."

Cajun says, "Sir, thank you very much for your hospitality. I would like to add that was the best food I have had on any military installation, I have ever visited, anywhere in the world."

Captain Burke says, "Yes, now you know what they say about submariner's food is true. I am going to head back to my cabin. Would you like to join me for a while, Chief Breaux?"

Cajun replies enthusiastically, "Absolutely, Captain, I'd love to see a little more of your ship."

As the Captain starts to walk off the Bridge, he says, "Ok, follow me but do me a favor, don't let any of my men hear you call our vessel a ship. We refer to it as the boat."

Cajun snickers at his own naivety. "Ahe, Ahe, Sir."

Once they settle in the Captain's quarters Cajun takes a seat across from him. There is a knock at the door. The Captain says, "Enter."

One of the personnel asks the Captain, "Sir, would you care for some freshly brewed coffee?"

Captain Burke replies, "Yes, I would certainly appreciate a little fresh brew."

The young man in the doorway ask Cajun, "And you, Sir?"

"No thank you, I just had a big breakfast," answers Cajun. The man turns and shuts the door.

Captain Burke looks at Cajun. "Don't think I'm going to talk your ears off asking you questions. I just brought you down here to my quarters to relax for another hour or so until we catch up with the U.S. Ronald Reagan." I don't care who you are, you and your men have just been through one of the most unusual military operations I have ever heard of. You must be mentally exhausted."

Cajun says, "Obviously I haven't had much time to reflect on everything that has happened in the last few hours. But now that you mention it, suddenly, I do feel tired."

There is another knock at the door. "Enter." The young man is back with the Captain's coffee, which is served on what appears to be a silver tray. The Captain takes the tray, placing it on a small table. Without speaking, the man leaves the cabin, closing the door behind him. "Please, Chief Breaux, feel free to lay your head back and catch a small power nap. You don't have to entertain me." Cajun does not say anything, he just closes his eyes and lays his head back against the wall.

"Chief Breaux, Chief Breaux, it's time to wake up." says Captain Burke as he gently shakes Cajun. "We are coming abeam the U.S. Ronald Reagan. You and your men will be transferring there in about fifteen minutes as soon as they can get a boat in the water."

Cajun snaps awake quickly and rises out of the chair and says, "Captain Burke, thank you very much for your hospitality to me and my men."

Captain Burke says, "Not at all, Chief. It was in fact a pleasure to meet you and your men. You will not be soon forgotten. Please follow Seaman Hayes. He will reunite you with your men then assist in the transfer."

Cajun can tell the submarine is on the surface of the Indian Ocean long before he climbs up the ladder onto the deck. He can feel the lateral back and forth movement as the waves beat against the submarine's hull.

His men have already been assembled. As Cajun joins the group, Wyatt ask, "Hey, Boss man, where have you been? Have you been hobnobbing with the Captain?"

"The Captain did show me his private quarters. However, no state secrets were revealed. I guess as soon as they get that small craft abeam this boat, we will be transferred to the carrier" ,answers Cajun.

Jack chimes in, "Yes, although I kind of hate to leave this boat, as I hear they are having shrimp for dinner tonight."

Two of the seamen are motioning for the men to board the smaller craft for the transfer to the carrier. Cajun and all his men are not as surefooted as the Seamen. These guys have their sea legs. As the boat rocks back and forth, they tentatively lower themselves into the small craft. In fact, by the time they all get onboard, the craft is full. It will not hold any more people.

The seamen drop the holding lines then the transfer craft slowly heads toward the carrier. Wyatt cannot help commenting as they draw closer to the carrier. "My Lord, had you ever told me that a U.S. Carrier was this big, I would never have believed you. Would you look at the size of this thing?" As they come along side, two large hoisting cables are attached. They are lifted-up, boat and all onto the carrier.

The boat has been raised to about midlevel. As they get off the boat they enter the interior of the ship. Cajun can see a welcoming party. The first thing he notices is a beautiful lady running his way. She is the most beautiful lady he has ever seen. He sees it is Savannah as she leaps into his arms. Standing twenty feet away with the ship's Captain, stands Ryan Clayborne.

The Captain of the carrier moves forward to greet Cajun and says, "Welcome, Chief Breaux. Welcome to you and all your men. I am Captain Jeff Kindrich. I just wanted to come down here to meet you in person and tell you how proud we are of all of you."

Cajun speaks up and says, "Thank you very much Captain Kindrich. On behalf of all these men, let me say that we are extremely happy to be here."

The Captain goes on to introduce his Executive Officer. He starts to introduce Ryan then thinks better of it as Ryan gives Cajun a big bear hug. He does the same with Jack and Wyatt. Ryan looks out at the other men and says, "I would give you all a hug but maybe it's better if we just go inside."

Cajun and Savannah walk arm in arm as the group proceeds towards the interior of the ship. Ryan takes Cajun and Savannah aside. "Why don't you two spend a little time together, but as soon as you can fit it in, I would appreciate it if you would meet with me so that we can debrief this mission. I have the brass in Washington breathing down my neck to know exactly what happened."

He looks at Ryan with a little gleam in his eyes and says, "Just give us thirty minutes and I'll meet with you. "Once we have both completed our debriefing, you won't need me or Savannah anymore until we go ashore, will you, Pigeon?"

Ryan replies, "No, once I have a preliminary report on what happened, we'll be satisfied until we reach shore."

Savannah ask, "Ryan, when we go ashore, where in the world will that be?"

Ryan answers, "We will go ashore in Osaka, Japan. From there, you will be flown to Hawaii, then to Washington, D.C. Your men can then fly to anywhere in the United States or Europe.

Savannah looks into Cajun's eyes. "Why don't you go ahead and get the meeting over with now, because it is a long way to Japan?"

Cajun says, "OK Pigeon, let's go do our thing."

As they start walking off together, Ryan says, "Why do you always call me Pigeon?"

"Relax, Pigeon, and Laissez Les Bon Temps Roulez!"

Glossary

Abeam	Position at a ninety-degree angle to an object or land mass
ADF	Automatic Direction-Finding beacon (navigational aid)
ATC	Air Traffic Control
BINGO	Almost out of fuel, with twenty minutes flying time remaining
Cleared in Hot	Cleared to open fire within a defined battle area
Chock Order	Refers to numbered position in a flight of military aircraft
Cyclic	Control on helicopter for controlling flight forward, backward, left, & right
C-4	Explosive charge
Duce and a half	Two- and one-half ton military truck

FARP   Forward Area Refueling Point

GPS   Global Position System

Feet Wet   A position over open water after having departed a
                        land area Having Had Means that a military
                        soldier will report already having had breakfast

Instrument Mode Refers to the operation of an aircraft in inclement
                        weather

Laissez Les Bon   (in Creole French) … Let the Good Times Roll
Temps Roulez

Land to Ground   Refers to a helicopter landing all the way to the
                        ground not to a hover

Land to a Hover   Refers to a helicopter landing to a three-foot hover

Mad Minute   All members of an infantry unit expend all their
                        remaining ammunition to keep the bad guys
                        heads down as they prepare to jump on helicopters
                        departing a "Hot Zone"

MRE   Pre-packaged Meal Ready to Eat

NVG   Night Vision Goggle

NOE   Nap of the Earth movement in helicopter hugging
                        the terrain

Night Hawk   Operation requiring the naked eye at night after
                        night adapting for 30 minutes

PDP	Pre-Departure-Pee
POW	Call sign of Wyatt Garrity, not Prisoner of War
Pull Pitch	Lift up on Collective to add power (lift) into the blades
Rally Point	Predetermined position where troops form after an action
Rotate	Refers to the manipulation of yoke on an airplane to cause climbing flight
Squawk	Transponder continuously transmitting identification code
Squawk 7700	Transponder transmitting Emergency identification code
Sweep the Cockpit	Excessive nervous movement of Cyclic Control
TOGA	Take-Off / Go-Around Button on Mode Control Panel of a Boeing jet transport aircraft, which is part of the automated flight control system.
VHF Radio	Very high frequency communication radio
V1	Airspeed on a jet aircraft at which, even in the event of an emergency, the takeoff roll shall continue till liftoff
V2	Critical airspeed on a jet aircraft for the best performance in the event of an engine failure

Winchester   Military term for "out of ammo"

Warrant Officer   Technical Officer in the military who has one
                     primary job